M000277946

Boyfriend Material

Boyfriend Material

Jon Jeffrey

KENSINGTON BOOKS
http://www.kensingtonbooks.com

KENSINGTON BOOKS are published by

Kensington Publishing Corp.
850 Third Avenue
New York, NY 10022

Copyright © 2002 by Jon Salem

All rights reserved. No part of this book may be reproduced in any form or by any means without the prior written consent of the Publisher, excepting brief quotes used in reviews.

All Kensington titles, imprints and distributed lines are available at special quantity discounts for bulk purchases for sales promotion, premiums, fund-raising, educational or institutional use.

Special book excerpts or customized printings can also be created to fit specific needs. For details, write or phone the office of the Kensington Special Sales Manager: Kensington Publishing Corp., 850 Third Avenue, New York, NY 10022. Attn. Special Sales Department. Phone: 1-800-221-2647.

Kensington and the K logo Reg. U.S. Pat. & TM Off.

Library of Congress Card Catalogue Number: 2002101745
ISBN: 0-7582-0102-8

First Printing: November 2002
10 9 8 7 6 5 4 3 2 1

Printed in the United States of America

ACKNOWLEDGMENTS

More than a few people helped me get this book out of my head and onto the page . . .

Rene Paul Barrilleaux—The Rain Man of contemporary art. We talked just a bit and not one but two characters were born. He guided me on the purchase and framing of an amazing Dianora Niccolini photograph, too. This has nothing to do with the book, except for the fact that the advance helped me afford it.

Ken Barton—A brilliant attorney. Not mine (can't afford him) but he did a little research for me on ethical issues regarding the lawyer/client relationship. I needed him desperately, as the extent of my legal mind is a few seasons of *L.A. Law* and whatever happened on *Ally McBeal*. Ken's wife Lea is a fabulous contemporary artist. Again, not related to the book, but we're all here, so why not give her a plug.

Linda Konner—My fabulous literary agent. She's a kitten in person and a tiger at the negotiating table. Jacqueline Susann brought us together! It's true. We met at a book party for the reissue of Barbara Seaman's biography of the *Valley of the Dolls* author. I co-wrote the foreword. Not much, but my first real credit and a spot on the podium. By the way, Barbara's dogged insistence and frequent flyer miles got me there. I was dirt poor at the time. Could barely scrape up the funds to dry clean my Dolce & Gabbana outfit. But I did. This was New York! This was Jackie! No way was I showing up in Macy's private label. Anyway, I said something obnoxious about Jackie prodding me from heaven to tell the assembled guests (an eclectic mix, even a transsexual lap dancer who ran away from home at seventeen was there) that I needed an agent. Suddenly, Linda's shoving her card in my face and telling me to send her my book. Completely insane. But this is how things happen.

John Scognamiglio—My intrepid editor. He gave me the title, told me I could do it, and sent encouraging e-mails in all caps with lots of exclamation points. I say he's publishing's version of Tony Robbins. Love our Monday ritual, which is to call each other and scream about *Queer as Folk*.

Charles A. Smith—The very talented (and very patient) photographer. It took two sessions to shoot the little author photo. The first time I refused to smile (wanted to give off a petulant model vibe). The result? Let's just say I lit a fire that evening. So I listened to Charles and smiled the next time, though I did pull a Streisand and complain about the lighting.

Sarah Jessica Parker—I'm already naming names, so what's the harm in plopping her in. Love her, love the show. And let me throw in Chris Isaak, Diana Krall, Kylie Minogue, and J. Lo for singing like angels while I hammered away at the keyboard.

If love is the answer, could you rephrase the question?
—Lily Tomlin

1

All-American Jock with an Edge

Carson St. John was slightly drunk, a little bit stoned, and being ravished against the television cabinet by a male escort who charged two hundred fifty dollars an hour.

I'm the gay Charlie Sheen. Before the multiple rehab visits and Spin City *comeback, of course.*

His peers were downstairs, listening to a panel of pundits drone on about why this magazine succeeded, how that one failed, whether Tina Brown's *Talk* would've triumphed had September eleventh been just a bad dream.

But Carson had made a stealthy exit, taken the Regal Biltmore elevator to his eighth floor room, and waited breathlessly for Brian to arrive for sixty minutes of midday, no last names, anything you want sex.

Brian, aka SexyLAModel, looked better in person than he did in the two photos he'd e-mailed—one striking a *GQ* pose in a Brioni suit, the other striking a porn pose in nothing at all.

Carson had imagined him taller. Maybe he was five-foot-ten on his tip-toes? But the rest was truth in advertising. Masculine, handsome, one hundred seventy pounds, dirty blond buzzed hair, blue eyes, lean muscular body, great smile. Definitely what the AOL profile promised—all-American jock with an edge.

"Like what you see?" Those had been Brian's first words as he ripped off his tie and flung it to the floor with the kind of brazen carelessness that makes certain men's hearts go bang.

"I feel like an adolescent," Carson had whispered. It was true. In the last hour he'd taken two showers, raided the mini bar, smoked half a joint, and brushed his teeth four times.

Brian had moved closer as he undid the buttons of his denim shirt. "Are there some adolescent experiences that you want to act out again? I love to role play. Maybe I could be your gym coach."

I'm not paying two hundred fifty an hour to relive the worst years of my life. That's what I should be paying a therapist one hundred fifty an hour for.

But Carson hadn't said this out loud. Instead, in a very soap opera move—say, Deidre Hall as Marlena in a rare moment of unstoppable passion—he'd just pulled SexyLAModel toward him and began kissing like mad.

They were still going at it, steel tongue to steel tongue, bulging crotch against bulging crotch, when the stud for hire suddenly drew back and, radiating a rude animal sexuality, looked Carson right in the face to say, "One hour's not gonna be long enough."

Carson discarded Brian's denim Tommy Hilfiger button down and peeled off the man's undershirt. "It'll have to be." He wasn't blowing five hundred bucks on some escort. Even a hot tanned one with perfect teeth, buff chest, ripped abs, and big veins wrapped around his forearms. He would, however, blow the escort.

It took about a minute for both of them to get naked, representing about four dollars, Carson estimated. But a wise investment.

Brian lay there on the bed, gloriously nude, stroking the tool of his trade. Seven inches. Cut. Rock hard. "How bad do you want to suck this?"

Very.

Carson was just getting into it when the stab of guilt came. He tried to cast it away, to concentrate on the delectable task before him.

"Oh, yeah," Brian moaned. "Take it all."

This helped. Carson got off on verbal encouragement. But the guilt stuck there in his brain like the chorus to "Oops! . . .

I Did It Again." Years later and he was still singing it. Go
Britney. Now he could even hear the sound of Rocco's voice.
If this relationship is going to survive, it needs to be casual.
I'm not ready to be monogamous. I meet too many hot guys
in my line of work.

Back home, Rocco was a DJ at Damage, the trendy dance
club of the moment. That particular announcement had come
somewhere between a hook up with the new bouncer and a
sleepover with a dancer from *Cabaret.*

Naturally, Carson wanted to leave Los Angeles and return
to New York with the secret knowledge of his own indiscre-
tion. He would just forget the fact that money had exchanged
hands. Cruising at a bar meant prolonged glances, body language interpretation, awkward small talk. If a meaningless
encounter was the goal, hiring a male escort just seemed . . .
well . . . *efficient.* Plus, you were assured a better-looking guy
who took care of his body and was a proven dynamo in the
sack.

They were rolling around on the bed when Carson's
Motorola Timeport two-way smart pager beeped. It was
Danny. The tone music of Madonna's classic "Holiday" gave
him away.

Carson stretched toward the nightstand to reach the gad-
get. "This will only take a second. Amuse yourself down
there." He gently pushed Brian's head to his crotch and read
Danny's text message.

WHERE R U?

Carson smiled. He could just see him. Danny Kimura, entertainment lawyer, clad head to toe in regulation Prada,
trapped in an endless negotiation meeting for his bread and
butter client, the bubble gum pop boy band Four Deep.
Laughing, Carson typed out a reply on the tiny keypad.

GETTING A BLOW JOB IN L.A.

"What's so funny?" Brian asked. He pulled a face and removed a pubic hair from his tongue.

"Nothing." Carson pushed the pager under the pillow.
"Just a message from a friend of mine."

There was a sexy gleam in Brian's blue eyes as he climbed

on top and kissed him hard on the mouth. "You know, I really want to fuck you."

Carson thought about Rocco. His *boyfriend* (granted, a loose term here) never took the high road, especially when Carson was out of town, at work, or, hell, even in the next room. It was noon in New York. Rocco was probably just waking up with some guy he'd met the night before. His idea of commitment was where he kept his treasured collection of vinyl twelve inches. Right now it was in Carson's apartment. Significant, yes, but still too soon to register at Pottery Barn and order invitations for the commitment ceremony.

Carson's eyes engaged for what seemed like a blissful eternity with the man on the clock. Then he felt a surge up from his loins. *Sorry, Rocco.*

He reached for the lubricant and a condom. Carson didn't have to close his eyes and pretend Brian was Chris O'Donnell with a really short haircut because the guy was a dead ringer.

And worth every penny.

Post action, Brian lay kicked back on the bed, cradling the back of his head with both hands, all the better to show off his impressive biceps. He glanced over to check the time. "I can stay, you know. My next appointment isn't for several hours."

Carson looked up. He was between Brian's legs, his chin on the man's belly button. "I can only afford one hour. I'm not David Geffen."

"Who's that?"

"Never mind."

A moment of silence. Slightly awkward but nothing to pop a Xanax over.

"So, did you enjoy it?"

Jesus. Carson *would* have the luck to hire an escort with self-esteem issues. "At one point I yelled out, 'You're the king of the world!'"

Brian grinned. "Yeah, I liked that."

An impulse raced up Carson's brain stem. "Do you by any chance keep a journal?"

"No, but I write poetry."

A terrible fear registered. Rocco had written a poem once,

and Carson had been forced to listen to it one morning in bed. It'd been like waking up with Jewel. Not a good way to start the day.

"Poetry's a tough sell," Carson said diplomatically. "I was thinking more along the lines of a diary." He waved a hand through the air. "*This Stud for Hire: A Week in the Life of a Male Escort.*"

Brian's eyes brightened with interest.

"It'd be perfect for *Throb.*"

"I love that magazine."

Carson smiled. "Well, you just rammed the editor in chief."

Brian swung out of bed and started hunting down his clothes. "For real? That's cool. It's a fun mag, like a gay guy's *Cosmo.* You don't bring us down with a bunch of political crap or scare us to death with health news."

"I wish you'd been in last month's focus group."

"What's that?"

"Never mind." He watched him slip on his underwear. "So what do you think about the diary? You could have a byline and a photo spread."

Brian hesitated. "Too many people read that magazine. I'm only up front about what I do with a few other escorts."

As Brian put on his pants and buttoned his shirt, Carson considered splurging for an extra hour, then discarded the idea. "Your business would soar."

The guy didn't wait so much as a beat. "No, thanks. I'm not in this for the long haul. Just trying to make some cash until my acting and modeling career take off."

Good-looking, great in bed, *and* a cliché. A true multitalent. "Have I seen you in anything?"

"I had a big role in an industrial video once. I played a supervisor who sexually harassed a secretary."

"Kind of like an after school special for adults with boring jobs?"

"Yeah." He scooped up his tie and stepped in front of the mirror to knot it.

"What about modeling?"

"I was in a catalog for workout equipment." He struck a jogging pose. "This was me on the treadmill."

"At least give the diary some thought."

Brian admired his reflection, smoothing his buzzed hair with both hands. "You can put me in the magazine after I win my Tony Award."

He was so sweet to dream out loud. Carson wanted to hug him and gently break the news that you had to work on the New York stage to get one of those.

"Time's up."

Carson picked up an envelope and walked it over.

Brian accepted the cash without counting and kissed him. "How about something extra for parking?"

Carson produced another ten dollars. A thought distracted him. "At the risk of getting too personal, how do you maintain a relationship in your line of work?"

"I don't. But that's not unusual here. L.A. is filled with flakes. People never expect others to live up to their promises." Brian shrugged. "I've got a secret life going on, plus acting and modeling to pursue. I'd make a terrible boyfriend."

Carson's idea wheels started spinning. He practically pushed Brian out of the hotel room, then retrieved his pager from underneath the pillow, typed in a message, and sent it to Danny. It was the perfect topic for the next gay summit.

Q: WHAT DO U CONSIDER BOYFRIEND MATERIAL?

2

Girl, You're in My Heart

The answer was Leo Summer.

Danny Kimura fought hard to control his lustful stare. He was, after all, legal counsel to the entire boy band, not erotomaniac to just one member. But every cell of Leo's white-hot, yes-I'm-a-star, even-the-way-I-sleep-is-cool heartthrobness demanded attention.

As did the situation at hand—a bruising negotiation to hammer out a deal regarding a Four Deep network special. With the group's manager sidelined by last minute tour details, Danny had been tapped to helm this meeting.

So far, so good. After bluffing the assembled Ivy League trio with an insane asking price, he sat ready to accept a huge sum to lock the guys in—much more than Four Deep was worth. Danny had forecasted this desperation with just the sort of cunning that had helped him leapfrog from clerk to junior associate to future partner at Ross, Orloff, & Dayan, an entertainment law firm with offices in New York, Los Angeles, London, and Tokyo. His clients ruled the multiplexes, starred on television's number one sitcom, sat atop the *Publishers Weekly* list, hoofed it on Broadway, and, in Four Deep's case, dominated MTV's *Total Request Live*.

Danny had known that the early season ratings for the network in question would be dismal. The new entertainment chief had signed off on one of the crappiest fall lineups in recent memory. An updated version of *BJ & the Bear* (still with the less talented Landers sister) had actually made it onto the air. That's why he'd stalled this formal talk until *after* the numbers were in. After all, a pressured executive's naked yearning for a guaranteed sweeps period blockbuster could be a beautiful thing.

"Where do you plan to schedule us?"

The network reps stared back in amazement because the question—a very relevant one—had come from Leo. Guys in slickly packaged, highly choreographed boy bands weren't supposed to *think*. They were supposed to demand Krispy Kreme doughnuts and blame farts on each other.

"We're not sure," the official spokesman murmured, his gaze on Danny. "Probably a Friday or Saturday in mid-November."

Danny glanced at Leo. This young man was nobody's studio puppet. The story of him leaving school at fourteen to move to Orlando and trudge through the teen dream factory was now a paragraph of pop history. Maybe he didn't know his trigonometry, but Leo definitely knew his demographics.

"My audience doesn't stay home on Friday and Saturday nights," he said. "Your mother does."

The top suit's face turned pink. Then he laughed nervously. "You've got a point there, Leo."

Danny studied Chad, Greg, and Damian, the more disposable members of Four Deep, three guys who would most likely be working at a car wash if they didn't happen to be in a successful boy band. Had they noticed Leo's bold pronoun choice? Did they even know why they were here? Could they tell you who the vice president of the United States was? No, no, and hell no, respectively.

"Tuesday," Leo said with authority.

Danny watched the network reps take in the savvy pop star, reassessing their preconceived notions about the uneducated, model-perfect commodity who sang banal ditties and danced with robotic precision. They didn't know that Leo had fought the brass at his record label over the first single release from Four Deep's sophomore album, *Twice Shy*. The execs wanted to unleash the up tempo "I've Got a Secret (And It's Loving You)," but Leo had lobbied hard for the power ballad, "Girl, You're in My Heart." They reluctantly deferred to his wishes, and the song hit number one within six weeks. It was still perched there, not only on the pop chart, but on the adult contemporary and dance charts as well. For the latter, it had been Leo's idea to record new vocals with DJ/remixer Abraham B. for an edgier sound.

"Tuesday it is," the network man promised.

After that, it didn't take long for Danny to close the deal for megabucks, a turn of events made all the sweeter by the fact that the teen pop boom was officially on life support. Still, as long as twelve-year-old girls roamed the earth . . .

They were in the elevator when Greg elbowed Danny to say, "Hey, man, I bet you can't guess how many times Damian jerked off yesterday."

He shot a disapproving glance to this beefy kid with the flop of red hair and the broad face. "You're right. I can't."

Chad extended his finger. "Pull it," he encouraged, laughing.

Danny just looked at him.

But Greg did the honors.

And then Chad let rip an explosive fart that immediately fouled up the air.

Greg and Damian broke up laughing in that way only idiot guys can.

"It's the chicken-fried steak," Chad explained. "Does it to me every time." He chuckled. "Who dares me to take a shit in this elevator?"

The doors opened into the parking garage, where a white stretch limousine waited.

Danny, Leo, Greg, and Damian exited.

Chad lingered behind.

"I dare you, motherfucker. I dare you!" Greg taunted gleefully.

Chad's fingers started to work on his button-fly jeans. He was actually going to do it.

"Get out of the elevator!" Danny shouted, suddenly feeling like a hall monitor at some alternative school.

Chad pretended to take offense. "I'll just take a dump in the limousine then," he said huffily.

Greg and Damian collapsed all over each other as they

tumbled into the car and barked orders at the driver to take them to the nearest Taco Bell.

Danny turned and regarded Leo sympathetically. "How do you tour with those guys and keep your sanity?"

Leo shrugged. "I've spent almost every waking minute with them for the last five years. They're like my brothers." A pause. "Retarded ones, of course. But still my brothers."

Danny laughed. In this light, in that outfit, it was uncanny how much Leo looked like Ryan Phillipe in *Cruel Intentions*. The same slightly curly, smartly cut blond hair, piercing baby blues, pouty lips, lean body, and if all that wasn't devastating enough, he had the impervious attitude down to a science.

Leo gave up a private, knowing smile and held it.

Danny shifted uneasily. This was the first acknowledgment of that chance meeting a few months ago.

The setting had been Manhole, a decadent gay bar in Chicago. Danny was in the city on business, helping a client (musical theater star on the decline) out of a bad real estate deal (originally brokered by stupid husband). So there Danny had been at this wild club, leaning against the bar, looking hot in his Prada techno pants and skintight Angry Little Asian Girl T-shirt by Lela Lee that rode up past his navel to give away just a hint of the great abs he worked goddamn hard for with his straight trainer at Hanson Fitness in SoHo. He could even remember what song had been thumping out of the sound system when he saw Leo. "Can't Get You Out of My Head" by Kylie Minogue.

At first he couldn't believe it. But Danny had focused his gaze, counted to ten, and realized it was him. Leo Summer. Shirtless, fearless, and dancing with ecstasy-laced abandon against a brooding, genetically gifted but utterly disposable hunk in full military dress.

The attorney and the client had shared a long, meaningful stare. And then Leo had just given Danny this devilish grin and disappeared into a back room with the major/colonel/ whatever. Gossip of the Four Deep singer's scandalous night *out* had spread like poison ivy, especially over the airwaves of Chicago's pop stations, but nothing ever took hold on a national level.

"You should come to Miami with us," Leo was saying. "We could sneak off to Salvation. Have you been there?"

Danny shook his head. The South Beach club was famous for its Saturday night pleasure orgies. He'd been dying to go but no business had taken him to the area yet, and he hadn't indulged in a vacation since finishing law school.

"I talked to our travel agent about putting me up in a different hotel," Leo whispered pointedly. "We could share the same room and no one would know."

Suddenly the limousine door flung open. "Hurry the fuck up!" Greg shouted. "We're hungry."

Leo rolled his eyes. "The Three Stooges beckon. You know how to get in touch. Let me know." He quietly slipped into the backseat and shut the door.

Danny watched the vehicle coast away, half shocked, half titillated. The offer was dangerous, professionally irresponsible . . . and incredibly tempting.

Maybe that's because he'd lived his entire life in such chained up duty. The perfect Japanese-American child—hardworking, studious, honorable. Over and over again his parents had emphasized getting a degree and a stable job. There had also been something about marrying a nice Asian girl, but he pretended not to hear that part.

For his mother, he'd gone through high school a weak, sexless, passive nerd, the dividend being a full scholarship to Columbia, where he'd graduated with honors, setting him up to attend law school at Yale. For his father, he'd taken up Tae Kwon Do, even qualifying for the Olympic trials. For his family legacy, he'd sought out a career in pushy corporate America, becoming the first in his family to do so.

Now Danny wanted something for himself. And ever since that night at Manhole, he hadn't been able to get Leo Summer out of his mind. The fantasy was infinitely desirable, the reality endlessly problematic.

But he called his assistant and asked her to book a weekend flight to Miami anyway.

3

The Soccer Mom's Husband

Nathan Williams checked his e-mail for a message from
WallStreetTop. *Every five minutes.* Some would call that
obsessive. He preferred passionately eager.

The telephone rang.

His heart raced with the possibility that it could be Mike.
Everything arrowed down to him now. Would Mike e-mail?
Would Mike call? Would Mike stop by?

"Frankovich Gallery," he purred into the sleek Bang &
Olufsen receiver.

"Nathan?"

His heart screeched to a halt. "Hello, Mother."

"Is this a bad time?"

"No, it's fine. Slow day here."

"I can't believe we paid all that money for Vassar just so
you could baby-sit paintings."

He held the phone away from his ear, made faces at it, and
then gave it his middle finger. "I know. Total waste. I
should've gone to junior college."

"Don't be glib, Nathan."

Since that was forbidden, he wondered if he should be honest. *Can I call you back, Mother? Any minute now I'm expecting an e-mail from a white man who lives in Connecticut
with his wife and two kids. Then I'm closing the gallery early
to go have sex with him.*

"I'm calling with good news," Audrey Williams went on.
"Tia Elliott has relocated to Manhattan. She just started with

Goldman, Sachs & Company. I have her number right here. I thought the two of you could have dinner."

Nathan just sat there and said nothing. Tia was the daughter of Dr. and Mrs. Arthur Elliott; he was the son of Dr. and Mrs. Patrick Williams. They were children of the black upper class. Of course they should have dinner. After all, the elite must stick together.

"We've got a new show opening soon," he started, hoping to beg off this intrusion. "I'm going to be very busy."

"Your brother's a surgeon, and he has time to date," Audrey said sharply.

Nathan wanted to throw the phone out the door and into the street with the hope that a double-decker tourist bus would run over it. His mother had mastered the art of pulling the big brother card. Henry had pursued a *respectable* career in medicine. Henry worked at the Mayo Clinic. Henry liked girls. It was all too perfect. Just the way his mother expected her children to be.

Nathan remembered Tia Elliott well. Growing up in Chicago, they were the same age and had done all the same things. Both had been in Jack and Jill, the national invitation-only social group for children, and both had headed off to Camp Atwater, the summer sanctuary just west of Boston that featured Senator Ted Kennedy and Washington power broker Vernon Jordan on its board of directors. But Nathan's most vivid memory of the Elliott family was Christian, Tia's brother. If ever there was a moment when Nathan realized that he lusted after boys, it had been the sight of Christian taking off his shirt to join a neighborhood game of pickup basketball.

"I promised Tia's parents that you would look after her," Audrey was saying.

Nathan sighed. "You should've talked to me first. There's so much going on. My schedule's insane."

Audrey seethed in a moment of silence. "Find the time to take Tia out to dinner." It was an order, not a suggestion. "As a favor to your mother," she added coldly.

Nathan transcribed the fantasy response in his mind.

Mother, I don't give a damn about Tia Elliott. She's a bitch. Now if you were calling to tell me that her brother Christian had moved to the city, I'd be all over it. But that was fantasy. And this was reality. So he took down the girl's number and promised to call.

With his mother out of the way now, he got back to more important matters. Such as checking e-mail. There were two new messages. The first was from Carson. That could be read later. But the second item required his immediate attention, and by the time Nathan finished scanning it, he had a raging hard on.

FROM: WallStreetTop
TO: NathanW
SUBJECT: Come Get This
Can't stop thinking about your talented mouth and great ass. Meet me at our special place about 6:30. Big Mike's got something for you.

How vulgar. And he loved it. Nathan had spent most of his life repressing his sexuality, uncertain of it, ashamed of it. Moving to New York changed all that. He wasn't just the son of Patrick and Audrey Williams anymore. Finally, at twenty-six, he was Nathan Williams in his own right. A hot black meteorite in the demimonde of the city's young and mediagenic art set. The fourth member of a hip clique that included *Throb* editor Carson St. John, lawyer to pop superstars Danny Kimura, and educator Rob Cahill, his roommate and more like a brother to him than Henry had ever been.

Yes, for the first time, Nathan was living *for* life and not in fear *of* it. Every day he felt like an anxious racehorse stomping to leave the gate. There were so many lost years to make up, so many lonely nights to take back.

Impatience burning, he watched the last customer shuffle out. It wasn't like like she was a potential buyer. He'd overheard the woman on her cell phone, talking about killing time until she met friends for dinner.

Now the coast was clear. He flicked switches, activated

alarms, locked doors, and ran like hell to the train station. All the people around him looked bored and depressed. Maybe that's because they didn't have a Mike in their lives.

He got off at Grand Central and made a beeline for the terminal's Oyster Bar. Then he pushed through the swinging doors of the Saloon and just stood in the entranceway, surveying the corporate America crowd.

And there he was, sitting in the corner, tie loosened, knocking back a three-olive Ketel One martini, not ready to go back to the suburbs to change diapers, check homework, and eat his wife's casserole.

The eye contact lasted a nanosecond.

Nathan knew the drill. He hit the men's room first and secured the last stall. Mike followed about a minute later. It was always quick, dirty, and strangely unsatisfying, but Nathan couldn't get enough. These interludes had become as essential as air.

The silence was the worst. Especially when Mike pumped him from behind. Nathan wanted to cry out—the pleasure, the pain, the danger of being caught. But Mike whispered warnings to stay quiet. Sometimes he even clamped a hand over Nathan's mouth.

The whole sordid scene ended the same way each time. Mike would give him a hard, bruising kiss and say, "That was good. I'll be in touch."

Tonight was no different. Except that Nathan lobbied for more. "We should have lunch," he said.

This wasn't part of the usual script, and Mike stared at him for a long time. "I like to keep things discreet."

"There are discreet restaurants. Even if someone does see us, maybe I'm just asking you about stocks."

Mike cupped Nathan's face and said, "Lunch is for pussies. I'll take you to Switzerland."

Nathan swallowed hard. "Are you serious?"

Mike slapped his cheek, laughed, and walked out.

Nathan stood there for a moment. He had no clue how to read this, and it would drive him crazy all weekend. Maybe Rob's assessment could provide some clarity. If only his roommate's view on Mike wasn't so negative. Regardless, Nathan wanted to talk things out and hear some advice, even if the chances of his actually heeding it were slim to none.

He pulled himself together and headed back into the bar, intending to find a pay phone since his cell had been missing for three days. If he called Rob now, they could still make plans to meet somewhere for dinner. And that's when he ran into Stella Moon.

"Nathan Williams. Oh, my God. How are you?"

From then on he was a goner.

She accosted him in a voice so loud, so thick in its Southern drawl, that you had to question its authenticity. But it was real. She captured him in an embrace and kissed him full on the lips, then clasped both of his hands and said, "People are talking about you, honey."

An immediate fear registered, that feeling you get when you think someone knows your darkest secret.

"Everybody's like, 'Nathan Williams is so gorgeous, and he knows so much about contemporary art.' And then I'm always like, 'He's my friend. And he *is*. And he *does*.' " She let out a throaty laugh.

Nathan just smiled.

"What are you doing here?"

"I met a friend." His gaze darted to Mike's typical hangout area. No sign of him. "I was just leaving."

"Stay and have a drink with me. I'm meeting a friend, too, and he's always late. I don't want to sit at the bar and get hit on by a bunch of losers stuck in middle management."

"Actually, I have—"

"Don't tell me no," Stella said, clutching his arm with both hands. She stopped a waiter passing by. "I've got drugs in my purse, and if I don't get a cosmopolitan right away, I'm going to have to take them."

The waiter smiled. Amazingly, he seemed to understand. He turned to Nathan expectantly.

"Just a Coke for me," Nathan said.

Stella regarded him curiously.

"I don't drink," Nathan explained.

"That is *so* adorable!" A pause. A worried glance. "You're not an alcoholic are you?"

"No."

"Because you're so young. That would be really sad. I wish I could stop drinking and taking drugs, but I just don't have the willpower."

Stella Moon hailed from Birmingham, Alabama. She was twenty-seven, blonde, beautiful, and possessed an overwhelming appetite for drink, drugs, designer clothes, sex, and, most of all, shameless self-promotion. Oh, and she was an artist. A very successful one—at least financially. Where the eighties art boom had been decadent but about the art, today's new boom was decadent but about the artist. That's how a minor talent like Stella Moon had fast forwarded from nobody to boldface name in Page Six.

Her looks and outrageousness were already the stuff of modern legend. When a *New York Times* critic excoriated Stella in a recent review, she'd tracked him down at another opening and said, "Honey, your tiny little five hundred word column doesn't mean shit to me. Next week I'm on the front page of the 'Styles' section—*above the fold*. So fuck you."

It was only a year ago that Stella had put her stamp on the scene with a series of Warhol-like miniature portraits of famous New Yorkers. The twist—she painted them with make-up pencils. Intrigued, Harold Starr had given her a show at his new gallery in the meat packing district. Every important name turned in an appearance, and every piece sold, including the one of Donald Trump, although that had been slyly purchased by his publicist to avoid the public embarrassment of being the only subject without a red dot.

Nathan had been like everyone else in believing that Stella would likely disappear after that auspicious albeit head-scratching debut. But her next project had defied all expectations, not to mention all elements of good taste. *Mango Cock* was a colorful painting of the tropical fruit with a phallus sticking out of it. An Internet e-millionaire paid fifty-five thousand dollars for the work. After that, nothing could stop her.

They were sitting down now, and she was scowling into her cosmopolitan. "The only reason I'm waiting around for this guy is because he's the *best* kisser." Stella put a hand on Na-

than's arm for emphasis. "There's a red velvet couch inside
the ladies' room. Last week he tipped the attendant, and we
made out on it for at least an hour. I gave him a hand job, too.
Can you believe that? I'm such a whore sometimes. And this
man is no good for me. Scott's married, he's got kids, and the
son of a bitch only meets me here to fool around before he
catches the train back home. How pathetic is that?"

Nathan didn't answer. It hit too close to home. So he tried
to imagine what Switzerland was like this time of year.

"If only I had listened to my psychic," Stella continued. She
didn't talk *to* you so much as *at* you. "The day I met him was
the day she told me not to leave my studio. Something about
a negative encounter. Do you have a psychic?"

"No," Nathan said. "But I read my AOL horoscope."

"I should put you in touch with Vandela. That's who I
work with. All you have to do is send her your birth date—
time, date, location—and a recent photo. She's amazing.
There were things she knew that I've never told anybody. I
swear. Just the other day she said someone close to me was
holding back my success. At first, I was like, she must mean
my mama. But she worked a little longer and said the person
was Harold Starr. I didn't believe her. I said, 'No, that can't
be! He's the man who changed my life!' And she goes, 'Trust
Vandela.' Does that not give you chills?"

Nathan agreed. It was so much easier that way.

Stella finished her drink and waved for the waiter to bring
her another. "Well, honey, I looked into it, and do you know
what that bastard was doing to me? Harold was letting some
friend of his take my paintings on approval. This guy had
Papaya Cock in his apartment for like two months. I checked
him out, and he never buys. He just gets all this work on approval and throws big parties so people will think he's a serious collector. I called Harold and cussed him out for at least
ten minutes. He got that piece back in the gallery, and it sold
the next day for sixty thousand. And do you know that he's
taking full commission on it, too? What a fuckhead."

"This riff sound serious," Nathan observed.

"Oh, believe me, it is. Did I tell you that I'm gonna be in a
fashion layout in *Vogue*?"

"That's great."

"An editor there commissioned me to do *Watermelon Cock*, and one thing led to another. I'm *so* excited. You know, I'm running out of fruits to do. I think the only thing left is boysenberry. I thought about moving on to vegetables, but something about *Green Bean Cock* just doesn't sound right. That would be overkill, don't you think? I don't want to turn into a joke."

"Of course not."

Stella gave him a shrewd look. "You're on my short list, honey. Frankovich is in a great location, it's got a fabulous reputation, and you're just as scrumptious as you can be."

Nathan really listened now. Granted, Stella Moon was one antic short of being a cartoon character, but her popularity seemed to be growing exponentially. It would be quite a coup to snare her for the gallery. "We would be thrilled to represent your work, Stella. On an exclusive basis, of course."

"Oh, *of course*. I believe exclusivity enhances value. My mama taught me that."

"Is she an artist?"

"No, honey, she's president of the Junior League back home. She was a Miss Alabama, though. That's artistic. Her talent was mime."

Nathan stared at the ice in his Coke. There was a chance here to close the deal. "Why don't you come by the gallery next week?"

Stella leaned in to kiss him on the lips again. "Oh, honey, I just had to do that. You are too much. I can't believe how laid back you are. I love it. Most gallery people give me the hard sell, and it just stresses me out, and I end up having to take drugs to zone out for a couple of days. But you are precious. I would love to come on over to Frankovich, but there's one little string I have to attach."

Nathan felt a sense of dread coming on.

"I have this friend. His name is Panther. He's an artist. He does the most incredible stuff. There's always a man with a big dick in his work. He's black, you know. But not like you. I bet you went to all the best schools and everything. Well, Panther dropped out of state college and never knew who his daddy was." Stella lifted up her Anna Sui top to reveal a taut stomach. She touched the area just above her belly button. "He's got a scar right here from where he got stabbed in the eighth grade. I mean, this guy is the closest thing to a thug I've ever known. He's brilliant! I think he could be the art world's answer to Tupac Shakur. Remember him? The rapper? People still look him up on the Internet. By the way, I have my own Web site now—Stella Moon dot com. Hopefully, when Panther makes it big, he won't get shot at."

Nathan jumped in. "What's the string, Stella?"

"I'll come to Frankovich if you give Panther his own show. He's got this new series called 'Nubian Nights' that is *so* hot."

"I'd have to see his work and pay him a studio visit before I could agree to that."

"Honey, all you have to do is meet *him*. It's not about the *art*. It's about the *artist*! Do you think anyone in this town would've given me the time of day if I'd just sent around slides of a mango with a dick attached? I'll bring Panther by next week. You're gonna love him."

A cellular jingled.

Stella reached into her D&G bag and pulled out a mirrored StarTAC that she used to check her lipstick before answering. "Hello? . . . Where are you? . . . Oh, fuck! . . . I don't care what's going on . . . Honey, I'm worth losing a job over." She hung up and looked at Nathan. "That asshole is stuck at his brokerage house dealing with some kind of emergency. I guess it's just you and me for dinner."

Nathan shrugged. He really wanted to spend the evening with Rob, but there was no getting rid of Stella Moon.

4

A Daddy for the Teacher

"**O**ther clubs have sued under the Equal Access Act. Most school boards surrender before trial. We'll get on the news and everything."

Rob Cahill regarded the outspoken teenage lesbian with the pierced lip. "Madison, there's no reason to go to the courts. Manchester High sanctioned the Gay Straight Alliance without resistance."

"Oh, well, that's what my friend in California had to do at his school. He spends most of his time fighting just to have the club." She looked genuinely perplexed. "What else is there to do?"

"Being on the news would be cool." Caleb, an out and proud junior, offered this. Then he chuckled. "I could wear my BOTTOM BOY T-shirt and really freak people out."

Everybody laughed except Justin, a quiet freshman who, judging from the expression on his face, had no idea what a bottom boy was.

"I heard they're trying to ban a gay history book from the library," Madison said. Her eyes narrowed conspiratorially.

Rob smiled. Oliver Stone had nothing on this girl.

She punched the air with her fist. "We can protest that!"

Suddenly the energy of the group—twelve members strong—lurched forward.

"I can wear my CUT OR UNCUT? T-shirt at the sit-in," Caleb said.

More laughter.

Frustrated, Rob finger combed his hair with both hands. As faculty sponsor for the new group, he'd asked Mrs. McElroy, head librarian, to order *Long Road to Freedom: The Advocate History of the Gay and Lesbian Movement*, planning for each member of the club to read a chapter and report on it for the rest of the group. But he was unaware that the book included several frontal nude shots of men, a fact that a scarlet-faced Mrs. McElroy quickly pointed out.

"Relax, guys. There's no reason to stage a protest against the school library."

In the back of the room, Brad Pike cleared his throat. He was an eighteen-year-old senior, six-foot-two, about one hundred ninety-five pounds, all of it chiseled good looks and corded muscle. At this morning's pep rally for the football team, girls had chanted his name as if he were a rock star.

On instinct, Rob decided to nudge the young man into participation. "Do you have something to add, Mr. Pike?"

"Yeah, first of all, I'm straight."

Rob grinned. "I'm sure some guys at Manchester will be disappointed to hear that."

This got bigger laughs than Caleb's jokes.

Brad took the ribbing in stride, as good a sport as he was an athlete. "I think the GSA's focus should be about spreading a message of tolerance and acceptance throughout the school. That's why I joined. I'm kind of a leader at Manchester. If other students see me respecting gay people, maybe they'll do the same."

"It's not just the kids, though," Madison chimed in. "I've seen *teachers* look the other way when gay students are being harassed. Some of them laugh along with the bullies."

Rob nodded somberly. This time she had a legitimate point. "I think this club can challenge those attitudes." He fixed a gaze on Madison, then Caleb. "In a constructive way." He checked his watch. "Time to wrap up. I'll see you next week. Same time. Same place. Everybody have a good weekend."

As the kids began to filter out of the room, Rob booted up his Apple iBook to check his e-mail. He hoped Nathan had sent a message about meeting for dinner because there was nothing to eat at home.

"Hey, Justin," Brad said, gently approaching the scared freshman. "If any asshole messes with you, just let me know. I'll take care of it."

The boy nodded, beaming. To be recognized by a jock like Brad was a major event. Within this sprawling brick and stone TriBeCa school, he was fame personified.

Rob typed in his AOL screen name and password.

"Mr. Cahill?"

He looked up. It was Brad. And only Brad. The rest of the students had scattered. "That was a nice thing you just did."

The teen dream shrugged off the praise. "Can I ask you a personal question?"

Rob felt his cheeks grow warm instantly. It was so hard to look at Brad and not pant with desire. Student or not, he was the kind of man that makes you look twice and then hold the stare. "I'd prefer that you didn't."

"Are you gay?"

Rob avoided eye contact, studying the laptop screen. There was one message from Carson with an attachment. Probably the new cover of *Throb*. Nothing from Nathan. "I'm not going to answer that."

"So you are," Brad challenged.

"This conversation is inappropriate. I'm sponsoring the alliance because a group of students asked me to. It's not a personal matter."

"My dad is gay."

Rob looked up, stunned.

"My parents got divorced when I was seven. A few years later, they sat me down on the couch, and we all read *Daddy's Roommate*."

Rob tried hard not to laugh, barely winning the fight. "That explains your mature attitude toward homosexuality."

"Yeah, I guess. Anyway, I've developed pretty good gaydar." Brad sized up Rob and nodded. "You're definitely in the family."

From his neck, Rob felt a flush begin to spread. "I'm not comfortable with this—"

"I think you and my dad would make a great couple."

Rob blanched. "Excuse me?"

"Are you dating anyone?"

Rob merely stared. This wasn't happening.

"Some people think my dad is my older brother. We look that much alike. He's held up well through the years."

"I don't—"

"You know Gigi Wagner?"

Rob nodded, wondering how the popular cheerleader figured into this.

"She came over to our apartment once to give me a blow job. Afterward, I got caught up with my PlayStation. Guess where she was? Downstairs coming on to my dad! It was just like Mena Suvari from *American Beauty*. She wanted him bad. Still does."

"Good. Fix *them* up," Rob said. Nervously, he began to collect his things.

"Just have dinner with him."

Rob snapped shut the computer and tossed it into his Jack Spade bag. "Not interested."

"At least meet him for coffee. His name's David."

Rob made a move to throw the bag over his shoulder.

But Brad had a firm hold on the satchel.

Rob's gaze blazed a trail from strong hand to muscled arm to tanned and gorgeous face. If the father looked even *half* as good as the son . . .

"This is weird for me, too," Brad admitted. "I've never done this before. You see, my dad's a great guy, and I hate to see him alone. He's always given so much of himself to me— never misses a game, helps me with my homework, the whole bit. But I'm off to college next year. He should concentrate on his own life. He needs a boyfriend. Are you a top or bottom?"

Rob reared back, horrified. "What?"

"Don't worry about it. My dad's versatile."

"This has to stop. Right now. I have no intention of dating your father!"

"I think the two of you would hit it off right away."

"Go home, Brad."

"He usually gets in from the office around seven."

Rob started to leave. "I have no use for that information."

"I take it you haven't graded the career campus tests yet."

Rob returned a suspicious look. Every two weeks he quizzed his business co-op students on media literacy, politics, and popular culture as a way to keep them informed about the world around them. His steadfast policy—a failing grade required parent/teacher contact. No exceptions.

"I bombed, Mr. Cahill," Brad said, feigning despair. "I know that I flunked that test. Looks like you're gonna have to call my dad anyway."

"I should change your name to Hayley Mills in my grade book."

"Who's she?"

"The Parent Trap."

Brad continued to stare blankly.

Rob sighed. He suddenly felt ancient. Maybe Brad should be fixing him up with the grandfather.

5

Whatever Happened to Martika?

The trouble started as soon as Carson returned from Los Angeles. Suddenly everything Rocco did got on his nerves. The way he breathed. The way he chewed. How he sat. Anything he said. It was maddening.

On their way to meet Danny, Rob, and Nathan at Big Cup, a coffeehouse in Chelsea, Carson gave Rocco an exfoliating stare, zeroing in on the Camel Light between the DJ's fleshy lips.

"God!" Carson shrieked. "Can you even go five minutes without a cigarette? You make me sick!"

Rocco stopped. He silently exhaled a cloud of smoke. "What's your problem?"

"I don't know. Emphysema maybe. I'll keep you posted." Carson kept on, halting once he realized that Rocco wasn't following. And then it hit him. What did he ever see in this guy?

Rocco slept around, never paid his full share of the rent, had no appreciation for reruns of *Saved By the Bell*, and listened to nothing but dance music. How could someone rebuke the occasional power ballad? Something like "Hero" by Mariah Carey or "I Turn to You" by Christina Aguilera. Only a poisoned heart could question the healing properties of such earnest ear candy. A dark memory flashed. Rocco had once professed a hatred for songwriter Carole Bayer Sager. That was pure evil. He could be a danger to children.

With this in mind, Carson made no move to double back.

DJ Darth Vader held his position, too.

On Eighth Avenue, there was a Mexican standoff. Totally *High Noon*. But without the guns, Western wear, smelly horses, and Gary Cooper.

Carson took a moment to really study Rocco. He wasn't even that good-looking, especially with clothes on. The true magic was underneath them. That body. God, it was fierce. When Rocco did his shirtless DJ thing at Damage, dancing all around with that eighteen karat gold chain, its SEXY BITCH charm banging up and down on his clavicle, he appeared much cuter than he actually was. Hence, the decision a few months ago—after three martinis, mind you—to practically knock him over the head and drag him home.

The sex had been amazing. So much so that at the end of the day, in spite of the sneaky credit card charges and all the affairs, some behind his back, some right in front of his face, even Carson had to admit—the screwing he was getting was worth the screwing he was getting. But there came a time to move on. That time was now.

"You should probably go back to the apartment and pack your things."

Rocco tossed his cigarette into the gutter. "Why should *I* move out?"

Carson shot back an obvious look. "Because it's my apartment, my name's on the lease, and you can't afford the rent." Then he continued on toward Big Cup, alone and strangely unaffected.

When he arrived, almost every pair of eyes watched him walk in. Very cruisey. Carson was in no mood for cruisey. He wanted coffee and mindless conversation with friends.

A strange-looking young man with glitter on his face gave Carson a hard stare, the kind you give someone at a bar when it's really late and you're horny and you want to wake up alone but not necessarily go to bed alone. That stare.

Carson ignored Glitter Guy, ordered a latte with chocolate orange biscotti, and joined the guys on the couch, sliding in beside Danny. "Will someone please tell the club kid over there that it's eleven o'clock in the morning. He's been watching too much *Queer as Folk*."

Rob smiled. "He was cruising me, too."

Danny exchanged a look with Nathan. "He must not like ethnic guys."

"And such a loss for us," Nathan said.

"Why did we meet here?" Carson asked.

"Because I don't get paid for another week and coffee was all I could afford," Rob said. "Last week's brunch almost wiped me out."

Carson gestured to Glitter Guy. "Say that again, only louder. I'm sure he'll get over you in a hurry."

Nathan scratched his crotch longer than traditional manners allowed.

Carson gave him a curious glance. "Sorry I'm late."

"You're always late," Rob said. "You should talk to a therapist about this Elizabeth Taylor complex."

Danny laughed. "Better than Faye Dunaway. Can you imagine? He'd be a monster."

"Don't fuck with me, fellas!" Carson cried, aping Faye aping Joan from *Mommie Dearest.*

Everybody laughed, except Nathan, who continued to scratch.

"Are you dying over the new cover or what?" Carson demanded without preamble. He always e-mailed them the advance cover proofs of *Throb.* The magazine had made its mark by attracting emerging and established talent for its provocative covers. Not just gay hunks like designer Tom Ford, *Real World* alums Danny Roberts and Chris Beckman, and Rupert Everett, but straight icons like Brad Pitt, Russell Crowe, and Lenny Kravitz. The upcoming issue featured the WB's next wonder stud—Ryan Law.

Rob's eyes lit up. "It reminds me of Matthew McConaughey's first *Vanity Fair* cover. Remember? He just came out of nowhere. I must have stared at that for three days."

Carson had just taken a bite of biscotti and munched fast to make his point. "Exactly! You know how our parents remember exactly where they were when JFK got shot? Well, we have the first Matthew McConaughey cover of *Vanity Fair.* The memory of that day is so vivid to me."

Rob shook his head and laughed.

Danny lobbed a crazy look over to Carson. "Excuse me? We have the deaths of Princess Diana and JFK *Jr.*, thank you."

"Okay," Carson conceded quickly. "But that *Vanity Fair* cover's at least third." He brought a hand to his cheek in a swooning gesture. "*Ryan Law.*" He intoned the name as if it impacted the world. "Isn't he gorgeous? The day of the photo shoot happened to be his twentieth birthday. We had a cake and sang to him, and when he blew out the candles, he closed his eyes really tight and made a wish. It was *so* cute."

Rob rolled his eyes. "And this was a hard day at the office?"

"Well, yes, now that you mention it. I was hard. But only when Ryan stripped down to his swim trunks. I was a total professional the rest of the time."

Nathan scratched his crotch again.

"Is something wrong with you?" Carson asked.

Nathan looked embarrassed. "I started itching in the middle of the night, and it won't let up."

Carson, Danny, and Rob traded knowing glances.

"What?" Nathan asked, paranoid.

Carson decided to go first. Nathan had only jumped into gay life about five minutes ago. Add his inexperience to his snotty, upper-class upbringing, and you had quite a case. "Not meaning to pry . . . but have you had sex recently?"

Rob stared at Nathan, as if daring him to lie.

"Yes. I have a boyfriend. I would've told you, but it's important that we're discreet."

Rob almost lost it. "*Boyfriend?* The guy's *married.* He's got *kids.*"

Carson and Danny traded guilty pleasure looks. A tawdry scandal among friends. Always fun.

Nathan glanced down. "It's complicated."

"Not really," Rob scoffed. "He sends you an e-mail, and you meet for sex in a public restroom. That's pretty simple."

Nathan's eyes didn't leave the floor. Reluctantly, he scratched again.

In silent acknowledgment of how delicious this was, Carson touched his Jil Sander shoe to Danny's Prada loafer. Then he took the plunge. "My guess is that you've got crabs."

Nathan looked up now, his face a mask of incredulity. "But that's an STD."

"A very common one," Carson pointed out. "But easy to take care of. You don't even have to see a doctor. Just go to the drugstore and buy some RID. It'll be gone in about a week. Oh, and remember to wash everything you've worn or slept in with hot water."

Nathan didn't so much as blink. "*You've* had crabs?"

Carson nodded. "Three times in college."

Nathan's eyes got big.

Carson shrugged. "I was going through a slut phase."

"I got them in law school," Danny admitted.

"Summer camp," Rob chimed in. "I had a crush on this counselor, so I stole his underwear and wore it. Big mistake."

Carson laughed. "That's so gross. You should never tell that story."

"I must have something else," Nathan said stubbornly. "I've only been with Mike."

"Mike is a closeted Wall Street prick," Rob snapped. Then he paused a beat and let out a big sigh. "Come on." His voice was softer now as he stood up and gestured for Nathan to take his hand.

"What?"

Rob pulled him up. "Let's have a look in the bathroom. I'll let you know if it's crabs or not."

And off they went.

"I'm glad he's not *my* roommate," Carson said as soon as they were out of earshot.

Danny grinned knowingly. "So how was Los Angeles?"

"I *love* L.A."

"Tell me about this guy."

"His name's Brian, and he looks just like Chris O'Donnell with a military haircut."

"Think you'll see him again?"

Carson thought about it. "Maybe. You could see him if you want."

Danny's eyebrows furrowed. "What do you mean?"

"He's an escort."

"Be serious."

"I am."

"You *paid* for sex?"

"I paid for time. We spent it having sex."

Danny shook his head. "What about Rocco?"

"He's history."

"Since when?"

Carson checked his watch. "About fifteen minutes ago."

"You don't seem upset."

"Rocco is not worth any drama."

"Well, just don't become one of those guys."

"What guys?"

Danny gave him an ominous look. "The guys who start making good money and then become escort junkies. They hire out hunk after hunk for sex as a way to avoid a real relationship."

"I've done it *once*. I spent an hour with the guy. I didn't pay for an overnight so I could hold him in my arms and pretend he was my lover."

Danny leaned back and drank deep on his espresso. He made a face that smacked of regret. "That was judgmental, wasn't it?"

"Uh, *yeah*."

"Sorry. Maybe I should hire an escort, too. It's obviously safer than having a boyfriend who works on Wall Street."

Carson laughed. The little spat was over. "I know Nathan is just *dying*. How much do you want to bet that he comes back here and swears off sex forever?"

Danny grinned. "Nothing more than a pack of gum because that's exactly what he's going to do."

"How's Leo the *Tiger Beat* fantasy?" Carson asked in a singsong voice.

Danny's sigh was heavy. "He invited me to join the group in Miami. They've got three sold-out concerts there." His voice dropped an octave. "He asked the travel agency to put him up in a different hotel. You know, to separate him from the other guys." A long pause. "For more privacy."

Carson began humming the chorus to Four Deep's ubiquitous hit, "Girl, You're in My Heart."

"I'm not sure if I'm going yet," Danny said.

Carson did a double take. "Why not?"

"I represent the entire group. I can't engage in a personal relationship with one member. Even if Leo was a solo act, it'd be unethical."

"I don't get it. Lawyers will think twice about fucking a client, but they'll fuck *over* clients without blinking."

Danny looked pissed. "That's nice. Like I'm an ambulance chaser."

Carson put a comforting hand on his arm. "You're not an ambulance chaser," he said soothingly. "You're a cradle robber. How old is Leo? Twelve?"

Danny couldn't help but laugh a little. "Fuck you. He's nineteen."

"And you are . . ."

"Twenty-eight."

"It's kind of romantic when you think about it. You're his Michael Douglas; he's your Catherine Zeta-Jones."

Danny laughed again. "You're such an asshole."

"Seriously. I think you should go. How long have you been harboring this crush? Get it out of your system. You can't jack off to Four Deep album covers the rest of your life."

Danny barely cracked a smile as he fingered the rim of his espresso cup. "It's not just the ethical dilemma. I think Leo's somebody I could fall in love with, but what kind of relationship could we have? Being outed would destroy his career. The other guys in the group couldn't know. My firm couldn't know. We haven't even hooked up yet and already I'm exhausted from the sneaking around."

Rob and Nathan returned to the scene.

Carson and Danny looked up with interest.

Nathan avoided eye contact.

"It's official," Rob announced. "He's got crabs."

"Congratulations!" Carson said, patting him on the knee. "You're now just as slutty as we are . . . . or have been in the past at least."

Nathan just sat there like a pile of laundry. Finally, he said, "I'm never having sex again."

Carson turned to Danny. "I prefer sugarless. Something minty."

"I can't go to the drugstore and put that stuff on the counter. The clerk will know. I don't even have the nerve to buy condoms yet."

"I'll buy it," Rob offered, exasperated. "We'll pick it up on the way home."

This lifted Nathan's spirits. But only a bit.

"I guess there's no point in playing the Mr. Fantastic game," Danny said. "Nathan has a lock on it."

Whoever had the most notable week—good or bad—was granted that dubious title. Carson surveyed the guys. He still didn't know what Rob had been up to. "Not so fast. I had sex with an escort in L.A. and broke up with Rocco. That's pretty competitive."

"What about me?" Danny broke in. "Leo Summer, lead singer of Four Deep, erotic fantasy to millions, invited me to Miami. And not just to go over contracts."

Rob leaned forward, not about to be upstaged this time. "A student is trying to fix me up with his father."

Carson, Danny, and Nathan just looked at him, not quite believing it.

"It's true. He even failed a test on purpose just so we'd meet at a parent/teacher conference."

Carson got quiet. Rob never even made runner up for Mr. Fantastic, but this was good stuff. "It sounds like the gay version of *Parent Trap.*"

"I'm way ahead of you on the Hayley Mills jokes," Rob said.

Carson and Danny turned to each other, then to Nathan.

"I know," Nathan grumbled. "Crabs is too normal."

Rob beamed. "Could it be? Am I Mr. Fantastic?"

Carson and Danny confirmed it with a nod.

"This is such an honor," Rob said, placing hand over heart. "First and foremost, I'd like to thank the academy."

Everybody howled.

"Hey, I almost forgot," Rob blurted. Reaching into his Jack Spade bag, he dug around for several seconds. "I brought something for show and tell. Ah, there it is." He pulled out what looked like a trading card. "I found this in the hall at school. It's a scream."

"What is that?" Carson demanded, grabbing the goody first. It resembled a baseball card, only this was no shortstop. Cody was a sixteen-year-old Virgo from Tennessee. He loved science, the movie *The Matrix,* and kindness and a sense of humor in girls.

Carson passed it to Danny. "If things don't work out with Leo . . ."

"Girls at school love these," Rob explained. "A few have some cyber romances going. You can e-mail these guys."

Carson swiped the card from Danny to take another look. "Did you get in touch with everyone about the question of the week?"

Danny just sat there.

Carson nudged him with an elbow.

"No, it's been a crazy week. I ate dinner at my desk every night—including Friday."

"Okay, you have a high pressure job. We believe you," Carson said. It annoyed him whenever Danny played the corporate martyr. The guy made an insane amount of money for someone his age. Now Carson addressed the group. "What do you consider boyfriend material?"

"Is this going to end up in your magazine?" Rob asked.

Carson gave a diffident shrug. "I don't know. Maybe."

"Then this qualifies as research. You owe me for the coffee."

"You need a better job," Carson snapped.

"I love teaching!"

"But it doesn't pay enough," Carson argued.

Rob jutted out his chin. "Everything isn't about money."

"So you wouldn't consider *wealth* boyfriend material?" Carson asked, skillfully bringing things back on point.

Rob paused, deep in thought. "Not really. For me, it's about intelligence. I want a smart man. One with a lifetime membership in MENSA would be nice."

Danny leaned forward, a teasing glint in his dark eyes. "What if a guy was really dumb, but he looked like Dean Cain?"

Carson smiled.

Rob wavered. "How much does he look like him?"

Danny gave Carson a sinister grin. "He's a genetic clone."

"Under those circumstances, I'd work past the stupidity. Maybe I could give him some books to read and tutor him on the side."

Carson decided to join in. "I want a guy with a real career. I mean, Rocco was a DJ, and my last boyfriend, Larry—"

"Lance," Danny corrected.

Carson looked at him. "Huh?"

"Your last boyfriend was Lance. Larry was seasonal help at Gucci. You had a crush on him last Christmas. He's the reason you spent eight hundred dollars on a pair of motorcycle boots."

Carson mulled this over. "Oh . . . that's right." No wonder he was still paying off his Citibank Visa. "Anyway, *Lance* was a bartender, which is fine. I have nothing against DJs and bartenders. They play great music and fix me drinks, but I want a guy who has a job that a college student can't get. Is that too much to ask?"

Nathan spoke up. "So the perfect man is smart, looks like Dean Cain, and has a great job?"

Carson, Danny, and Rob nodded in agreement.

"That's not realistic. It's no wonder the three of you are single."

"Ooh," Carson trilled. "I see the crabs have made you itchy *and* bitchy."

"For instance, take Mike," Nathan began.

But Rob held up a hand to stop him. "No, let's not take Mike. I don't know which is worse—the pubic lice or the wife and kids."

"The wife and kids," Carson answered. "For five dollars you can get rid of crabs in a week or so."

"I'm not absolutely sure that the crabs are Mike's fault," Nathan protested. "Maybe he got them from his wife. Maybe she's a skank. He likes me. I know—"

Now Carson interrupted. He couldn't let this shit go on another second. Nathan needed to start riding the gay life bike without training wheels. "Mike doesn't like you in a romantic way," he said gently but matter-of-factly. "You're his dirty little secret. I bet you don't even have his real e-mail address. It's probably some lame screen name like WallStreetStud."

Nathan's mouth fell open. His eyes looked suddenly heavy. That's what an instant of tough realization could do. "Wall-StreetTop," he whispered miserably.

"Here's another test—do you have his number at work?" Danny asked.

Nathan shook his head. "He says it's hard to talk there. Things get crazy with all the stock trading."

"Move on," Carson advised. "When you pick up RID, use it in the physical *and* metaphorical sense." He focused in on the trading card again, not studying Cody so much as the concept. Suddenly his heart picked up speed, the idea engine revving up. "This could be brilliant," he murmured, primarily to himself. Carson's mind began to spin. The possibilities were endless. Oh, God, it could be huge! He put a hand on Danny's knee to steady himself. With great flourish, he slapped the Cody card on the table.

Danny looked at it. "I'm having impure thoughts. Put it away."

"Wouldn't it be great if you could sift through a pack of cards for an available man? Think about it. A card like this could tell you whether a guy was boyfriend material or not. Everyone I know needs help on that front." He gestured to Nathan. "Case number one." He thrust both thumbs in his own direction. "Case number two—myself. Rocco was *so* not boyfriend material. I broke up with him and felt nothing, not even a second of regret. I mean, he was still within spitting distance, and I was already itemizing a shopping list in my head. Which reminds me. I want a new hat from Burberry's. Who wants to go shopping after this?"

"I'll go," Danny volunteered.

"That's ridiculous," Rob scoffed.

"Burberry is hotter than ever!" Carson shouted.

"Not that. This trading card idea. It would never work," Rob said.

Carson sat ready to debate this to the death. "Why not?"

"That gimmick is cool for thirteen-year-olds, not thirty-year-olds."

Carson scooted forward and with his index finger tapped Cody's forehead three times. "There is an intense psychic connection between the thirteen-year-old girl and the adult gay man."

Rob slumped backward, still unconvinced. "Speak for yourself."

Carson sat up straight. "Raise your hand if the new Four Deep album is in your CD player."

Danny's hand went up first.

Then Nathan's.

And, reluctantly, Rob's.

Carson grinned. "Keep your hand up if the screen saver on your computer is your favorite movie, TV, or pop star."

Not a single hand went down.

Carson's smile widened. "If your savings account is fair game for a shopping spree, keep that hand up."

Everybody remained frozen.

Carson beamed triumphant. "I know your arms are getting tired, but I have one more question. If you thought to yourself, 'That guy at the counter in the Gap T-shirt is really cute,' don't you dare move."

Rob closed his eyes in wrenching defeat. "Oh, man, I'm such a *girl*!"

Danny and Nathan laughed.

Carson was too busy planning his future to join them.

From out of the blue, Danny asked, "Hey, whatever happened to Martika?"

Rob pulled a face. "Where did that come from?"

"I don't know," Danny said. "She just suddenly came to mind."

"Didn't she sing 'Toy Soldiers'?" Nathan asked.

Danny nodded.

Carson sighed and stood up to leave. "Okay, boys, I'm out of here before somebody starts asking about Stacey Q."

6

What It's Like to Wake Up
with a Pop Star

Pop stars don't have morning breath. When Leo rolled over to kiss Danny, it was like a Big Red commercial come to life. Danny's sample size for this survey wasn't large. Just one to be exact. Granted, it would be nice to throw Justin, J.C., both Nicks (Carter and Lachey), Ricky, Enrique, and the guy in O-Town named after the lead actor from *CHiPs* into the experiment, but, if, at the end of the day, he had to settle for Leo Summer and Leo Summer alone, then what the hell. He could live with that.

"Can I ask a tacky question?" Danny ventured.

"No, I haven't hooked up with any of the guys in the band."

"That's not what I was going to ask."

Leo playfully bit down on Danny's lower lip. "Yeah, right. I read the online message boards. All the queers have fantasies about us in one orgy and circle jerk after another."

"I don't think people *really* fantasize about Chad, Greg, and Damian. They're just trying to be polite."

Leo rolled over and stared at the ceiling. "You'd be surprised. There's a mother/daughter groupie team that kicks it regularly with Greg. They followed us to almost every city on the last tour. Now he refuses to have sex with just one girl. He says it feels like masturbation."

Danny laughed. "Are you serious?"

Leo reached over and stroked Danny's inner thigh. "Of course, I am. This isn't the button down world you're used to.

In fact, you're the first person in months who's made it into my bed without blowing one of the roadies first."

"You know, that'd be a nice lyric to a country song."

Leo smiled. "God, it's nice to wake up with someone who doesn't want me to autograph their dick or their ass or their tits. Groupies are so boring."

"You're bisexual?"

"Not really. I just sleep with enough girls to control the gay rumors." He sighed. "So what's the tacky question? I won't think any less of you. I promise."

"How much does this room cost per night?"

They were at the Shore Club in South Beach, nestled inside a six thousand square foot, three-story penthouse with its own steam room, sauna, and pool. The night view of Miami Beach was the stuff of gasps and infinite gazes. The other members of Four Deep were staying at Ian Schrager's Delano Hotel a few dunes down. Danny felt like he and Leo were in another world.

"Regular people pay ten thousand dollars," Leo said.

"Isn't that a bit oxymoronic?"

"What do you mean?"

Danny checked himself. Leo had stopped going to formal school after the ninth grade. "How could a regular person afford to pay ten thousand a night?"

"I guess I mean to say *nonfamous* people. The manager promised to comp me a few nights if I called his daughter on her birthday. Not a bad deal. After she stopped crying, it only took about five minutes."

Danny spooned into Leo and snaked his hand down the naturally smooth chest that right now was pinned up on millions of adolescent bedroom walls. A giddy feeling came over him. He tried to suppress a laugh but lost the fight.

Leo rubbed against him. "What's so funny?"

"I was just thinking."

"About . . ."

"All those people screaming for you at the concert last night. And you end up here with me. It's wild."

Leo groaned, extricated himself from Danny, and got out of bed. "Don't make noises like a fan." He was nude, his well-kept body a golden bronze from just a single day napping on one of the giant mattresses around the main pool.

This smug, mercurial quality would normally cause Danny to lose interest, but Leo wore it so well that Danny found himself more intrigued than ever.

Leo lit up a Marlboro Light and dragged deep. "I need another fan like I need a fucking hole in my head."

Danny watched this perfectly arrogant bitch god in almost amazement. He'd come off so sweet on that MTV *Diary* special. "You said groupies were boring. Well, so are whiny teen idols."

Leo turned around and stared at Danny for a long time, puffing curls of smoke, glowering with sleepy eyes, growing impressively erect.

Danny gave him a knowing smirk. "You're probably going to tell me that you hate your own music."

Leo opened his mouth to answer.

But Danny cut him off. "Wait. Let me take a shot at it. Rock's where your heart really is, and you want to write your own songs, too."

Leo crawled back into bed and straddled Danny's chest. "Yeah. Me and Leif Garrett." He leaned in and braced his hands against the wall to feed Danny his impressive cock while singing "I Was Made for Dancin'" all the way to heaven.

That was the last time Danny saw Leo for the remainder of the weekend. There were media appearances, sound checks, a studio session to record Spanish vocals for "Girl, You're In My Heart," and, of course, another sold-out concert.

To pass the time, Danny amused himself with every available luxury. He ordered insanely expensive items from room service, booked a facial and massage at the Sundari spa, purchased a new watch that he didn't need at Me & Ro on the Shore Club's ground floor, and leafed through the *Miami Herald* on one of the sherbety-colored leather couches in the lobby.

Bored and more than a little lonely, he meandered through the property's paved orchard, taking in the white-flowered ligustrum trees with a ho-hum attitude. Glancing at the time, he made a face. Still hours to kill before his flight out. He thought about heading over to the St. Augustine Hotel. A hot bartender there had been written up in *Ocean Drive*. But those kind of missions were no fun without Carson. Impulsively, he hit the first speed dial number on his cell phone.

Carson answered singing Four Deep's first big hit, "All My Love 4Ever, Girl."

"Guess what I'm walking on," Danny teased.

"The bodies of the twelve-year-old girls you killed to have Leo all to yourself?"

"No, smart-ass. The soles of my Prada slip-ons are currently atop Portuguese cobblestone at the Shore Club in South Beach."

"How lovely. My brand-new Adidas just stepped in gum on Prince Street. So, tell me, are you *Mrs.* Leo Summer yet?"

Danny could hear Nathan laughing in the background. He felt an instant's pure envy. "Is Rob there, too?"

"Hell, no. We're shopping designer retail, and he only buys at outlet stores."

Danny let out a morose sigh. "I suppose I'll just go up to the penthouse and detoxify in the steam room."

"Hey, why don't you call up the Hilton sisters. Maybe they'll come over and play."

"Now I know how Barbara Hutton and Christina Onassis felt. A three-story hotel suite is kind of creepy if you're alone."

"Oh, the poor little rich girl. You could go see that cute bartender at the St. Augustine and tell him all your problems over an Absolut Kurant kamikaze."

"Believe me. I've thought about it."

"Listen," Carson began distractedly, "we just hit D&G, and I have to stay with Nathan every second. Otherwise, he'll walk out of here with a fagged out Lenny Kravitz costume. Call me later." *Click.*

Danny kept the phone to his ear, not quite ready to let the connection go. Then he cleared the line, and, rebuking every voice in his head that told him not to, called Leo's cellular.

"How much do you miss me?" Leo asked.

"Lots," Danny confessed. "I can hardly stand being in the

room. And then I'm in one of the gift shops and find you staring at me from the cover of *Rolling Stone*. I believe the headline was 'The Six Million Dollar Hunk.' "

Leo scoffed. "Just the word 'hunk' is gross. It's not part of my reality."

There was a meaningful moment of silence.

"I shouldn't even be talking," Leo said. "I have to save my voice for the show."

"I fly back to New York in a few hours."

"Next weekend we play two nights in Vegas."

Danny knew it would be the same scenario all over again. He'd watch the concert from the VIP section, wait at the hotel for a few hours, and finally get Leo for a night of incredible sex and a quick breakfast the next morning. As relationships go, you couldn't get more shallow. Even so, Danny heard himself say, "I'll be there."

7

Out for Dinner

Nathan arranged to meet Tia Elliott at Pastis, a hot Parisian-style bistro in the meat packing district. She arrived a half hour late with a slim Nokia attached to her ear like an unsightly growth that needed to be removed.

"See where Andre is with the regression analysis. I'm just grabbing a quick bite, and then I'll be back."

Nathan stood up, waiting to be acknowledged.

Tia signed off and hugged him. "Oh, Nathan, why did our mothers make us do this?" She leaned back and really looked at him now, taking in his new D&G ensemble with patronizing amusement. "Interesting clothes. Are they wearing you, or are you wearing them?"

The waiter swooped in to inquire about drinks.

Tia glanced at her watch. "This is going to be a fast meal. I need caffeine. Bring me coffee *and* a Coke. Don't bother with appetizers. I can't even concentrate on the menu, so I'll take the chef's special, as long as it isn't red meat."

"Tonight we have a wonderful—"

Tia raised a hand to stop him. "Don't bother with the script. My nerves can't take it. Just surprise me. I'm sure it's great."

The waiter turned to Nathan.

"I'll have the same, I guess," he murmured, embarrassed, wondering why Tia hadn't just ordered her meal to go, or better yet, canceled altogether. Audrey Williams had painted this picture of a meek young woman alone in the big bad city. But it was fairly obvious that Tia Elliott had the capacity to eat her young without spilling a drop of blood on her Armani wardrobe.

"Did you really want to do this, Nathan? Be honest."

"Of course," he lied. "It's been—"

"Because I didn't. Blasts from the past don't do anything for me. I believe in looking forward." She drummed her neat, closely trimmed nails impatiently. "Where the hell is the waiter with my drinks?"

"He just left the table. Give him a chance."

Tia scowled, taking a moment to check her reflection in the antique mirror that lined the wall.

Nathan attempted a smile. "I'm trying to think of the last time we saw each other."

"Sophomore year. Christmas brunch at the country club. You had braids, a goatee, and had just denounced medicine as a career. Your parents barely spoke a word."

Nathan's eyes went wide.

Tia shrugged. "I'm a detail person."

"So you're working at Goldman—"

"Let's not do the small talk thing. I just might choke on the bullshit. Do you even know the Heimlich maneuver?"

He remembered Tia as bossy, rude, and generally impossible to deal with, but he'd never wanted to push her down the side of a mountain. Like he did right now.

The caffeine fixes arrived.

Tia knocked hers down like a gunslinger in the Last Chance Saloon.

Nathan stared at the fan pattern in the mosaic floor.

"It'd be so much easier if you'd just come out to your mother. Then she'd tell my mother, and they'd stop trying to set us up."

Nathan looked at her, stunned.

"I'm sure she already knows. Deep down. It's just a matter of putting the issue on the table."

"Tia, I don't know what—"

"Nathan. Please. I suspected long ago. And I knew for sure the night of the junior prom."

It was an eerie feeling to know that the secret which had

taken so long to accept himself had been obvious to other people. Even an Antichrist like Tia Elliott. At this point, it seemed futile to go into denial. "How did you know?"

Tia laughed at him. "You went with Veronica Ash, and all you did was kiss her cheek! That girl was so easy. I knew guys who could get a feel between classes. Prom night would've been a definite score." She paused a beat. "And I saw the way you used to look at my brother, Christian. He's gay, too, you know."

Nathan's mouth dropped open. Christian had been the proverbial golden boy—perfect grades, star athlete, boyfriend to the prettiest girls. Everything about him smacked of rock-ribbed heterosexuality.

"You can close your mouth now," Tia said, rolling her eyes. "He's got a boyfriend."

Dazed, Nathan could hardly think. He drank the coffee too fast and practically scalded his mouth. He tried to play it off, casually asking, "Where does he live these days?"

"Basically everywhere. But he keeps an apartment here. It's in Chelsea Heights. He's a personal trainer and travels a lot with his clients."

Nathan thought of Christian's body, the one that had been the inspired visual for a thousand or more self-gratification sessions. "Anyone famous?"

"I don't keep up with celebrities, so none of the names mean anything to me. He does train the lead singer from Four Deep. I remember that much."

Nathan leaned forward excitedly. *"Leo Summer?"*

Tia gave him a strange look. "I think so."

"One of my best friends is Leo's attorney."

"Like, wow," Tia snarled, mocking him in a vacuous teenage white girl voice.

Her cellular jingled. She glanced at the screen. "I can't get away for a fucking minute." There was more self-importance than misery in her complaint. Tia rose, walking away to take the call. A few minutes later, she returned and downed what remained of her Coke without taking her seat. "I have to go. Cancel my order when you see the waiter."

Nathan experienced genuine relief. He would much rather

dine alone than sit across from this bitch. "I hope everything's okay."

"It will be. As soon as I fire my idiot assistant. Listen, I'll tell my mother we had a nice time. You'll do the same with yours?"

Nathan grinned. "Consider it done."

Tia waved him off and started to walk away, then suddenly doubled back. "When do you plan on telling your parents that you're gay?"

Nathan mulled the thought and shrugged. "I'm on my own now, and it's really none of their business. I don't plan on making some big announcement."

Tia gave him a frustrated look.

"Why?"

"I'm dating a white guy, and it's getting serious. So I was thinking that if you told your secret and I told mine, then our parents could console each other. And since my parents would be getting the better bad news, maybe I'd get less shit from my mother."

Nathan couldn't believe Tia's audacity. "Well, that certainly works for you. I take it your parents don't know about Christian."

"Are you kidding? He's so deep in the closet he needs a survival guide to help him find his way out."

Nathan laughed. "I think his secret's safe. I never would've pegged him as gay. I'm still shocked."

"I better run. I'd say call me and we'll try dinner again sometime, but I'm really not interested in doing that."

Nathan wasn't offended. "Good. I'm not either."

Tia smiled. "Well, I can't exactly say that it was nice to see you again."

"I know," Nathan agreed. "This was awful." He paused a beat. "But I'll pay for your drinks if you give me Christian's phone number."

Tia dug into her purse and threw down a ten dollar bill. "I just got off cheap. I would've paid every drink tab in the whole restaurant to avoid that."

8

The Heloise Effect

Rob saved the grading of Brad Pike's career campus test for last. The teenager's answers were ridiculous. He knew better than to say that Enron was an antianxiety medication, that Halle Berry had won the Best Actress Oscar for flashing her boobs in *Swordfish,* and that a 401(K) had something to do with a man's sperm count.

Beyond failing the quiz, though, Rob had a more serious issue to discuss with the boy's father. Brad had been fired from his off campus job at a sports marketing firm for hooking up with a receptionist in the copy room.

This is why Rob tried to avoid approving students like him for the business co-op program. Brad had solid grades, enough core academic credits to graduate, and was well on his way to a good college. He just wanted a laid back senior year with all the enviable schedule trappings.

Rob thumbed through his current semester files until he found Brad's contact sheet. There were home and work numbers for his father. He tried the former first.

The voice that answered sounded just like Brad's.

Rob hesitated at first. "Brad?"

"No, David here. Brad's upstairs with a girl from school."

What else? Rob cleared his throat. "This is Mr. Cahill, his co-op teacher."

David laughed a little. "He told me you'd be calling. Can you give him a makeup on that test? You have my word that he won't write down answers from Mars next time."

"Has Brad talked to you about what happened at The Janssen Group?"

"That's the sports marketing firm he works for, right? I hear it's going well. Thanks for lining up the job. He loves it. Good money, too. I never saw checks like that in high school."

Rob allowed a beat to pass. "He was fired on Friday."

"Shit! Are you serious? Why'd they do that?"

Rob explained the transgression.

David didn't appear concerned. "Women have been throwing their panties at Brad since he was fourteen or fifteen. Can you get him on at another company?"

"It's not that simple, Mr. Pike."

"Call me David."

"Okay. David. It's policy that any student terminated for cause be expelled from the program."

"Oh, I see. So that's the end of it? He's kicked out?"

"I wish there was something I could do."

"How about not kicking him out?"

"Mr. Pike—"

"Oh, we're back to that now?"

"I'm sorry. David. Brad's a great kid. I—"

"At least give me a chance to get Brad's side of the story. Are you free for coffee tomorrow? We can talk this over then."

"My day starts very early."

"No problem. I'll skip my morning workout. How does seven o'clock work for you?" He suggested a Starbucks location near the school.

Rob agreed, hung up, and suddenly began obsessing over what to wear, how long it'd been since he exercised, and whether or not it was true when people told him that he favored a young Kurt Russell from *The Computer Wore Tennis Shoes* years.

He burned nervous energy by going on a cleaning binge, putting the Heloise treatment to everything. This included folding out the sleeper sofa and making up the bed for Nathan.

Rob had purchased a one-bedroom apartment in the City-lights building for one hundred sixty thousand. A good deal.

But it meant living in the Long Island City neighborhood of Queens. Still, it felt good to watch his monthly salary go out the door in the form of a mortgage note instead of a rent check. Plus, with Nathan paying him a tidy lodging fee, Rob had been able to squeeze in an extra payment last year.

Nathan's temporary stay had gradually morphed into something semi permanent. The living space was small, but when Rob first moved to New York, he'd shacked up with two other guys in less square footage than this, so Nathan's presence didn't bother him. In fact, he rather enjoyed it. From his Houston home with two brothers and two sisters to dorm living at the University of Texas in Austin to his New York digs, first with two closeted jocks, now with an out-and-a-danger-to-himself gallery manager, Rob had never lived alone.

Why? For reasons like this one: the apartment was spotless, and he was standing in the tiny kitchen eating saltine crackers with grape jelly, Ben & Jerry's Concession Obsession, and Jose Olé mini taquitos, washing each course down with water, swearing to himself that he would stop, and then starting all over again, merely killing time until Nathan arrived home.

Rob's heart lifted when he heard the key in the door. "How was dinner?"

"Tia had to leave, so I ended up eating by myself. But it was great."

"Why didn't you call me? I've never been to Pastis. I would've joined you."

"I didn't think of it." Nathan shrugged and looked around. "You must've talked to that student's father."

"Why do you say that?"

"You always clean when you're sexually insecure."

"If that's the case, maybe I should quit teaching and become a maid. I'm meeting him for coffee in the morning. Do you think a pink Oxford and khakis is too gay?"

"No, I think it's too frat boy goes home for Easter, but you look great in that, so wear it. Have you talked to Danny?"

Rob shook his head no. "I talked to Carson, though. Danny had a great time with Leo in Miami, and he's meeting him in Las Vegas this weekend."

"He's just like that woman who wrote *I'm With the Band*. What's her name?" Nathan took the spoon from Rob's hand and stabbed a generous bite of ice cream.

"Pamela Des Barres. That book made me fall in love with Don Johnson all over again. It's no wonder Melanie Griffith married him twice. He's hung like a—"

"I just found out that the love of my life is Leo Summer's personal trainer. If I write a letter and give it to Danny, do you think he'll give it to Leo to give to Christian?"

Rob grabbed the spoon. "I have no idea what you're talking about, but as a high school teacher, I must go on record as saying that your plan sounds very seventh grade."

9

Notice the Ring

In the midst of a messy breakup, it's better to inform every-one as soon as possible to avoid an awkward situation. With this in mind, Carson instructed his assistant to send a change of address card to his personal mailing list. It read:

CARSON ST. JOHN REGRETS TO INFORM YOU THAT DUE TO A SIGNIFICANT SHORTAGE OF REDEEMABLE QUALITIES, ROCCO TOCHES CAN NO LONGER BE REACHED AT THIS ADDRESS. HE NOW RESIDES AT AN UNKNOWN LOCATION.

"You really want this to go out?" Plum Kinsella asked. She was Madonna British (originally from Michigan but game enough to fake an accent and front an attitude), a perfect size zero, and slumming at the *Throb* offices until something like a fact checker position opened up at *Vogue*.

Carson gave her a dumb look. "Yeah, I really do." This tickled his memory. He rifled through his Louis Vuitton shoul-der bag (obscenely expensive, still paying for it eighteen months later) and pulled out a Palm Pilot. "Send one to every address you can find on this, too. Then messenger it over to Rocco at Damage."

Plum shook her head disapprovingly.

"At least I'm giving it back. If I were a real asshole, I would've chucked the stupid thing into the Hudson."

Plum rolled her eyes. "I stand corrected. You're a class act."

Carson smiled tightly. "Just get them out today. Okay, Plum?" He turned his attention back to the rough concept samples of boyfriend material trading cards. The art department had done a great job on such short notice.

"Carson St. John?" A man's voice and three fast knocks hit the air in concert.

Carson looked up to see a dream of a guy standing in the open doorway. *Thank God that's my name.* "Before you serve me with papers, I should say that I fully intend to buy a CD at regular club prices before the end of the year."

The man grinned. "Sorry, I'm not here on behalf of Columbia House." He crossed the room to Carson's desk and offered a large hand. "Gil Bellak, Full Picture Associates."

Carson blanched. His eleven o'clock appointment. Naturally, Plum had done nothing to even resemble a marginally competent assistant—remind him, print out the day's schedule, etc. And he'd been too busy all morning with his anti-Rocco correspondence to check his own calendar.

Gil had an Owen Wilson vibe going strong—athletic build, blond hair, a badly broken nose, killer lips, and a laconic drawl that sounded sexy as hell. His shake was firm, and he offered intense, confident eye contact.

"Here," Plum said, passing Gil one of the postcards. "Everyone else is getting one."

Gil scanned the offering and laughed. "Didn't work out, huh?"

"Can't keep anything from you." Simultaneously, Carson tried to shield his embarrassment and figure out a way to transfer Plum to a magazine even less to her choosing, like *Field and Stream.* "Can we offer you anything to drink?"

"Coffee would be great. With cream and sugar."

Carson turned to Plum with an obvious look.

"The machine's broken again," she said, as if the matter were closed now.

Forget *Field and Stream.* He would FedEx her to one of Larry Flynt's rags. "There's a coffee shop on the first floor. I'll take a hot water with lemon."

Plum hated any task that smacked of a Hazel existence. She gave him a little glare, snapped, "Answer your phone," and then left.

Carson gestured for Gil to have a seat in the cozy conference area adjacent to his desk. A sudden nervous energy settled in his stomach. Matthew Redmond, the publisher of *Throb*, had scheduled the appointment and insisted that Carson meet with this guy, a celebrated media consultant with a notorious reputation for swooping in to tell magazines, radio and television stations, and Internet companies what they were doing wrong. His notoriety came from the fact that he was so right so often that the words "After Gil . . ." had become a coveted industry phrase. It meant you were better off than before.

None of this mattered, though, because Carson hated consultants. They made too much money and were always waiting on an urgent fax. Hotel workers should get special combat pay for all the consultants who stalk the front desk to ask, "Did I get a fax?" How does one go about becoming a consultant? What are the qualifications? Why couldn't Carson be one for, say, the Academy Awards? Don't let Whoopi Goldberg host the show ever again. There. He just consulted. Two thousand dollars, please.

It didn't help that Gil Bellak was so fucking attractive. Now Carson actually wanted to listen to everything he had to say, if only to look at him and hear his voice for a few hours.

"I've analyzed the last twenty-four issues of *Throb*. You've done a great job," Gil began.

"But?"

Gil gave him a defensive look.

Carson glanced down at Gil's shoes, which revealed a lot about a man. More than the contents of his wallet sometimes. Black Ferragamos. Nice. Expensive, too. But they could stand a polish. And as a general rule, Carson had big problems with men who refused to wear Gucci loafers. "There's always a but. This is the part where you tell me everything that's wrong with the magazine."

Gil sighed. "Try to think of me as an ally, not an adversary."

"That's a tough order, Gil. You see, I did some analyzing of my own. Every magazine you work with ends up with increased ad sales, higher circulation . . . and a new editor."

Gil shrugged. "Some people have difficulty accepting new ideas."

Carson stalled a moment, realizing he had few options. The publisher was paying Gil Bellak an enormous sum just to be here. Top consultants were like supermodels. They didn't get up in the morning unless you paid them ten thousand dollars. So if he wasn't willing to work with this guy, then he better be willing to resign. And he loved *Throb* too much to leave. At least right now.

"Let me tell you a little bit about my background," Gil began.

Carson fought back an audible groan. He couldn't stand it when people talked their resumes. Gil got a pass, though. But only because he was so great-looking. Carson watched him blather on, barely taking in a word, too mesmerized by the delicious shape of his mouth. There might've been something about studying photography and comparative literature in Paris at American University. He couldn't say for sure.

Plum returned with the drinks and a fresh copy of her resume. "If you happen to know anyone at *Vogue* . . ."

"Actually, I had lunch with Anna Wintour last week," Gil said, taking a quick peek at Plum's paper history.

Carson silently mouthed the words, "Get out."

Plum gave him a fuck you smile and exited, closing the door behind her.

Carson laughed a little. "I don't know what to do with her. She came highly recommended from *Teen People.* I think they just wanted to get rid of her."

Gil drank deep on his coffee.

For the first time, Carson noticed his ring—a simple gold band on the meaningful finger. "You're married?"

Gil nodded. "Three kids." He smiled. "Two girls and a boy."

"Of course."

"Why do you say that?"

"Three is the new two. Your line of work obviously keeps you apprised of all things state of the trend." He squeezed juice from the lemon wedge into the hot water. "Can I ask you something?"

"Shoot."

"Why should I be interested in hearing a straight married man's notes on a gay magazine?"

"Let me put it this way: I'm not a young urban black male, but last year I took *Chill* off the chopping block. Advertising's up thirty percent. Circulation's up ten."

"There must be some affinity. Maybe you dream about being a rap star."

"I'm into classic rock."

"Well, for my own peace of mind, at least tell me you're a closeted bisexual."

"Sorry."

"Mildly curious?"

Gil shook his head no.

"I don't believe you," Carson said. "Let's play a short game. I'll say a word or phrase, and you respond with the first thing that pops into your mind. Ready?"

Gil grinned. "Fire away."

"Calvin Klein."

"Christy Turlington."

"Locker room."

"Body odor."

"Sale at Barney's."

"Boring."

"Matt Damon."

"Good Will Hunting."

"Cutest member of *NSYNC."

Gil hesitated, as if raiding his memory file for a name. "Shit, I get those guys confused . . . Chris."

Carson let out a frustrated sigh. Not a single ambiguous answer. "You *are* straight."

"Told you. I never lie to my clients."

"Okay, Jedi Master. What do we need to do to make *Throb* beat faster?"

Gil smiled. "Spend more money."

"I have no problem with that. But *you're* going to tell Matthew. Last month he banned us from making directory assistance calls. And he hates working lunches. There are ten-year-olds on the Upper East Side with allowances larger than my expense account."

"Don't worry. I'll make the case to Matt." Gil leaned in, propping his elbows on his knees. "*Throb* is struggling to find its voice in a crowded field. Look at your competition. *Out, Genre, Instinct,* a number of British imports—almost all of them are obsessed with style and hard bodies. Gay men in their late twenties and thirties have outgrown that."

Carson raised his hand slightly to stop him. "You're speaking from the depths of your heterosexual heart now."

Gil gave him a bullish look. "I think there's room for something new. The magazine business is volatile. Your ad sales are slipping. Subscriptions are down. Keep targeting *Throb* to twenty-year-old gym bunnies, and you'll be packing boxes this time next year."

Carson glanced over to his desk. The mock-ups of the boyfriend material trading cards were right on top. His great idea to jump-start the magazine felt very *YM* right now. Rob's voice rang inside his head. *That gimmick is cool for thirteen-year-olds, not thirty-year-olds.* Gil would laugh him out of the room if he pitched that concept.

"I think *Throb* should relaunch in a format to *enhance* the lives of its readers. There's an essential quality to magazines—the smell and feel of the paper, the caliber of the writing and photography—it's a real craft. My recommendation to Matthew will be this: pump enough cash into *Throb* to make it the most luxurious magazine in the marketplace for gay men."

Carson regarded Gil for a moment. Here sat a rich, smart, handsome, straight guy with a great sense of humor and not a trace of homophobia. It just wasn't fair that a woman woke up next to him every morning.

"This could mean going smaller in terms of circulation," Gil continued. "The key will be establishing a stronger connection to the reader while staying ahead of the mainstream."

Carson nodded to the beat of Gil's enthusiasm. He had no

qualms about putting his career in someone else's hands, provided those hands were brilliant and well manicured. "What
about our online presence? I've been trying to convince
Matthew for months to overhaul the Web site."

Gil shook his head no again. Emphatically. "Online readers
are fat and old. Why invest in a free product for the cubicle
set just looking for a quick escape? The offline audience is
your bread and butter. They're loyalists, and they'll save back
issues like souvenirs. Besides, you can't take a computer to the
john." He laughed. "I do think we should generate some sort
of Internet companion to *Throb*. Maybe a subscriber-based
daily e-mail. Ultimately, I see *Throb* lifestyle conferences in
major markets across the country. This could be a huge revenue stream and really build the brand."

Carson was nothing short of amazed. "If you weren't already married, I'd propose to you right now."

Gil laughed. "I suppose you have too much dignity to settle
for being my mistress."

"Actually, I don't. If you put me up in a better apartment,
I'm yours."

Gil shook a finger at Carson. "You're funny. That doesn't
resonate in your letter from the editor. We need to boost your
profile. Tina Brown transformed the editor in chief position
into a glamorous role. You should be a boldface name in the
columns. Brendan Lemon wrote about his closested baseball
player boyfriend in *Out* and turned up everywhere. That's
what we need for you."

"I'm more than willing to have an affair with Derek Jeter
and then write about it."

Gil gave Carson a long, intense stare. "You need a column.
Something like Candace Bushnell's original 'Sex and the City'
pieces for the *New York Observer.*"

"Boyfriend Material," Carson said quickly, hoping to salvage at least part of his plan. "The universal gay obsession—
finding one, keeping one, getting over one, living without
one."

Gil smiled broadly and punched the air with a triumphant
fist. "That's fucking brilliant." He stood up and assumed the
high five position.

Carson went through the motions, but it was all too NFL Sunday for him.

"Give me an idea for the first one," Gil said. "Fast. Off the top of your head. For a column to work it has to come organically."

"I just got back from L.A. where I shelled out two hundred fifty bucks for my first male escort."

Gil liked this. His eyes sparkled. "I've got an idea. Road test an escort here in New York. Compare the two. Make it an East Coast/West Coast comparison."

"That could be dangerous," Carson said. "Remember what happened with the rappers? The escorts might start killing each other."

10

Black Cat

SELL SOME GODDAMN PAINTINGS!

This note was neatly printed onto a Post-It and affixed to Nathan's computer screen. At least it was clear. No ambiguity to sort out. The last show by a British artist whose work centered around Monopoly game pieces had sold poorly. Nathan had known that it would only be a matter of time before John Frankovich turned up the heat.

Managing an art gallery was like any sales profession. It demanded a lot of lunching, dining, partying, all of it with an eye toward networking, making connections, convincing collectors to spend megabucks. This was on top of installing the exhibits, negotiating artwork loans, dealing with shipping and insurance.

To land an exclusive arrangement with Stella Moon would definitely boost sales in a hurry. Nathan thought about last week's encounter. Stella was famous for bullshitting people just to pass the time. Maybe if he pushed her a little . . .

He searched his database and found her cross-referenced under Contemporary Visual Artists and Beautiful People, Female. This system always proved useful when assembling the perfect invitation list for a big opening or a salon.

She answered on the fourth ring, her drawl distinctive even with a short, groggy, barely audible, "Hello."

"Stella? It's Nathan Williams from Frankovich. I'm sorry. Did I wake you?"

"What time is it?"

"A few minutes after ten."

"Oh, fuck. Honey, I'm so glad you called. I would've slept straight through my therapy session. I've got the worst hangover. I think I drank six or seven cosmopolitans at Passerby last night."

Nathan knew the bar. It was adjacent to Gavin Brown's Enterprise and a major haunt for gallery managers and art collectors. If they hadn't already, everyone in Manhattan's art set knew now that Stella was looking for a new place to call home. "I won't keep you," Nathan said easily. "I just wanted to encourage you to stop by the gallery this week if you have a chance." He hesitated, remembering the string. "And bring your friend, Panther. I'd like to learn more about his new project."

Stella Moon yawned. "Oh, honey, we will. As soon as Panther gets out of jail."

"Jail?"

"He waved a gun around at some club. It wasn't loaded, so I don't see what the big deal is. Don't worry. His lawyer will get him out this morning."

"Okay." But Nathan was worried about what he might be getting into.

"I had an epiphany when I was throwing up on the sidewalk last night," Stella said. "I'm going to do a limited series of vegetable cock paintings. I started thinking about eggplant and cauliflower and broccoli and squash. Suddenly, I was inspired! What do you think about that for my first show at Frankovich?"

Nathan saw visions of red dots. "People will love it."

"I think so, too. My therapist believes I stopped drinking, so I better get in the shower and try to put Humpty Dumpty back together again. Look for us later this afternoon."

Nathan spent the rest of the day trying to reach Danny, calling every half hour to no avail. He was in a meeting, on a conference call, at lunch, or out of the office. But finally, Nathan caught the legal eagle. "Are you trying to avoid me?"

"Of course not. Your crabs are gone now, right?"

Nathan groaned. He had actually forgotten about that particular humiliation.

"According to my assistant, you're officially stalking me. What's up?"

"Rob says that you're going to Las Vegas with Leo."

"I promise to bring you back an autographed picture of Wayne Newton."

"Very funny." Nathan paused. "Listen, has Leo ever mentioned his personal trainer? A black guy about my age. Looks like a young Denzel Washington with an Usher body. His name's Christian."

"Never heard of him."

"I think he travels with Leo."

"Maybe. A lot of people do." Danny sounded distracted. Nathan felt certain that he was reading something. "Are you listening to me?"

A long silence.

"Danny!"

"What? Oh, sorry. I've got a stack of contracts to go through before I leave today."

"Then I'll make this short. I want to tag along to Vegas with you."

"Absolutely not."

"Please, please, please!"

"No, no, no!"

"You won't even know I'm there."

"Exactly. Because you won't be."

"Don't be such an asshole."

Danny sighed. "I'm not comfortable in this relationship yet. Who knows where it's going? And I'm not bringing a friend along to entertain me while I wait around for my rock star lover. That's bordering on *I'm With the Band*, and—"

"Rob and I were just talking about that book."

"Yeah, well, don't even think about nicknaming me Pamela."

"Would you object to Penny Lane?"

"Fuck you."

"I'm just teasing. Seriously, you can count on me for support. This must be an awkward situation."

"Thanks."

"So . . . do you mind if I come along?"

"Yes."

"I can?"

"No. I mean yes, I mind."

"Danny!"

"I'll ask Leo about . . . what's his name?"

"*Christian.* Christian Elliott."

"And if I happen to meet this Christian, I will tell him that you inquired about his welfare."

"No!"

"Okay, I'll relay a message slightly less Jane Austen."

"No, I mean, just find out about his boyfriend. I want to know what he does and how serious they are."

"I'm impressed. For a twentysomething black guy, you really know how to maneuver at *Sweet Valley High.*"

"Rob said seventh grade last night. At least I'm maturing." Nathan saw Stella coming through the door. "I have to go. Think about me going along. I'll call you back."

"Honey, I was practically killed in the street!" Stella announced, charging toward him in an all white ensemble (could be Jil Sander), eyes eclipsed by enormous Chanel sunglasses. She hugged him tightly and kissed him on both cheeks, smelling of fresh gardenias (had to be the new Marc Jacobs fragrance). "A fat woman in a beat-up Chevrolet almost ran me down!"

Nathan smiled. "She must have been insane with jealousy. Look at you. You're radiant."

"I'm flushed! Feel my heart!" She grabbed Nathan's hand and brought it down to her cleavage.

It was racing. And rubbery. Definitely implants. "Can I get you anything? Tea, bottled—"

"My Paxil will kick in any time now."

"Where's Panther?"

"He had to stop by his dealer's place first." Stella removed her sunglasses and really gave the gallery a studied appraisal. "Honey, I've always loved this space. It's going to be so much fun working together. Remember those makeup pencil portraits that put me on the map?"

Nathan nodded. "Of course."

"What do you think about that as a show after vegetable cocks?"

"Did you have a theme in mind?"

"Manhattan socialites. Every one of those bitches will show up for the opening. And think of the publicity advantages—*Town & Country, W, Bazaar, Gotham.*"

Once again, Nathan visualized a wall full of bad art and red dots. "You are brilliant."

"I am!" Stella Moon said. "I am so fucking brilliant. And *you!*" She pointed at Nathan accusingly. "*You* are going to hang my fucking show in this fucking gallery!"

Nathan got caught up in the moment. "You are so fucking right!"

They laughed and hugged again.

"Can I get in on some of this love?" The voice was deep and rough.

Nathan turned to see a young, bad boy thug type—do-rag, jeans off his ass, white sleeveless undershirt, jail tattoos on his muscled arms, and brand-new Iversons on his feet.

"Panther!" Stella squealed. She pulled Nathan closer to the fine as hell gangsta. "Meet Nathan Williams."

Nathan extended his hand.

Panther's larger one put it through the brother shake that Nathan had never quite mastered. "Nice joint you got here, man."

Nathan swallowed hard and wondered if this hand had ever handled a gun, drug money, a blade . . . another man. "Stella tells me your work is very provocative." Suddenly, he hated the way he talked, cursed the privileged upbringing. Right now he wanted to be down, but it was beyond his reach.

Panther nodded smugly. "My shit is tight." He gestured to a large portfolio. "Wanna check it out?"

"Absolutely." He led them over to his sales desk, quickly clearing it off to accommodate Panther's work.

The badass unzipped the case to reveal a large canvas painted pitch black.

Nathan looked twice, thinking at first that it might be a

trick of the mind. But the piece was simply what it looked like—a canvas painted black.

"I spray painted that motherfucker," Panther said.

Stella clutched the roughneck's arm. "Isn't it sick?"

Panther hooked an arm around Stella's waist. "I got twenty-two of these. And for the opening, I got twenty-two ballers to stand next to them. Buck naked. Dicks as long as your forearm. I call the shit '*Nubian Nights.*' "

Stella practically jumped up and down. "It's so wicked!"

"So," Panther began arrogantly. "Do you want me?"

"Yes," Nathan said, in answer to the show . . . and the artist.

II

Boy Crazy at the Hudson Bar

"I have to ask," Gil said. "What the hell are you up to?" This question came after the second round of apple martinis with a brown sugar kick. Carson and Gil were at the bar on the second floor of the Hudson, another Ian Schrager hotel slash place to be seen. Carson couldn't stop squishing the technogel chairs. "I have a question, too. What the hell are you talking about?"

Gil reached inside his coat pocket and produced the sample art for the Boyfriend Material trading card concept. "I came across this sample in the art department. They said it was a new project."

Carson wanted to crawl beneath the underlit glass floor. "You weren't supposed to see that."

"But I have seen it," Gil said.

"It was just an idea."

"I'd like to hear more about it."

"Why? So you can tell me to file it away on the off chance that a *Teen Throb* sees the light of day?"

"I'm intrigued."

Carson gave Gil a ray gun gaze. There really was an earnest expression on his face. "A friend of mine is a teacher and found a similar card featuring a high school guy. His name was Cody, by the way, and he was a Virgo who loved *The Matrix*. Anyway, I thought it would be clever to develop a similar concept for gay men. Something beyond the online dating bullshit where everyone subtracts ten years and adds two inches. Think of all the bad first dates that could be avoided with something as simple as a trading card. I mean, even if a man looks like Ricky Martin, I would know not to bother if, for example, his favorite TV show was *America's Funniest Home Videos.*"

Gil laughed. "You wouldn't even meet the poor guy for coffee?"

"No. I'd rather alphabetize my CD collection."

Gil zoned out for a moment, then bounced back to earth. "Are you up for another round?"

"That would make me officially drunk."

"Don't worry. I promise not to take advantage of you." Gil signaled the waitress for two more. "I really like this trading card idea."

Carson was stunned. "I thought we were going for a more sophisticated reader."

"That's true. But there's a subversive camp element to this. I can see readers being amused yet at the same time secretly hopeful. It would be a great companion gimmick to your Boyfriend Material column. We could feature four guys each month and perforate the cards. That way they could be collected or passed around."

The third martini arrived, and Carson took a generous hit. "I think I love you."

Gil smiled. "You *are* drunk."

Carson shrugged. "Hey, you like my ideas; you're rich and handsome. What's not to love?"

"A wife and three kids."

"Not a problem. The only holiday I'll ask for is New Year's Eve. And the occasional three-day weekend in the Hamptons. I hate the drive, though. Do you have access to a helicopter?"

"No, but I have my own seaplane."

Carson did a double take. "Seriously?"

Gil laughed. "No." He fingered the stem of his martini glass. "Why is a guy like you single? You must be quite a catch in the demimonde of gay culture."

"I'm too goddamn picky. You see, I've been waiting for a man who can actually use a word like *demimonde* in a sentence."

Gil drank up. "Stop hitting on me."

Carson leaned in to whisper, "Why? Are you tempted?"

Gil wavered. "The truth? Mildly curious. I lied earlier today. But I'd never act on it."

"So you've *never* experimented with a guy?"

"No."

"Not even once? A summer friend? A frat brother?"

"The closest I've come to being with another guy is high school wrestling."

"Not far off the mark. All that rolling around is a form of sexual aggression. I firmly believe The Rock is an erotic fantasy to millions of teenage boys."

Gil shook his head and grinned. "You've got issues."

"I know. I've considered therapy, but it's too expensive. My clothing budget would take a major hit. You choose your battles, I guess. But at this point in my life, I'd rather have a fabulous wardrobe and be fucked up. It's a good thing that I'm functionally dysfunctional."

Gil raised his glass in salute. "I like that. Mind if I steal it?"

"It's yours. Do you see a shrink?"

"No time. But I listen to Dr. Phil tapes."

"Happy marriage?"

"For the most part. It's hard with three young kids. Sometimes we go days without having a real conversation. Everything is 'We're running low on milk' or 'Ally didn't sleep through the night again.' The traveling I do causes resentment, too. I get the most quiet time to myself, and that makes me the villain more often than not."

Carson was struck by the sudden intimacy of the conversation. And it only heightened the level of his crush. "I take it your sex life is not the stuff of *Red Shoe Diaries*."

Wearily, Gil rolled his head back and sighed. "Lately, my sex life has been showing up on my hotel bill."

"Ah, the joys of pay-per-view porn," Carson said.

"Is there anything more lonely or pathetic?"

"You know, Gil, you really shouldn't drink. You're much more attractive when you're sober and arrogant."

Gil looked at Carson with slightly red, open-to-anything eyes. "Don't tell me the magic's gone."

The sharpened, animated energy of flirtation had reached a new level. Carson experienced a flush of desire. Just the idea of what could happen next left him craving.

"I probably shouldn't mention the fact that I have a room here," Gil said.

"Is that why you chose this bar? So you could seduce me?"

"I think I'm the one who's being seduced."

"And quite easily, too. I thought it would take five or six drinks. It's only been three. Have you ever cheated on her before?"

As soon as the question hit the air, Gil stiffened. "I'm not perfect." There was a long stretch of silence. "I've strayed a few times. Nothing serious. Mostly models and editorial assistants." He stopped the waitress as she passed by and asked for the check.

"I'd be a step up the food chain at least."

Gil signed his room number and left a generous tip. "Let's get out of here." He gave him direct eye contact. "You can prove it."

The elevator ride up was a tightwire of sexual tension. Carson's gaze stayed on Gil like a laser, studying his hands, trying to will their touch. The space around him was pure desire, so absolute, so intense, that if he didn't surrender to it he could be driven mad.

Gil's room was small, less than two hundred square feet, the focal point being a freshly turned down bed. Carson flung himself onto it and loosened his tie. "Strip for me."

Gil, just drunk enough to oblige, seemed eager for Carson to see his body, which was in great shape—naturally smooth, taut, muscular, the athletic build of a professional tennis player in peak condition . . . and growing steadily aroused.

Gil dove on top, pinning Carson to the mattress. His first kiss came down hard, almost bruising. For a straight guy new to gay love, he seemed to be a natural.

Carson drew up a mental ledger of his recent involvements. There was Rocco—a serial adulterer, a smoker, and nobody's ideal partner for Trivial Pursuit. Great sex; terrible boyfriend.

That one afternoon with Brian, aka SexyLAModel—the escort with Broadway baby dreams. Great sex; the world's oldest profession.

And now Gil—the very married Owen Wilson clone with the super brain that could take *Throb* to the next level. Great sex (presumptuous, yes, but all signs were pointing that way); his magazine's paid consultant.

Jesus Christ, only Lana Turner had made worse choices in men. But Carson was digging this one. It wasn't just sexual blood pumping; it was psychic blood, too. He felt a real connection, and even though there were so many reasons to stop, Carson ignored them all, giving in to his damn-it-all, devil-may-care nature.

If Gil Bellak really wanted to know how good one man could make another man feel, then he was one lucky bastard tonight . . .

12

The Tree Doesn't Stand Far
from the Apple

"**L**ook, Dad. The shirt's straight from the dry cleaners, and the pants are pleated. I think Mr. Cahill's trying to impress you."

The father gave the son a playful macho punch to the gut and pressed a twenty dollar bill into his hand. "Just get me my regular, smart-ass."

Rob was mortified. First, David had the bad manners to show up thirty minutes late. Second, he'd brought along Brad, making an already awkward situation downright tortuous.

"David Pike." He extended a strong, nicely manicured, masculine hand.

Rob winced under the bone crushing grip, staring back in almost amazement. David's resemblance to Brad was uncanny. Men this hot were usually names above the title at the multiplex or staring back at you in print ads for cologne and designer underwear. "Uh . . . Rob . . . Rob Cahill." Already he could feel his palm start to sweat. He pulled his hand away before it became obvious.

David smiled. "Brad said you were cute. I'll say this much—the kid may be straight as a board, but he knows a good-looking man when he sees one."

In response, Rob simply drank his latte and wondered if the pools of sweat under his arms had formed large crescent moons onto his pink Oxford shirt. "I have to say," Rob started, nervously at first, but anxious to let his feelings be known, "I'm a little surprised that you showed up with Brad."

David looked genuinely stunned.

A sudden wave of humiliation washed over Rob. What if he had it all wrong? What if this wasn't a date before the date? What if this was only a meeting about Brad's status in the co-op program?

"You want me to get rid of him?" David asked, gesturing to Brad with his thumb as the teenager made his way over.

"It just makes it difficult to discuss—"

"Oh, don't worry about that. As of today, The Janssen Group is reinstating Brad."

Now it was Rob's turn to look stunned.

"Turns out someone at my agency plays golf with one of the partners. He invited me to join their scramble yesterday. We worked out the problem over thirty-six holes." David laughed a little. "Hell, I even got my kid a raise. How's that for negotiation?"

Brad approached the table and set down his father's coffee. "You don't mind if I keep the change, do you? I've been un-employed for a few days." He glanced at Rob and winked. Then his expression turned serious. "The way they fired me was so bogus, Mr. Cahill. If anything, I was a victim."

"A victim?" Rob's tone was incredulous.

"Of sexual harassment. *She* came on to *me*." Brad grabbed his crotch for emphasis. "That woman wanted this dick bad. She was always making jokes about me being in my sexual prime, rubbing up against me, telling me she'd like to show me some tricks in bed that high school girls don't know about yet. What was I supposed to do?"

"File a report with your supervisor. Or come to me."

Brad laughed.

Ditto David.

"Come on, Mr. Cahill," Brad said. "This babe was begging to get Piked." He grabbed his crotch again. "I'm not going to *complain*. I'm going to bend her over the copy machine and give her what she's asking for. It's a hormone thing, I guess. I mean, I've got a regular girlfriend, a few babes on the side, and I still jack off about six times a day. Why would I turn down a good-looking woman who's waving her pussy in my face?"

David beamed at his son as if he'd just won first prize at the science fair. "He's got a point."

"Actually, I think you're both missing the point," Rob said. "No matter who made the first move, carrying on in the copy room of a business office is unprofessional behavior." He rolled his eyes. "You must have been absent that day."

Brad shrugged. "Okay, I'll give you that. Just don't make me file a formal complaint. A lame move like that would ruin my chances with the hot girl in the PR department."

"No hooking up at the office," David scolded. "Mr. Cahill's right. Get a room somewhere or go back to her place."

Rob was shocked. "Actually, that's not what I—"

"I can live with that," Brad said.

An awkward moment of silence.

Brad sighed. "Well . . . I'm going to head on to school and give you ladies some time alone." He placed a hand on Rob's shoulder and squeezed. "Mr. Cahill, I plan on stopping by your room to check your breath before first period, and if I smell cum, I'll know that this meeting went as well as can be expected."

Rob just sat there, speechless, lost in a catatonic state of embarrassment, wishing he could exit via astral projection.

Brad laughed and took off.

David shook his head, laughing a little, the way a normal father might do if a son had squirted him with a water pistol. "Isn't that kid something else?"

Rob managed a vague nod. "The way he talks doesn't bother you?"

David shrugged easily. "I'm not like these other parents who live in denial about their teenager's sex life. I fucked around just like Brad when I was his age. As long as he's safe—that's all I care about. I know he uses condoms because he's always asking for some of mine." He smirked. "Lately, I've had no use for them."

Rob sipped on his coffee. Thank God he had a prop. It amazed him that David could have any trouble attracting a one night stand, a date, even a life partner—not only in the general sense but before the close of business today. Just here in Starbucks he was garnering coveted looks from both genders. But there had to be something wrong with him. Maybe it was like finding an unbelievable clothing bargain at an outlet shop. You had to inspect it down to the microfibers to discover the imperfection, then decide whether anyone would notice. Frightening thoughts began beaming into Rob's mind like laser fire. What if David had a bipolar disorder? Was HIV positive? Got into the whole come-into-my-dungeon-so-I-can-tie-you-up-with-duct-tape thing? Listened to Garth Brooks music? He shuddered.

"What about you?" David asked. "How's your condom supply?" The smile that came next made one thing clear: if this man was out of practice, it was true what they said about riding a bike.

Rob had never been good at fast encounters. Those were Carson's specialty. He preferred a get to know you meeting like this, then dinner and a movie, and a third no strings outing (bookstore browsing, a museum exhibit, a long run in Central Park) before, in the poetic words of the old Shalamar hit, "Dancing in the Sheets."

Of course, few men shared his patience and more often than not moved on, usually making it to the stage of scheduling platonic date number three but canceling before it happened or simply not showing up. And of those who did run the gauntlet, too many thought that merely waiting to have sex was itself foreplay for a *serious relationship* and were ready to live together, buy matching rings, stop going to clubs, and get fat. He didn't want a man too casual, and he didn't want a man too needy. One of Carrie Bradshaw's funny lines came to mind. Just call him "Goldicocks."

David waved a hand close to Rob's face. "Still with me?"

He captured a whiff of David's cologne—hints of cedarwood, cinnamon, and cloves. In the same millisecond that this brought Rob back from his personal reverie it almost spun him off into a brand new one.

"I was asking about your condom supply," David said.

"It's holding steady," Rob said. "Has been for a long time." He glanced up to see a colleague standing in line.

Lisa Birley stared straight at them, a question in her eyes. She taught English, served as faculty sponsor for the newspaper, and functioned as the school's answer to Matt Drudge. Her take on this would be old news before the first lunch bell rang.

Rob waved.

So did David.

Lisa narrowed her gaze suspiciously.

David leaned in. "That's Mrs. Birley, right?"

Rob gave him a discreet nod.

"She taught Brad's creative writing class last year and called me a few times to complain about the sex in his stories." David laughed. "I think she really liked them, though, especially the one about the jock and the school nurse."

"I remember that one. It actually got circulated around the faculty lounge. Pretty steamy stuff. For a while there he was the Jackie Collins of Manchester High."

David smiled at him. "Have dinner with me on Thursday."

Rob ran a quick mental calendar. That was television night. It meant Chinese takeout, *Friends, Will and Grace,* a half hour to clean up and shower, then hopping into bed to watch a recording of *CSI.* TiVo was a beautiful thing.

But so was David Pike.

13

Thug Love on the Down Low

The music stopped, the lights went up, and a mass of hard-core hip-hop fans began shouting, pushing, and throwing punches.

Nathan was scared out of his mind.

A menacing, villainous roughneck with a just-out-of-prison body lunged toward him. "Hey, pretty boy! Bitches go upstairs!"

Nathan tried to focus, but three rum and cokes had him buzzing strong. The floor was crammed so tight that he could barely move.

The DMX wannabe got right in his face. "You ignoring me, bitch?"

Suddenly, Panther cut in and shoved the asshole several feet backward. "Step off, motherfucker!"

Security rushed by, escorting two do-rag wearing linebacker types toward the exit door. Almost instantly, the chaos subsided, and the music resumed.

Panther scowled at the hefty duo being bounced. "It's always the fat girls stirring up shit!"

Nathan's heckler gave Panther a cool nod and a hard smile. "You got that right." There was a meaningful look. It said, "I don't want to fuck with you." It also said, "But I do want to fuck with you." And then he disappeared into the throng of the tall, the muscular, and the ultra masculine.

There were at the Warehouse at 141st Street and the Grand Concourse in the South Bronx. For Nathan, it was like an alternative universe. He'd never been in a situation with so many black men in one place before. It was a hot, wild, and crazy feeling. A strange thought occurred to him. What if his mother could see him now? The image in his mind broke him up. Audrey Williams would definitely need a Depends for a sight like this.

Panther glared at him. "What's so goddamn funny?"

Nathan's laughing fit faded fast. As he stood there and smiled at Panther, he glanced around and realized how out of his element he must look. Everybody on the floor affected major attitude and gave off tough, unfriendly, ready to rumble vibes.

His clothes didn't help him blend in either. The uniform here was wife-beater tanks, baggy jeans, work boots, and flashy jewelry, while Nathan had come straight from the gallery in a Rene Lezard shirt and Donna Karan stretch fabric pants. No matter, he moved his body to the hard bass beat, thrilled by the subversiveness of it all, and shouted, "I feel like Alice in Thugland!"

Panther just stood there at first, a masterpiece of forbidding, dark, and mysterious sensuality. Finally, he gave up a hint of a smile.

For Nathan, it was as if the earth had opened up and shown him a pathway to paradise. He wondered if he could handle a fourth drink without falling over. Heavy-duty chemical assistance was necessary because Panther was the sexiest man Nathan had ever encountered. So sexy, in fact, that it frightened him. Panther was the kind of man who could come along and within five minutes lay claim to everything you owned. And Nathan was already poised to put his life up for grabs.

The music blasted so loud that Nathan could feel it in his chest. Nelly's vulgar growl on "Hot in Herre" faded, and the DJ pumped Mary J. Blige's "Family Affair" into the mix.

The precise moment that Panther had loped into the Frankovich Gallery was the precise moment that Christian Elliott had ceased to exist. Snap. Just like that. Nathan had known he was a goner when he heard himself agreeing out loud to host Panther's "Nubian Nights" show. Spray painted black canvases and nude thugs? It wasn't an art show so much as a freak show.

After Panther's initial visit with Stella, Nathan had managed to hold out for a few days before calling him. Under the pretense of going over logistics and publicity for the show, Nathan had asked for a meeting and scheduled it late in the day, hoping to coax Panther into a dinner as well.

When Panther never showed up, Nathan had not been surprised. He was intuitive enough to know that men like Panther operated on their own clock. That's why he'd stayed late at the gallery to catch up on paperwork too long ignored. It had been almost ten o'clock when Panther knocked on the front window.

"Let's roll," Panther had said, then turned and started down the street in the direction of the train station.

Nathan had moved feverishly to lock up and raced to catch him. "Where are we going?"

"Be cool. You'll see."

And so the descent into this exciting new world had begun. Nathan didn't even know that it existed. The Warehouse was hardly distinctive, just a nuts and bolts club with bi-level dance floors, a lounge, and an outdoor patio. House music thumped on the upper level, leaving the first floor as a hip-hop haven for hard-ass brothers.

It had been clear upon entry that level one was Panther's sanctuary and that anyone who wanted to kick it with him had better be able to deal there. Nathan had thought he was doing well until that ignorant ex-con had started up. *Bitches go upstairs.* Not tonight, hardrock. Nathan had every intention of staying right here with Panther.

"Follow me."

Nathan trailed Panther into the bathroom and inside one of the stalls. The whole scene brought back memories of Mike, and Nathan wondered if he would ever meet anyone who wanted to have sex in a bed like normal people.

"I'm on the DL," Panther said. "You know that, right?" His fingers began to work on the button fly of his jeans.

Nathan gave him a strange look. He had no idea what Panther meant.

"DL. On the down low," Panther said impatiently. "I'm no faggot, okay? I just mess around."

Nathan was drunk but not that drunk. Same story, different cast. But at least this guy wasn't married.

Panther finished undoing his jeans and pushed them down to his feet, leaving him in a pair of boxer briefs that left little to the imagination. "Damn, I wish I had a bump of Tina right now."

More confusion. "Is that your girlfriend?"

Panther laughed at him. "Boy, you don't know shit." He used both hands to cradle Nathan's head and guide him onto his knees. "Tina means crystal meth. Ever tried it?"

Nathan began to feel slightly dizzy. The stall started to spin. Somehow he managed to shake his head and murmur, "I can barely handle liquor." A wave of nausea sent him reeling, but, for the moment, he recovered.

"Well, when I get my hands on a quarter, you're in for it, nigga. You haven't been fucked until you've been fucked with a crystal dick." Panther peeled down his underwear. "That's what you want, isn't it?"

Nathan struggled to remain upright. The nausea intensified. Perspiration beaded on his forehead.

"You know what I want you to do for me?" Panther asked in a thick voice.

Nathan couldn't respond. He was too busy fighting against the inevitable.

"I want you to suck this big dick and swallow my cookies."

It was the last part that sent Nathan over the edge. He tried for the commode but missed it and ended up vomiting onto Panther's boots. All of a sudden he remembered. This was the reason he didn't drink.

14

Candlelight & Them

"I look like a dork," Rob said, grimacing at his own reflection in the Melrose floor mirror from Crate & Barrel.

"Come closer," Nathan croaked. He was beached on Rob's bed, nursing a killer hangover.

Rob stepped toward him, sighing impatiently. "You wouldn't feel so bad right now if you'd just done what I told you to do."

"Eat a big hamburger and fries?"

Rob nodded. "It always works for me."

"The mere thought of food makes me too weak to stand. How do you expect me to get dressed and walk to a bad restaurant?" He touched his forehead with the back of his hand.

"Believe me, it can be done. It's no way near as impossible as those idiot millionaires who try to travel around the world in a hot air balloon." Rob shifted uncomfortably and splayed out his arms.

"You don't look like a dork," Nathan assured him. "You look like a college guy on his way to a friend's wedding."

Hardly placated, Rob stomped back to the mirror and took inventory of his ensemble. Kenneth Cole shoes, pressed Gap khakis, J. Crew white Oxford shirt, navy sport coat from the Brooks Brothers outlet, and a boring tie of indeterminate origin. Maybe a graduation gift from one of his aunts? He undid the knot and attempted to tie it again. "I do!" Rob shouted.

"I look like some slacker who woke up at eleven-thirty and realized I had to be at a noon wedding."

Nathan shook his head in disagreement. "You're freshly shaved, and your hair looks great. You at least woke up by ten-thirty."

Rob pulled off the tie and threw it down, then sank onto the edge of the bed. "David's in advertising. He dresses like Danny, only a little more conservatively. I think everything he wears is Hugo Karan."

"Hugo *Boss*," Nathan corrected. "Or *Donna* Karan. Either way, he has great taste." He paused. "In clothes and guys."

Rob turned back to face Nathan, a reluctant smile on his face.

"Don't try to dress like someone you're not. You have a very relaxed style that works for you. David obviously likes it, or he wouldn't have asked you to dinner in the first place. But . . ."

Rob tensed.

"That tie is hideous. It looks like something you would find at Small Town Bankers R Us. You can borrow the new one I just picked up at Hermes."

"Really?"

"It's still in the box. But you'll have to cut the tags off and promise not to spill anything on it."

"Consider it done."

Rob darted into the living room and sorted through Nathan's latest shopping stash until he found the Hermes box. He opened it to find a beautiful floral patterned tie made of fine silk. The price tag alarmed him.

"Did you find it?" Nathan called out weakly.

Rob marched back into the bedroom. "I can't wear this! It cost almost two hundred dollars!"

Nathan waved away his concern. "Oh, please. It's just a tie."

Rob stepped over to the mirror and held it up against his shirt. It did bring some serious pizzazz to an otherwise unremarkable outfit.

"*That* looks great," Nathan said. "Now put it on and let me sleep. Your wardrobe drama has depleted my energy."

Rob knotted it quickly before he changed his mind. "What about cologne?"

"I have a new bottle of Michael Kors in the bathroom. Help yourself. And then please go."

"Thanks." Rob started out, then halted at the door. "One more thing. Do you like that silver ring I sometimes wear on my thumb?"

"Absolutely not. I thought Carson told you to put that down the garbage disposal."

"I thought he was kidding."

"He wasn't. No rings, no bracelets, no necklaces. Unless you become a rock star, and then all the rules change. A guy like you should limit jewelry to a nice watch."

Rob pushed back his sleeve to glance at his old Fossil. "I need to work on that." And then he noticed the time. "Shit. I better go. Otherwise, I'll have to blow good money on a cab."

He took the train to the Upper East Side and made it to Daniel with a few minutes to spare. The restaurant—one of New York's selected haute eateries—was all soaring ceilings, damask walls, and gilded limestone columns—very Venetian Renaissance.

David had already arrived, and the maitre d' escorted Rob to his table.

Upon seeing Rob, David smiled broadly and stood up to embrace him, then gestured for him to take the seat next to him at the four-top.

Rob thought this odd. He would've much preferred to sit across from David, but he chose not to make an issue out of it.

"You look nice." David's brows perked up. "Good enough to eat."

Rob grinned, feeling an instant warmth go to his cheeks. And it had nothing to do with the run down Park Avenue to make it there. "Whatever you do, don't eat my tie."

"It's not yours, is it?" David asked.

Rob pretended to be shocked. "How did you know?"

David flipped the tie over to read the label. "Ah . . . I was going to say Gucci or Chanel . . . did you put this on to impress me?"

"No, I put this on to avoid *embarrassing* you. You should've seen the first one I had on."

David laughed. "Pretty bad, huh?"

"I don't dress up very often."

"Well, you'll be glad you did tonight. The food here is incredible."

A waiter approached the table and addressed David. "May I interest you and your guest in a drink while you wait for the rest of your party to arrive?"

Suddenly, Rob zeroed in on the two place settings opposite them. *Rest of your party?* Jesus, the waiter knew more about this date than he did. Who the hell . . . and then Rob spotted Brad Pike, strutting his way toward the table, pulling along an older girl (quite beautiful, actually) in a clingy black cocktail dress with a beaded Hello Kitty evening bag in her free hand.

David was busy quizzing the waiter on wine selections.

Rob, still dismayed, managed to stand up to greet Brad and his date.

Brad embraced him warmly, surreptitiously whispering in his ear, "She thinks I'm in college, so the story is you taught me two years ago. Got it?"

Rob nodded vaguely.

"Rob Cahill, meet April Bradlee. She's in PR at The Janssen Group. Rob used to be my co-op teacher in high school."

"Really?" April cooed excitedly, shaking hands firm and fast. "It must be so weird to date the father of one of your former students." She punctuated this with an annoying giggle.

"You have no idea how strange it is."

April giggled again.

David finished up with the waiter and rose to kiss April's cheek. "Just hold on, gorgeous. A nice bottle of wine is on the way."

Rob secretly wished a family therapist was headed to the table instead.

"Have you been here before?" David asked April.

"No, but Mexican food is my favorite."

"They serve French cuisine here," Rob pointed out.

More giggling. "I always get those two confused. They taste the same to me."

David snaked a hand down and squeezed Rob's knee.

Rob jolted, knocking the table and causing the silverware to clink.

"Dad, are you giving Rob a hand job over there?" Brad asked.

"Not yet," David said easily. "I thought we should at least order appetizers first."

April was really giggling now, her ample breasts bouncing up and down.

Brad watched her boobs with all the speechless wonder of a *Star Wars* geek catching bootleg footage of the next George Lucas opus.

Rob removed David's hand from his knee and said, "This is a big surprise. You never mentioned that Brad and April were joining us tonight." He laced his delivery with just enough acid to let David know that *big surprise* was code for something else.

The waiter arrived with a bottle of expensive Merlot, making quite a show out of removing the cork. He offered David a sample to taste.

"It's perfect," David announced.

Everyone's glass—including Brad's—was filled in short order.

Rob leaned in toward David to murmur under his breath, "It's okay for Brad to drink?"

"I don't see why not," David whispered back. "He's going to be doing things to April later tonight that are equally adult."

Rob blanched.

"I've never been on a gay/straight date before," April said. "This is fun." She giggled.

That stupid laugh was getting on Rob's nerves. In a serious way, too. If she did it again, he just might have to take the cluster of yellow roses in the center of the table and shove them into her mouth. To calm himself, he drank deep on the wine, then turned his attention to the menu.

David leaned over to say, "You should try the—"

"I can order for myself," Rob snapped.

Brad glanced up, smirking. "Mr. Cahill . . . uh, I mean, Rob, that was pretty bitchy. You must be establishing your fem role in the relationship."

April giggled again.

Rob's eyes focused on the flowers. The impulse was there . . .

David whispered, "What's your problem?"

"Nothing," Rob muttered. "Everything's fucking perfect." He decided on the roasted lamb medallions with a citrus-rosemary glaze. And for dessert—milk chocolate mousse bombe with ginger cream center and orange marmalade. Then he reached for the wine and refilled his own glass.

After all, the only way he could imagine getting through this meal was to get drunk and eat well.

15
Siegfried and Roy Slept Here

Danny was burning hot with jealousy. He sat there, alone in the corner, knocking back a weak Scotch and water as he watched Leo lick whipped cream off the navels of at least half a dozen strippers with long legs, big tits, and powerful lungs. Their screams of delight practically drowned out the turgid rock music.

Chad bulldozed his way in to turn the girls around and squirt more whipped cream, this time onto their bare bottoms. "No one can say I don't know how to kiss ass!" And then he proceeded to wash them clean with an eager tongue.

Leo, Greg, and Damian cheered him on, whooping like frat boys after tapping the first keg.

Other club dwellers demonstrated vocal support, too, but mere pedestrians were kept at bay by a flank of thick, no-neck, no-nonsense bodyguards.

Danny tried to make himself believe that it was all just for show, that Leo hated every second of this macho carousing. But if Leo really was, in fact, *miserable,* then he was the best fucking actor to come along since DeNiro.

Disgusted, Danny signaled the waitress for another rip-off drink, waved away her suggestion to go for a lap dance, and thought about calling a cab to get the hell out of there.

He was somewhere in the bowels of Las Vegas, far from the cocooned glitz of the MGM Grand, marooned in this sleazy strip club with four pop stars who were alternating Red Bull with hard liquor. The party was on. And it showed no signs of letting up anytime soon. If anything, Four Deep's sold-out concert just a few hours ago had only adrenalized them into superhuman chaos machines.

What the fuck am I doing? Danny dug deep for the answer, even though he knew he wouldn't even be asking the question if he and Leo were, say, back in their hotel suite and huddled beneath the satiny cotton sheets of the king-size bed. The son of a bitch should be licking whipped cream off *his* navel. Yeah, that would be a reason to stick around.

The truth was, Danny had no business being in Las Vegas at all. Four Deep was in the throes of a major contract renegotiation with their recording label. Only three projects remained in their original agreement—a Christmas set already in the can and pending a late fall release, a live album culled from the Miami shows, and a remix collection already in development, featuring overhauled versions of their biggest hits with special guest rappers to give their sound a tough urban edge, à la J. Lo's monster hits with Ja Rule, "I'm Real" and "Ain't it Funny."

Danny had to admit that, in the face of teen pop's current death spiral, Four Deep's continued success was nothing short of remarkable. The Backstreet Boys were imploding. Those 98 Degrees hunks had been out of sight so long they should be on a milk carton. O-Town might have risen to mini stardom via *Making the Band,* but the reality series had now been axed twice, first by ABC, then by MTV. Britney Spears, though still a ubiquitous superstar at the tabloid and advertising level, had become a pariah to radio programmers. They simply didn't spin her records anymore. Only *NSYNC had managed to hold onto the ledge. But without Justin's white boy soul act, they probably would've fallen hard and fast, too.

The same could be said for Four Deep. Leo Summer was carrying the whole group on his beautifully sculpted back. Rumors of a breakup and a bold solo move were rampant, though Leo maintained that such talk was only junk being stirred up by the press. No matter, the powers that be at Rhapsody Records were hesitant, fully aware that a singular spotlight for Leo was inevitable but wanting to take the group to the next level first. After all, the industry was littered with solo-too-soon casualties. And by the time they hit rock bottom and decided to get the old band together for that last ditch attempt at glory, they were a rehab weary *Behind the Music* cliché with nothing but small casino showroom gigs in their future.

Danny experienced an anxious feeling. He should be in New York right now, staying on top of the deal and making Rhapsody sweat by flirting with other labels. Instead, he was here in Vegas, scowling from afar like some tight ass girlfriend who hated her man to have a little fun.

The boys had given up individual drinks and were swigging straight from the bottle now. There was a torrent of commotion as they made their way to one of the club's private rooms, happy strippers in hot pursuit.

Danny made a mental note to have their road manager force feed them a dose of antibiotics tomorrow. Abruptly, he stood up to leave, throwing down some cash to cover the cheap drinks. He lingered for a few minutes, vacantly watching a bootylicious black girl bump and grind to Pink's catchy smash, "Get the Party Started." Some party. It was for shit. Still, Danny lingered, hoping Leo would appear. But when the minutes ticked by and another dancer took the small stage and began working the pole to an old Whitesnake number, he made his move, silently bitching at himself for not exiting sooner.

Leo caught him at the door. "What the fuck? Are you leaving?"

"Why the hell shouldn't I?" Danny snapped. "I'm the only one not having any fun in this dump."

Leo's bloodshot eyes flashed angrily. "Nobody runs out on me!"

Instantly, Danny knew what he was up against—a mean, irrational drunk who could upgrade a minor disagreement to full-scale drama faster than Winona Ryder could swipe a jeweled hair clip from Saks. Danny could telegraph the escalation, from the shouting to the shoving to the breaking up to the making up. Predictable. Boring. Emotionally immature. But at least the bullshit was passionate. Relationships could be worse.

"I'm not running out," Danny assured him. "It's just . . . I like spending time with *you*. I hate being a hanger on. That's not my style."

Leo held out his arms. "Look, I'm all yours. Damian's passed out, Chad's getting a lap dance, and Greg's got two girls going down on him at the same time. They'll never miss me."

Danny grinned, shaking his head. The dumb luck of those three assholes amazed him. Somehow they had stumbled upon a pop group that hit big. Now the jerks were multi-millionaires for doing little more than learning a few dance routines. It's not like they sang live. All their vocals were pre-recorded to accommodate the high energy choreography. Half the time they didn't even perform on the albums. The goons goofed off so much that it had become more efficient to bring in session singers to record their background vocals. As if anyone would ever notice.

Leo eyed the limo with a secret smile. "Let's take a drive. We can cruise the strip and watch the freaks. I'll even suck you off in the backseat with the windows down."

Danny felt a stir in his loins. "You're crazy."

"It's the least I can do for the man who's going to get me a killer new deal."

16

His Other Man

Carson was practically living at the Hudson Hotel. That first night with Gil had turned into two, then three, and now . . .

The hardest part was sitting in guilty silence whenever Gil talked on the phone to his wife and kids, which happened twice a night, once before Ally, Jordan, and Graham went to bed (oh, God, he actually knew their names!) and a second time before Claire (it helped to imagine her as an ugly, manic-depressive bitch) turned out the light.

What did you call a male mistress? Besides a bastard, of course. That word was appropriate but not quite specific enough. For instance, an exceptionally rude loser selling subway tokens could easily be classified as a bastard. There had to be a better turn of phrase. Carson was putting his mind to work on the issue just as Gil stirred, spooned closer and gave him the benefit of an impressive morning erection.

Except for the fact that Gil was married with three children, Carson realized that he could get used to waking up with him on a regular basis. Intellectually, Gil was a refreshing challenge, which made for some serious electric chemistry. He wasn't merely smart; he was *brilliant,* and Carson had never done brilliant before. Now he was hooked.

Gil's hand was resting on Carson's naked thigh.

Carson found himself staring at Gil's wedding band. Suddenly, he was playing back the things he'd said to Nathan. *Mike doesn't like you in a romantic way. You're his dirty little secret.* Granted, this situation was slightly more respectable. After all, he knew Gil's last name, they only stepped into public restrooms to use them for their intended purpose, kissing was not on the forbidden list, and they grew closer post climax, as opposed to running for their lives like any number of hard up actors in those Irwin Allen disaster films. But, at the end of the day, Carson had to admit: he was a dirty little secret, too.

He grabbed Gil's hand and pulled it to his chest. A heartbeat later, that beautiful hand came to life, moving up to massage Carson's neck, then traveling farther to trace the outline of his lips, teasing his mouth as he gently sucked on its index and middle fingers.

Gil let out a little groan and pressed inward to demonstrate just how ready he was.

Carson smiled to himself. "I've spoiled you rotten these last few days," he whispered.

"What?"

Carson flipped over to face him. "You know what I'm talking about."

Gil shrugged helplessly. "But I don't."

"Okay," Carson said easily. "Let's order room service then. I can get an earlier start."

Gil's face registered alarm now. "Wait."

"For what?"

"We usually order room service after . . ."

He grinned, triumphant. "After what?"

Gil hesitated. "After you . . . you know." He directed his eyes to the tented sheet and the serious pole action going on down there.

"Do you actually expect me to give you head first thing every morning?" Carson put an incredulous top spin on the question.

Gil blushed a pretty pink. "No . . . of . . . of course not," he stammered.

Carson gave him a fierce stare. "Because I fully intend to live up to that expectation." And then he ripped off the cover and went to work.

Gil's laugh turned into a guttural moan. "I was playing

along," he sighed dreamily. "I knew you were just . . . oh, damn, I'm close . . . fucking with me."

Carson stopped. "Such a bad liar." He started back, finishing the job. It was obvious that Gil rarely got head at home, because not only did he come quickly every time, but he behaved as if a little oral attention was the best thing to come along since the voyeuristic train wreck of *The Osbournes* on MTV.

Carson had no problem swallowing. Gil restricted himself to macrobiotic foods, so his semen always tasted clean and kind of sweet. By comparison, Rocco must have been on a steady diet of sewer rats.

He jumped out of bed and showered first, leaving Gil to order coffee, fruit, and bagels, as was the routine. Then while Gil showered, Carson would loaf around in a towel, swoon over Matt Lauer, receive the room service cart, and give the hotel guy a generous tip from Gil's wallet (he made much more money).

The telephone jangled.

Carson was enthralled by an interview with Richard Gere, and, only half thinking, picked up on the second ring. "Hello?"

"Gil? Is that you?" A woman's voice. Claire, no doubt. *Claire Bellak.*

Carson froze. His heart pounded wildly in his chest. *Shit!* He hadn't meant to pick up the phone. But now that he had, there were several things he wanted to say. For starters, something along the lines of, "If you don't want your husband, then I do." No. He'd need big hair, shoulder pads, a drink in one hand, a cigarette holder in the other, and considerable shares of Denver Carrington in his stock portfolio to get away with that. So he said nothing.

"Gil?" A shrill voice this time. Clearly an unstable woman. Gil was better off without her.

"This is the Hudson Hotel," Carson said, finally.

"I know, I'm—"

"You must have been transferred to the wrong room," he said curtly. "There's no Gil here." *Click.*

A few moments later, Gil's cell phone jingled.

Carson stared at it, full of fear, as if it might come alive and attack him.

After several rings, it stopped.

Carson told Gil what happened the second he stepped out of the shower.

"Good save," Gil said. He kissed Carson full on the mouth and checked his cell, nodding. "That was her, too." A big sigh. Not a satisfied one. "It's not like her to try to reach me in the morning." His brow creased with worry.

"Call her back," Carson said. "I'll get your coffee ready."

Gil dialed home, and after the perfunctory hello-how-are-yous dropped, he was engaged in a full-scale domestic spat. Something about a broken washing machine. "What the hell do you want from me, Claire? I'm in Manhattan . . . Even if I *was* home, I don't know how to fix a fucking washer. . . . Call the guy . . . Okay, forget the guy. Buy a brand-new one . . ."

Gil liked his coffee with two creams and one sugar, so Carson busied himself with that task, wishing he could sink into the carpet fibers. He hated being exposed to this side of Gil's life. Here was a media consultant of legend, a man who had singularly saved failing magazines from ruin, getting bitched out over a stupid household appliance. It humanized him in a way that Carson found oddly unsettling.

"Jesus, Claire, why are you giving me this passive-aggressive bullshit? You're not pissed about the washer. You're pissed at me. . . . Oh, for Christ's sakes . . . Most of my work is in New York, and you knew that when you insisted we move to Chicago to be closer to your parents. . . . I'm not throwing it in your face, Claire. I'm just reminding you . . . Fuck this . . . Are the kids okay? . . . Because I'm not going to argue with you . . . No, I'm not . . . I need to be fresh for my meetings . . . Yes, I'm serious . . . I'm not going in any more pissed than I already am . . . Yeah, you're right, I'm a selfish asshole. Good morning to you, too. I'll call you later tonight."

Gil signed off, threw the phone onto the rumpled bed, and pulled at his wet hair with both hands. The towel looped around his waist came undone and fell to the floor, leaving him naked. He didn't bother picking it up.

"Let me guess. Trouble at home." Carson started toward him, slowly, but with purpose.

"That's the understatement of the century."

Carson got down on his knees and proceeded to lick Gil's cock, swirling his tongue up and down the shaft until it was hard and throbbing for more attention.

Gil laughed a little and half moaned, half murmured, "Twice before work? I think I'm in love."

And then Carson took him deep into his mouth. He planned to take his time, to make it a long, soul searing suck session. It would drive Gil crazy. It would cause him to be late for his first appointment of the day with Matthew. And it would make him forget about the life outside their decadent fantasy world of creative fusion, drinks after five, insanely expensive restaurants, and fabulous sex.

I think I'm in love. Clearly that had been Gil's dick talking.

He wondered what the rest of Gil was feeling, because speaking of love, Carson was three-quarters of the way there. And the realization scared the hell out of him.

"I should have married *you*," Gil whispered thickly.

Carson could almost feel his heart break a little bit, knowing their relationship didn't stand a chance beyond this hotel room. *That's right, you son of a bitch. You should have.*

17

Meow Mix

"You look like shit," Carson told Danny.

"Keep in mind that I came straight from the airport after a night of no sleep, not from Elizabeth Arden."

They were all gathered at the Cosi Sandwich Bar on 13th Street and Broadway for the first time in two weeks. Everybody appeared to be running on empty and in desperate need of a Prozac prescription.

"This is supposed to be *fun*," Carson whined. "We missed last week because *somebody* was molesting a child star in Miami."

At least that got a chuckle out of Nathan and Rob.

Danny merely glowered and picked at his scrambled eggs.

"This isn't group therapy," Carson went on, "nor is it the official meeting of the Kristy McNichol Fan Club. All of us . . . all of *you* . . . were happier when you didn't have a guy."

Danny's eyebrows shot up. "Freudian slip?"

"No," Carson snapped. "I never moped around thinking guys were the answer. I have too much empirical evidence to support that they're the problem."

Rob leaned in and spoke urgently. "Did I tell you what David's son said to me the morning we were introduced? He goes, 'Mr. Cahill, I plan on stopping by your room to check your breath before first period, and if I smell cum, I'll know that this meeting went as well as can be expected.' Right in front of his father! And David just laughed. Don't you think that's weird?"

Carson got a chuckle out of it. "Actually, it's kind of funny."

Rob shook his head. "I don't get it. All this open talk about sex with a parent. It's not normal. My mom and dad don't even know that I've lost my virginity. And I intend to keep it that way."

"Maybe it's because—"

Rob cut Danny off. "Oh, it gets worse. We met for dinner Thursday night—"

"Where did he take you?" Carson blurted.

"Daniel."

Carson, Danny, and Nathan, each one of them a shameless restaurant whore, traded nods of approval.

"And *Brad* joins us. With a girl. It's like a double date. Nobody from school, thank God. He brought along some twenty-four-year-old who works in PR. But guess what dominated the dinner conversation?"

Carson took a stab at it. "Kevin Costner's career choices followed by a detailed account of Liza's wedding."

Rob was not amused. "Sex. What else? Specifically, strange places they've had it. I wanted to crawl under the table when Brad announced that he'd once done it in my classroom while I met with the principal during my off period. I remember picking up that condom. All this time I thought it was a practical joke. I'll never feel comfortable at my desk again. I'm requesting a new one on Monday."

Carson pushed his omelet away. "I remember a family like that when I was in high school. The mother and father walked around naked, they kept condoms in a big bowl by the door, and they let their kids have sex in their rooms. They just believed in being really open and nonjudgmental about sexuality. Very European. They had a great-looking gay son, too. I was over there three or four days a week and twice on Saturdays. It didn't faze them one bit."

Danny looked over at Nathan. "Oh, shit. I just realized that I forgot to ask Leo about Christian."

Nathan shrugged.

"Who's Christian?" Carson asked. "I thought the new guy's name was Leopard."

"*Panther,*" Nathan corrected. Miserably, he shoved a slice of bacon into his mouth.

"Well, at least I knew he was named after a large cat. Can we meet him, or is this another one of your public restroom relationships?"

"You're one to talk. Or is agoraphobia the reason you stay cooped up in that hotel room with Tuna."

"*Gil,*" Carson hissed.

Nathan's smile talked of thrilled comeuppance. "Well, at least I knew his name had something to do with fish."

Danny broke up. "It's like the gay version of Alexis and Dominique Devereaux. If only there were a lily pond nearby."

Rob was laughing, too. "He's learned every bit of his bitchiness from you, Carson." He squeezed Nathan's shoulder. "You think he's an innocent, well-bred black boy, but he's really quite the Eve Harrington."

Carson tried to be a good sport. No need to cause a scene. Besides, there were few who could take him down. Nathan might score a few jabs here and there, but basically, he was a lightweight.

"Panther would not gel with our group," Nathan said, eager to change the subject. "Trust me on that."

"Are you ashamed of us?" Danny asked, feigning indignation.

"Panther is a thug on the DL," Rob explained.

Carson gave him a quizzical look. "I thought he was a bad artist. And what's a *thug on the DL?*"

Rob appeared delighted by Carson's ignorance. "Mr. Hip has not heard of this! Ten trendy points for the public school teacher."

"Don't get too excited," Carson warned. "You're already minus twenty for thinking every teenager should be like Sandra Dee."

"I'm lost here, too," Danny said. "I've never heard of a thug on the DL."

"It's a new generation of young black men who idolize rappers, dress like homeboys, and want to be *real,*" Rob said. "They seek out other guys for sexual pleasure but don't view themselves as gay. There are some DL thugs at Manchester

High. Students have approached them about joining the GSA. One kid got the shit beat out of him just for suggesting it."

Carson chimed in, relieved to know that he didn't have to take notes from Rob's mini lecture. "Wait a minute. I've heard about this. The hip-hop style is a form of drag. The only difference between these fags and RuPaul is that it takes her longer to get dressed."

Nathan let out a reluctant laugh. "If the right people were listening, you could get killed for that."

Carson rolled his eyes. "Oh, please. It's all about marketing. These guys are packaging themselves in the tried and true image of the tough, angry black man who's sexually aggressive. The scary part of all this is that they're actually believing the hype. If they're not really gay, then they don't have to protect themselves against what they think is a gay disease. That's why HIV cases are way up among black gays and bisexuals. It's at thirty percent now." He zeroed in on Nathan. "Drop this loser. He's nothing but trouble. And I wouldn't even accept a phone call from him unless he was wearing two condoms."

Nathan took instant offense. "Isn't *Gil* experiencing a bit of denial? I mean, he doesn't plan on coming out at the next PTA meeting, does he?"

Danny made a show of removing all forks within reach.

"Gil is not dangerously delusional," Carson said hotly. Nathan was really getting on his nerves. A few weeks ago he couldn't identify the crabs crawling around in his pubes. Today he had smart-ass answers for everything. "And he's not using me, either."

"And Panther is using me?"

"He colors a canvas with a can of spray paint and calls it art. My five-year-old nephew could do that." One beat. "But he's moved on to more complicated creative projects. I can't believe you're giving this fraud his own show. There's not a gallery in the city that would give him the time of day."

"It's not just the piece itself," Nathan argued. "There are nude models, too. This is high concept. It's basically performance art."

"Oh, really?" Carson scoffed. "A homeless man flashed me the other day. How about giving him his own show?"

"Look, just because Gil is in another income bracket doesn't mean your situation is that much different. He's in denial about who he is. He's living a double life. What you're doing isn't a relationship to him. It's an out of town fantasy."

Carson knew that his face registered the hit. Nathan's jeremiad had practically drawn blood. "Whatever the fuck it is, it's not likely to turn me into a statistic."

Abruptly, Nathan stood and threw down his napkin. "Go to hell." He started to leave.

"Is this your way of skipping out on the bill, drama queen?" Carson hollered after him.

Nathan stopped and spun around.

"Because your roommate can barely afford his own breakfast, and I'm not in a treating mood."

Danny waved Nathan off. "Don't worry. I've got it. Go cool off." Then he turned on Carson angrily. "We should do this more often. And since you cleared the room so fucking well, I guess you're the new Mr. Fantastic. Congratulations."

18

All Saints

Forget Carson St. John.
Days had gone by, and Nathan was still royally pissed. Rob had tried to defuse the situation and negotiate a truce, but Nathan wanted no part of it. He was fed up with Carson's impossible princess attitude.

Drop this loser. He's nothing but trouble.

The audacity to just announce something like that! The nerve was unreal. Especially since the oh-so-perfect messenger was in bed with a married father of three. At least Panther didn't have any kids. If Nathan had learned anything from Wall Street Mike, it was that. No wives, no children, no thank you.

He checked his cell phone for the fiftieth time, just to make certain the battery was still charged. Exactly twenty-four hours ago, he sent Panther a brand-new pair of Timberlands by courier. A polite replacement gift for the ones he threw up on. But still no call. Maybe he was out of the city or in the throes of creating his new show. Some artists got into a zone and didn't come up for air until days later.

The stinky cab jerked to a stop in front of the old sweat-shop building, and Nathan anxiously paid the fare and stepped out onto the curb. He took an old freight elevator up to the fourth floor and knocked on the second of three steel doors.

"Oh, honey, thank God it's you!" Stella Moon exclaimed breathlessly. Her hair was pulled back, revealing a high-gloss complexion and Paul Newman baby blues. "I think I'm being stalked!"

She pulled him inside her studio, an enormous loft space, and led him to a white leather sectional strewn with bills, magazines, CDs, and workout clothes, leaving up to him the chore of clearing a place to sit down.

At first, Nathan was genuinely alarmed.

"I think Harold Starr has someone following me," Stella said. "He's furious that I left his gallery."

And then he knew not to give the matter another thought. Typical Stella paranoia. Once she had convinced herself that she was pregnant with Mick Jagger's baby following a ten-day drug and alcohol bender.

Nathan gave her a vague nod as he noticed six huge canvases leaning against an iron pillar—all of them shockingly, significantly, blank. The sight triggered a central nervous system response. Stella's first show for Frankovich was approaching fast, and here she was freaking out over an imaginary stalker.

She seemed to pick up on his concern. "Don't worry, honey. I paint fast, like I draw." A self-satisfied grin. "Like I fuck, too." Suddenly, her eyes went wide, and she took in an excited breath. "Oh, I've got a surprise for you!"

Nathan braced himself. Surprises from the Stellas of the world were rarely trips to Zanzibar.

"I'm adding a film installation to the vegetable cock show."

Nathan felt an inner panic. "What kind of film?" Panther's live nude thugs could be loosely classified as performance art. But porn was porn.

Stella fell over with laughter, steadying herself on Nathan's arm. "Not one of *those* films, silly. A real one. Nothing elaborate, of course. It's just a short movie of me and one of my girlfriends talking about dicks. We're smoking cigarettes and drinking and going on about big dicks, small dicks, straight dicks, curved dicks, thick dicks, skinny dicks, hard dicks, soft d—"

"I get it," Nathan cut in snappishly.

"*Really?*" Stella's tone was all-knowing. "That's not what I heard." She pretended to gag herself with her finger.

Nathan shut his eyes, paralyzed by humiliation.

Stella cackled and began a bad impression of Panther when she said, "That motherfucker was supposed to be taking *my* cookies, but he tossed his all over my goddamn boots."

Nathan refused to open his eyes. "I sent him a new pair yesterday."

Stella gave him a supportive pat on the knee. "Honey, I thought it was hilarious. When he told me, I almost peed in my pants I was laughing so hard. At least you were in a bathroom. I threw up in a guy's brand-new Porsche once about ten minutes after he'd driven it off the lot." She giggled. "And no, it didn't work out between us." Stella got quiet for a split second, then gasped. "You must think I was raised by a street whore. I haven't offered you anything. Can I get you a drink? All I've got is vodka and Tang. There might be some Dr. Pepper, but I'm almost sure it doesn't have any fizz left."

"I'm fine. But thanks."

"So what do you think about the film idea?"

"I like it."

"Do you know Pamela Gross?"

The name registered nothing. Nathan shook his head.

"She just graduated from Hunter College, and she's my new best friend. Pamela says all the smart artists are doing installations and video and photo-based work. That's why I'm adding this film to the show. I don't want people to think I'm just a stupid painter."

Nathan didn't know what to say. Footage of two drunk girls on a penis rant was hardly *A Beautiful Mind*. "Your show will be great on its own. The film will only enhance it."

Stella clapped like a little girl. "Did I tell you that a gallery in Berlin called? My first overseas show! What's German for cock?"

Nathan merely shrugged. He was alternately amazed and unfazed by Stella's success as an artist, or, some critics would argue, as a provocateuse. If nothing else, though, her work was seductive. People felt guilty about being drawn to it, but they simply couldn't help themselves. They had to look and whisper and gawk and gasp and, almost always, *buy*. Every serious collector of contemporary art had ultimately come around to the notion that owning at least one Stella Moon original was as essential as air.

She halted and peered at Nathan with a puzzled expression. "What's going on? It just dawned on me that I didn't invite you here. You called and asked to come over."

"I need a favor," he said matter-of-factly.

Stella gave him a flirtatious nudge. "Anything for you, honey, even if it's illegal."

Nathan leveled a serious gaze. "Actually, it is."

The look on Stella's face was pure delight.

He decided to just lay it on the line. "Can you help me score some crystal meth?"

Stella took in a sharp breath. "Honey, are you a Tina junkie? I never would've guessed. Not in a million years."

"It's not for me. It's—"

"*For a friend,*" she finished. "Please. Don't bullshit me."

"I'm not," Nathan insisted. "If I truly was an addict, Stella, wouldn't I have my own dealer?"

She let this point sink in. "I guess you're right about that."

"I don't know the first thing about buying drugs. That's why I came to you."

Stella smacked him on the cheek with her Bobbi Brown–painted lips. "That is so sweet. I feel honored." She dug between the cushions until she pulled out a worn address book emblazoned with the Korean animation character Mashi-Maro. "There's a guy," she began, somewhat distracted as she thumbed through the pages that were covered in scribble from top to bottom, from left margin to right. "His name's Shep. He usually hangs out at Saints. It's a little bar tucked away at 109th and Amsterdam." She glanced up. "I can call him and vouch for you. Sixty dollars will get you a quarter gram."

Nathan's heart picked up speed. He was actually going through with it. "Fine."

Stella really looked at him now. "Are you sure about this?"

"Yes." And he was. There's no doubt that Panther thought him a lame-ass punk. Who wouldn't? He sucks down a few drinks at a club, and the next minute he's hugging the commode like some middle school girl who stole too many sips of Boone's Farm at a slumber party.

But that had been the old Nathan Williams. The new and improved version was ready for action. Screw Carson's know-it-all commentaries. Forget Rob's watchful eyes. Panther was the man for Nathan. And the only way to get a brother like that was to come at him hard, fast, and wild, which is exactly what he planned to do.

Stella rose up to search for her cell phone, growing more frustrated as each unsuccessful second passed. "I don't know where the fuck I put that thing. Quick. Call my number."

Nathan punched it in on his mobile and waited for the connection to make. All of a sudden his ass started ringing. He stood up and retrieved the slim device from between the cushions.

Stella giggled, grabbing it. "I swear, honey. I wouldn't be surprised if they found Jimmy Hoffa down there." She hesitated. Conflict clouded her face. "You know, I have a bad feeling about this. Let's call Vandela. She's the psychic I told you about."

"I don't need a psychic."

Stella started to dial. Then she stopped. "Crystal is no joke, honey. Don't get me wrong. It's a great drug. But it can really fuck you up. It makes you hornier than a college boy on spring break."

Nathan knew this. And he intended to be there with a smile and all the time in the world when Panther got that way.

"I know a girl who got hooked. She used to act in those little plays they put on in the subway station after midnight. Anyway, she was taking crystal like it was a multivitamin and went on a year long sex binge. Before it was over, she'd had an abortion, a bout with gonorrhea, and tried to commit suicide. Oh, honey, it was awful. But now she sings contemporary Christian music. She let her hair grow long like Amy Grant and everything."

"That's not going to happen to me."

"How do you know?"

"For starters, I can't get pregnant."

Stella rolled her eyes. "Smart-ass." She made the call, assured Shep that Nathan could be trusted, and set up a time for the exchange. Signing off, she looked at him and shook her head. "If you end up like Diana Ross in *Lady Sings the Blues,* then I'm going to drag you kicking and screaming to CMA."

Nathan stared at her blankly. What did the Country Music Association have to do with anything?

"*Crystal Meth Anonymous,*" Stella explained. "Duh. There are several groups that meet at the Community Center on West 13th. My colorist goes every Wednesday."

"I appreciate your concern. Really, I do. But I'll be okay."

"What's happened to you? Not long ago you didn't even drink. Now you're trolling around for drugs."

"Maybe I'm growing up."

"Honey, you were plenty grown up before. That's why I turned down bigger galleries and went with Frankovich. It was all because of you. So don't go backward on me."

Nathan flashed her his best smile and held up his right hand. "Scout's honor." He left Stella's studio and took a cab to Saints, stopping at an ATM along the way for more cash. Carefully, he folded three crisp twenties in half and slipped them into his front pocket.

Shep looked more tweedy English professor than drug dealer, and he greeted Nathan at the bar like a cruiser aching to bag a one nighter before closing time. "Stella told me to watch for a gorgeous young black man. Stupid me. I thought she was loaded."

Nathan smiled politely. "You're Shep, obviously."

"Remember the name. You might be screaming it later. Especially after you get a sniff of what I've got for you." Shep hooked his arm around Nathan's neck and walked him over to a remote corner of the smoky bar. "It's not like coke and X, my friend. The first crystal high isn't the best. *Every* crystal high is."

"Do you mind if we do this quickly?" Nathan asked, in the interest of time and his growing disgust. "I have to be somewhere."

The trade was smooth. Sixty bucks for what resembled shards of broken glass in a small bag. But Nathan knew better. This party favor was more than that.

It was his ticket to heaven.

19
Rambo's Girl

"**Y**ou can count on me to rumble," David said. "I'm just like those guys who went down on that plane in Pennsylvania on September eleventh. How about you?"

Rob just looked at him. They were eating cupcakes at Magnolia Bakery, and the manner in which David Pike might respond to a terrorist attack was not exactly at the top of Rob's things-I-want-to-know-by-the-third-date list. Finally, he gave him a diffident shrug. "I've never really thought about it."

David leaned across the tiny two-top and spoke in a low, intense voice. "Well, you should. You have to prepare yourself, Rob. Mentally *and* physically. Do you have any idea what a trained hijacker could do with a small knife?" He paused a beat to gather impact, then jerked his arm back and forth in a crude gutting pantomime. "He could slice out your organs like a butcher. Heart, kidneys, liver—you name it."

Rob had only eaten half his cupcake, and now he didn't want the rest. "Can we talk about something else?"

"Ever had a gun pointed at you?"

He sighed and glanced about, envious of the other conversations going on around him. "No. Have you?"

David shook his head, disappointed. "If it happens, though, I want the guy to stick it right in my face. The closer an enemy points a weapon, the more of a psychological advantage he thinks he's got." He stomped one foot and threw a powerful underhanded sucker punch into the air. "POW!"

Rob jolted in his seat.

"The bastard wouldn't know what hit him."

If David were merely average-looking, Rob would've already helicoptered out of there. It's amazing the kind of shit you'll put up with from a breathtaking guy. And David was truly that. Rob imagined that this must be what it's like to sit across from Brad Pitt and have him all to yourself. Hopefully, the conversation would be better, but in the case of a lull, you could always ask Brad about his fabulous wife, Jennifer. With David, there was nowhere to turn.

"You should learn some moves," David was saying. "You're in a pretty dangerous occupation."

"I'm a teacher."

"Exactly. Think of all the school violence. Who knows? Manchester could be the next Columbine. But with the proper training and the right set of circumstances, you could be the one to stop it."

Rob fought to contain his annoyance. Just what America needed. Another dope who wanted to be Chuck Norris. "What are the chances I'd ever put that training to use?"

"I could ask you the same thing about a fire. But I bet you've got a smoke alarm in your apartment."

Rob had no argument for that point. Since talk of disembowelings had cooled, he finished his cupcake.

David crinkled his eyes and smiled in secret amusement.

"What?" Rob asked, feeling the heat of self-consciousness rise.

"You've got some frosting on your lip." He tapped the corner of his own mouth with his index finger.

Rob attempted to rub it off.

David smiled again. And it was a killer smile. Devastatingly sexy. "Almost. Go like this." He demonstrated with a slow, deliberate tongue.

Rob swallowed hard. "How does that go again?"

David performed an encore. "I'd lick it off for you myself, but I couldn't stop there, and I don't think these people in here could handle all of that."

Rob found himself wildly turned on. There was no getting up from this table anytime soon. He felt a little flushed and turned away from David's gaze, wiping his mouth with the back of his hand. "What do you think about seeing a movie later?"

"Sounds good."

"There's a new Hugh Grant—"

"*Hugh Grant?*" David tossed back the actor's name like a wrong fast food order. "He does chick flicks. I like loud movies where stuff gets blown up."

Rob decided right then that if David liked golf or hockey, he just might have to end this now. Or come up with some arrangement where they only had occasional sex.

"Is there a new Vin Diesel picture out?"

Actually, there was. Not Rob's first choice, but staring at Vin for two hours sounded okay, so he agreed to ditch Hugh.

There were strolling down Bleecker Street when David suggested another plan. "We could skip the movie." He raised his eyebrows lasciviously.

Rob halted. "Are you serious?"

"This is our third date. Do you want my class ring or something?" His voice was gentle, and the zinger came off as affectionate teasing.

Rob laughed. "Either that or your varsity jacket. I can't very well jump into bed with every hot guy who comes along. People will talk. I've got a reputation to uphold."

David slapped Rob on the ass and started walking again. "And all this time I thought you were a sure thing." He let a beat pass. "How about my place? I should warn you. This was Brad's week to clean . . ."

"So everything's a wreck?" Rob finished.

David nodded. "Pretty much. But my bedroom's presentable. And the sheets are clean. Don't worry. Brad will leave us alone. We have a system. A sock on the door knob is the signal for getting your groove on."

Rob didn't even crack a hint of a smile. He bit down on his lower lip, inner turmoil mounting, the image of walking out of David's bedroom and running into Brad flashing in his mind.

"You're not comfortable around Brad, are you?" David asked.

Since he was perceptive enough to raise the issue, Rob decided to just put his feelings out there. "I guess I'm a bit of a prude, David. I mean, you're looking at a guy who's never watched a gay porn movie from start to finish. Brad is fine, but his sex jokes really bother me. And frankly, I think the way you encourage him is a little strange."

"I don't encourage it," David argued, not so gentle this time. Third date. First fight. Bad sign.

Rob stood his ground. "Nothing is off-limits—not his sex life, not yours, not even ours, which doesn't even exist yet, and judging from the expression on your face probably never will."

David stewed in a long second of silence.

They were standing in front of Marc Jacobs. Rob noticed a SALE sign in the window and made a mental note to pass this bit of news along to Carson, who routinely stopped feeding his mutual funds to pay for something ridiculous like a six-hundred-dollar shirt.

"Maybe I overcompensate," David began quietly. "For breaking up the family, for being better known as Brad's gay father than simply Brad's father. I didn't want to lose him. So I became the coolest dad in all of fucking Manhattan. It started with *Playboy* and *Penthouse* when he showed signs of curiosity. And then I let him stay up late to watch Cinemax. Soon I was buying him condoms and giving him all the privacy he wanted with his girlfriends."

Rob thought of his own father, who kept *National Geographic* in a locked cabinet. The dichotomous parenting values were hilarious.

"I understand and respect his physical needs," David continued, less apologetically now. "And he understands and respects mine. Sex is no big deal to us. He's not grossed out by the fact that I want to sleep with men. I think that's pretty amazing. I know fathers like me who haven't spoken to their kids in years. Or if they do, it's a shallow relationship and awkward as hell. Brad's my best friend. It might seem weird to you, but I'm goddamn proud of the way we interact."

At first, Rob said nothing. He just let the shame and regret being telegraphed all over his face speak for itself. Who was he to judge the way David chose to raise his son? It's not like Rob was responsible for the growth and development of a living thing. He didn't have a dog or a cat. Not even a plant to care for. They were all the silk variety. And he had to admit, Brad was a great kid. So what if he was sex crazed? What eighteen-year-old guy who looked like that and could pull any woman within sight range wouldn't be?

"I don't know what the hell I'm talking about," Rob finally murmured.

David stared back, his expression half stern, half forgiving. "Unless you've raised a boy from cradle to prom night, you really don't."

"You've done a great job with Brad. Other students look up to him. He's like a celebrity at Manchester."

David beamed. "I know. He's a star to me, too."

Rob was suddenly more attracted to David than ever. He found the whole proud papa thing insanely sexy. It gave him a new depth beyond the itchy trigger finger terrorist bravado and lover of brain dead action flicks. There was definitely substance beneath the calendar guy package. "Does that offer to go back to your place still stand?"

In answer, David pulled him in for a tight embrace right there on the sidewalk. His breath was hot and sweet in Rob's ear. "It's a good thing you're going willingly. I'd hate to throw you over my shoulder. But I would if I had to."

Rob's desire for David gave him a lightheaded feeling. He clung to him, like a drowning victim to a lifeguard, hands glued to the firm set of David's muscular back. It'd been a long time. The last encounter had been a fumbling drunken one with a meaningless pickup from Chances Are. This was real. He wanted to be good. Borderline adequate wouldn't do. But he had a stirring sense that David had lived a thousand sexual lives to Rob's one. The insecurities piled up and started tumbling all over themselves. "I think you're out of my league," Rob whispered.

David snaked both hands under the waistband of Rob's Gap jeans. "All you have to do is lie back. I'm going to give you the best fuck of your life. Trust me on that." He drew back and whistled for a cab. It was loud, piercing, and amazingly effective.

Two taxis screeched to a halt.

Rob looked at him in awestruck wonder. "I can't believe you just did that. Sometimes the only way I can get a cab is to throw my body in front of one."

David cradled Rob's head with both hands and kissed his forehead. "Has anyone ever told you that you're adorable?"

"There was this one guy. He gave me his class ring. You might know him."

20

If a Boy Answers, Don't Hang Up

Carson couldn't stop staring at Gwyneth Paltrow. "Who do you think is better in bed?" he posed to Gil in a whisper. "Brad Pitt or Ben Affleck? She actually knows the answer, and it's based on firsthand experience. Plus she has an Oscar and millions in the bank. Bitch. No one deserves that much."

Gil, so caught up in his turkey and shiitake mushroom meat loaf, was barely listening.

There were at the Hudson Cafeteria. Carson wondered if the hot spot's chic boarding school mess hall vibe, complete with communal seating and visible kitchen, was stirring up his inner mean high school girl.

A few seats down sat Jennifer Lopez, but Carson paid her little attention. Too overexposed. No, tonight's celebrity focus was Gwynnie. "Something tells me that Brad would be better during the actual act but that Ben would be more fun to cuddle with. He's got a sharp sense of humor. I imagine a lazy Sunday in bed with him must be very entertaining."

"Should I be jealous?" Gil asked with his mouth full as he devoured the last bite.

"There's no reason to be jealous. You don't stand a chance against those guys. Why waste the energy?"

Gil put down his fork and clutched his heart with both hands. "You're killing me."

"No, *you're* killing *me*. Tomorrow I have to go back to my apartment and deal with my loud neighbors again."

The waiter rushed by to inquire about dessert. They ordered coffee and a cappuccino pudding to share. Just as quickly, he flitted away.

"It can't be that bad," Gil said.

"It is. Plus, there's no room service, and I have to make my own bed."

"What do you want me to say? It's time to go. My work is done here."

Carson looked at him meaningfully. "Not all of it."

Gil averted his gaze. "I'll be back. You know that. I make it to New York at least seven or eight times a year."

"So you just expect me to be your guy on the side?"

"Only if you want to be."

"Suppose I want more? What if I demanded that you divorce Claire and marry me?"

"That would make you an instant stepfather to three kids."

Carson took in a sharp breath. "Okay, guy on the side it is. Just give me a few days notice before you arrive. I might have to break up with someone."

"You would do that for me?"

"Believe me, it's no big deal. I've done it for far less. Once to just get out of a night at the opera. Another time to avoid a boyfriend's cousin's bar mitzvah. I could go on."

"Hold that thought." Gil excused himself to visit the men's room.

The dessert and coffee arrived just as he left. Absently, Carson set about preparing Gil's coffee. All of a sudden it struck him that this was a very boyfriend thing to do. The realization of how much he would miss it came next. For the first time, Carson had found himself in a romantic relationship that he didn't want to end. The irony was bitter. Because here was one that never should have started up in the first place.

"I want you to promise me something," Gil said the moment he got back. "If you've got a question about anything or just want to run an idea by me, pick up the phone. You've got my cell number, right?"

Carson nodded.

"I want *Throb* to succeed. Normally, I stay on site through production of a magazine's first revamped issue, but Matthew couldn't afford me that long."

"By the way, Plum called on my way here. Three thick FedEx packets arrived this afternoon from Atlanta, Dallas, and Los Angeles. Lots of eligible bachelors to scrutinize. You work almost as fast as you come."

"Life's too short. Why dawdle?" He winked. "What you got should be top quality. I told them to weed out any entries average or below. There should be a fantasy element to the trading cards."

Carson marveled at Gil's ability to capture the details that separated great ideas from merely good ones. For a rapid turnaround of Boyfriend Material candidates, Gil had called in favors with current and former clients in all the major markets, primarily city magazines and network affiliate news departments. Local bachelor and bachelorette themed stories were routinely strong newsstand sellers and ratings winners. To Gil's credit, he'd pushed his clients to include gays and lesbians in recent months, so instead of starting at the beginning of the race, *Throb* was already sprinting toward the ticker tape. ABC's gag fest *The Bachelor* had every single man with an ego stuck in hyperdrive—straight or gay—wishing on a star to be the next Alex Michel.

"I agree," Carson said, harboring a secret desire to skip out on Gil and head for the office to start shuffling through the potential studs. "I've been thinking about additional revenue streams for *Throb,* too."

Gil grinned, shaking his head in upbeat approval. "I've taught you well."

"We could select twelve of the hottest guys for a Boyfriend Material calendar."

"Brilliant."

"That's not all. We fly all of them in and host a huge VIP launch party at one of the gay clubs."

"Beyond brilliant." He gestured to the cappuccino pudding. "Mind if I start?"

"Be my guest."

Gil dug in, consuming almost half in just a few bites.

"There's more," Carson began, grabbing Gil's spoon to get his own fair share. "We need something for the gay man who's not going to experience the occasion of someone walking up to him to say, 'Damn, ain't you Tom Cruise?'"

Gil started to laugh.

"I'm serious," Carson pressed. "Think of the bald men, the guys who have intentions of going to the gym but end up eating fried foods, the ones who need serious dental work, or—and this really makes me thankful for my own good fortune—the boys who don't tan well. They deserve a shot at finding that special someone. How about expanding the brand across the country? We could conceptualize and trademark a Boyfriend Material night for gay clubs. Call it something short and catchy like BFM Thursdays. I pick that day because it's a big night out and leads into the weekend. Guys with no date for Saturday night would pick out their tightest T-shirt, program TiVo to record *Will and Grace,* and run out the door with too much cologne on. We could market these clubs as exclusive members and offer them special section advertising space in the magazine and BFM collateral materials for one price. I asked the art department to work up a sample blank trading card for this. My instinct was to go with an oversized laminated, dry erase version. You know, something that could accommodate a Polaroid and ample space to fill in answers to the same questions that will appear on the collectible cards." He reached into his Vuitton bag. "Here. I filled out the prototype. Take a look."

BOYFRIEND MATERIAL IN NEW YORK

Name:	Carson James St. John
Born:	April 17, 1974, in Scottsdale, Arizona
Star Sign:	Aries
Hair:	Brown
Eyes:	Brown
Height:	5'11"
Weight:	170 lbs (add 5 to 7 after the holidays)

	Likes	Dislikes
Restaurant:	Le Cirque 2000	Loud eateries
Drink:	Lychee martinis	Cheap wine
Snack:	Gummi bears	Cashews
Taste:	Spicy things	Fleshy things (hate sushi)
Smell:	Vanilla	Cigarette breath
Animal:	Dogs and cats	Reptiles
Sport:	Any sport with tight uniforms	Golf
Designer:	Don't make me choose!	Jean Paul Gaultier
TV Show:	*Sex and the City*	*Survivor* (let them die)
Cologne:	Creed Silver Mountain Water	Anything you can find at a drug store
Diva:	Cher	Whitney Houston
Movie:	*The Way We Were*	*Forrest Gump*
Author:	Jackie Collins	Anyone you can't find at a drugstore

First Time I Fooled Around with a Guy: Eighth grade sleep-over

What Makes Me Really Mad: People who can't get over themselves

Phobias: Being trapped in a place where talk radio is playing

Strange Habits: My morning grooming routine takes an hour, and no, I'm not a drag queen

Gil studied the sample as if it were hard science, then turned to Carson quite seriously.

"I think I sound pretty interesting. I would ask me out."

Gil grinned. "I didn't know half this stuff. I feel like I'm falling for you all over again."

"And imagine all the time being saved. If you're a smoker who hates to shop, adores literary fiction, and frequents sushi bars, then there's really no point in even saying hello."

Gil drank deep on his coffee. "Carson, this idea is a masterpiece. You don't need me. You could be doing my job. I mean that."

Carson was genuinely stunned. "An independent consultant? Really?"

Gil nodded. "You're a clever son of a bitch. I'll give you that."

"Well, I'm not going to have any business cards printed up quite yet. Before you dub me the gay Helen Gurley Brown, let's make sure this concept takes off."

"I don't see how it can fail." He scanned Carson's BFM card again. "It really takes you an hour to get ready in the morning?"

"Have we ever left the hotel at the same time?"

"Now that I think about it, you do have a sneaky habit of hanging back. Whatever the routine is, it's working for you." He finished his coffee and sighed deeply. "Look, I know it's early, but I leave tomorrow, and I'd rather spend our last hours together in bed. Any objections?"

Carson experienced a mini storm of ambivalence. He wanted nothing more than to tumble into bed with Gil, but deep down, he knew that one more night, one *last* night, would only compound the emotional hurt. "I'm going to miss you," he said quietly.

Gil charged the check to his room and left an enormous tip. He always tipped well. Another reason why Carson thought him suitable for marriage. Of course, Claire had beaten Carson to the altar and tricked Gil into having three children. True vixen maneuvers that smacked of Sammy Jo's best schemes against Steven Carrington on *Dynasty.*

Gil stood up, avoiding eye contact, so anxious to leave he almost bumped J. Lo, who was stunning in a Miu Miu ensemble, her skin flawless. But back to Gil. He was displaying a sudden new talent as a track star.

Carson stopped him directly beneath one of the fiery stained-glass photographs by Jean Bapiste Mondino. "Hey, where are you going so fast? No need to run. Courtney Love isn't in the building."

The tension in Gil's strong jaw relaxed a little.

"Does telling you that I'm going to miss you make you that uncomfortable?"

"Let's not do this."

Carson glanced around. The atmosphere of the place had

an Ivy League feel to it, casting them as two star crossed college lovers. "You don't have to say it back. It's just something I wanted you to know."

"What do you expect me to say?"

"You don't have to say anything. This isn't a test. It's just—"

"I'm going to miss you, too," Gil said quickly. "This is the happiest I've been in a long time. If I could, I would leave Claire tomorrow."

Carson just stood there, speechless.

"But I love my kids too much. And they're too young to put them through a divorce and long distance split custody. In about sixteen years I'll have them all in college. Wait for me." His lips curled into a wry smile. "That's something I wanted *you* to know." He took a deep breath. "I'm going for a drink in the bar. I need to clear my head. If you don't want to stay tonight, I understand . . . so . . . I'll give you some time to gather up your things in the room."

Carson watched Gil walk away, almost hating him for letting the truth gush out of his mouth like that. He loved the screwed up family man even more now. And no way was he packing up and ducking out like some war bride who didn't have the strength to see her soldier man board the train. Carson would take every millisecond that Gil had to offer.

He took the elevator up to the room, determined to be bathed, naked, and in bed when Gil came moping through the door. Gratefully, he jumped into the shower, scrubbing head to toe with a travel packet of Brown Sugar Body Polish, an erotic weapon that would leave his skin so soft, smooth, and delicious that Gil would lick his way around the world and back again.

The telephone jangled.

Carson ignored it. He was still rinsing under the steaming jets, and the J.F. Lazartigue hair conditioner from France still needed another five minutes. He wouldn't have reached the receiver in time anyway. Besides, it was probably Gil.

He tried to imagine the look on his face when he opened the door and saw him there, ready, willing, waiting. Tonight would be amazing. Definitely an evening to remember. He stepped out of the shower and into one of the plush Hudson robes when the phone rang again.

Carson's first instinct was to ignore it, to make Gil think the worst, to build up the surprise. But then he thought about him in that bar with the yellow illuminated floors. Christ. If Gil didn't have a reason to come up, one drink might turn to two, then three, maybe four. Drunk sex was only fun if both parties were wasted.

He dashed over to catch it in time. "I had you worried, didn't I?"

There was a cold silence on the other end.

Carson felt a moment's pure dread and shut his eyes.

"This is Claire Bellak. Are you the faggot who's fucking my husband?"

21

Hit Me with Your Best Shot

A total stranger shoved Danny in the chest and started barking. "Oh, you're so big now, you won't talk to me?" "I don't know you!" Danny shot back. "So fuck off!"

Fast as lightning, one of Leo's ubiquitous bodyguards stepped in and escorted the asshole out of sight before he had a chance to respond.

Danny watched them go, still trying to place his harasser. Suddenly, a faint memory tickled his brain. There *was* something oddly familiar about him. But the idiot had no manners, so he dismissed the incident and returned to skulking in the periphery as Leo deflected effusive praise from a cadre of fawning fans desperate to be in a pop idol's orbit.

Greg and Chad had gone to Orlando for a few days to visit their clueless girlfriends. This left only Damian to represent the three disposable elements of Four Deep. At the moment, he had his head bent backward on the bar as people took turns pouring tequila down his throat.

They were at a CD release party for dance sensation Anastacia at Thom's Bar in SoHo's 60 Thompson Hotel. The guest of honor's soulful rhythm smash, "One Day in Your Life," thrummed from state-of-the-art speakers.

Danny tried to enjoy the music, to keep the drinks coming, to lose himself in conversation with others in the mix—the music executives, the PR power girls, the usual scene makers, and assorted hangers on.

The only high point so far had been being hit on by Joel,

the latest model of the moment, a former Queens construction worker discovered by a T Management scout when they
were both in line at a hot dog stand. A few test shots later, he
dropped his last name (Joel was real; Wyczawski too difficult
to spell), then found himself booked for Tommy Hilfiger's
spring ad campaign, smiling in the sun with his Pepsodent
perfect teeth, looking like the most beautiful fraternity boy
God had ever touched.

In fact, Danny had actually stuttered when Joel first engaged him in conversation. His presence was that arresting.
But he radiated a certain peaceful quality that had quickly allowed Danny to regain his equilibrium.

"Are you as bored with this party as I am?" Joel had asked.

"It's not so bad."

"I hope you're not an actor. You're a terrible liar."

"I'm a lawyer."

"Shouldn't you be better at lying?"

Instantly, Danny had liked him. Joel had an easy, confident
charm, full of spunk, energy, and cuteness. He wondered how
old he was and then recalled skimming a recent Page Six item
about Joel's twenty-first birthday party at Damage, where he
dirty danced with go-go boys until four a.m.

"You're not going to start in on bad lawyer jokes, are
you?" Danny had tilted his three-quarters down drink. "Because I'll need another one of these to get through something
like that."

Joel had just smiled, standing there, seemingly unaware
that he and Leo had a firm lock on the night's raging hottie
quorum. He wore a simple striped Dolce and Gabbana cotton
shirt untucked over a pair of dark Levis. "I'm driving you to
the bottle already? Maybe we're no good for each other."

Danny had laughed. "Do you know Anastacia?"

"We did a charity gig together a few weeks ago. I was one
of her back-up dancers." He had hesitated a few seconds to
listen in on the hit blaring at top volume, pumping his slim
hips a bit. "To this song, as a matter of fact. I only messed up
twice. But I looked good doing it."

Danny had no doubt.

"Are you here for the duration? Because I've seen Anastacia, and she's seen me. I'm ready to duck out. For some reason I've got a craving for a greasy cheeseburger, fries, and a milk shake from T.G.I. Friday's."

Danny had wanted so badly to say yes. "I'm sort of with someone."

Joel had given him a quizzical look. "For real? I hate to break it to you, dude, but you're being *seriously* ignored. I've been keeping my eye on you and just assumed you were alone."

Danny had stolen a glance at Leo, still surrounded, talking and laughing animatedly, nothing about his body language suggesting that he was looking for the next opportunity to extricate himself.

"Tell me you're not with Leo Summer," Joel had said, a cautionary tone in his voice. "You've been watching him all night."

Danny felt his body grow hot. The last thing he needed was for the rumor mill to start grinding. "He's just a client. I represent the group."

Joel had laughed. "If you were my lawyer, would you look at me that way? Maybe I'll change firms. Do you have a name?"

"Ross, Orloff, and Dayan."

"What? Your parents couldn't decide?"

"That's my firm's name. In case you want to switch over. Ask for Danny Kimura."

Joel had nodded and darted a gaze around the bar, rolling his eyes. "I'm over this. Sure you don't want to come pig out with me?"

"Another time maybe. I need to stick around."

Joel had shrugged and zeroed in on Leo with a poisonous stare. "You're wasting your time. Mr. MTV over there is a United Nations slut. Did you know that?"

Danny's heart had tripped a little faster. He could feel a ditch run down his forehead and settle right between his eyebrows. "What do you mean?"

"Leo Summer is a United Nations slut," Joel had repeated, as if everyone knew this and Danny had spent the last year in a coma. "He likes to *collect* exotic boyfriends. There's an

Arab model named Abu Awan. We did runway for DKNY last month. He's been with Leo for about a year, I think. There's a Balinese guy, too. You must be the trophy Asian dude."

Anger had swept over Danny in a scalding wave. "You're an insulting little prick, you know that?"

Joel had raised his hands in mock surrender. "Hey, don't shoot the messenger."

Danny had been unable to control his temper and lit into Joel with an aggressive, rapid fire delivery. "Why don't you do us all a favor and go stuff your mouth with that cheeseburger! Do you even realize that you're spreading the kind of vicious gossip that could ruin someone's career?"

Joel had laughed in his face. "Have you listened to Four Deep lately? The music will ruin Leo's career before gossip has a run at it."

Danny had stood there, dumbfounded. He knew Joel's back story. Serendipity had transformed him from construction worker to model virtually overnight. He preened in white boxer briefs and frolicked on the beach for coke-fueled photographers. He danced poorly at disease of the week benefits and craved junk food from bad chain restaurants. Since when did a guy like that have a clever comeback arsenal that rivaled Lorelai on *The Gilmore Girls*?

"And why do you call it *vicious* gossip anyway?" Joel had challenged. "Isn't all gossip vicious? It's fine to spread rumors about drugs and lip syncing and rude behavior and crazy rider demands at concerts. But the second someone talks about a closeted star being gay, they're suddenly *ruining* a career. That's a load of crap. Like being gay is worse than being an addict or a cheap dickhead who never tips."

Danny had truly hated himself by the end of Joel's tirade. The fantasy of shutting up this motor mouth by shoving his hardening cock in his mouth had distracted him from forming any sort of rebuttal. "I think we're off point," he'd finally said.

"I guess you're right. Let's get back to the U.N. slut. Go over there and ask him about Abu."

"I'm not going to dignify that bullshit by repeating it."

"Oh, I see. You won't dignify it, but you will lose sleep over it. That makes sense."

A rage to flee had surged through Danny's nervous system, so he simply compressed his lips and walked away without a word, finding himself back in Leo's rarefied atmosphere. If the bastard realized Danny had been gone, nearly assaulted, and definitely flirted with, he gave no indication.

Now, with just a half hour or so of distance, Danny sensed all his frustration toward Joel evaporating. He chuckled to himself. Here they were at a VIP function, pretentious attitudes choking the room, and supermodel Joel's pick up line had been to join him for a calorie assault at Friday's. You had to give the man credit for being down to earth.

And then Joel's words surged back into Danny's brain, inciting an emotional riot there. *United Nations slut.* Could it be true? His gaze honed in on Leo like a laser. Now he was chatting up King Jackson, his label mate at Rhapsody and an up-and-comer on the urban scene with his barbed wire tattoos and Lenny Kravitz abs.

Danny scowled at the jungle fever in the making. King Jackson was going nowhere. His first single, "All About the Bling Bling, Baby," had fizzled on the charts until P. Diddy saw fit to remix it, adding so many samples and guest rappers and new beats that not even a note of the original song remained. King had been relegated to little more than a background crooner. Yet here he was strutting around Thom's Bar like he had something to do with the song's reincarnation.

Danny was no longer aware of anything outside his own head. He became feverish with doubt and suspicion. Had Joel called it right? Was he just a trophy boy? Did Leo have a stable of international lovers? Arab, Balinese, Asian, African-American, French, Latin, Italian. Christ, Danny could go on forever. Maybe Leo had thrown in an Alabama redneck, too.

Some clumsy fool bumped shoulders with Danny, causing him to spill the last swallow of his drink. He spun around.

Inches from his face stood the same squat-nosed jerk who'd pushed him earlier. "Still got amnesia?"

And then it dawned on him. Danny couldn't place the name, but he remembered the face now. This blast from the past had been part of a three-man alternative rock band called Aunt Brenda's Garage. Danny had negotiated their first deal with Sony a few years ago.

"I'm sorry. Your name escapes me. But I know the group. Aunt Brenda's Garage, right?" He fought back the urge to scratch his head. "Whatever happened with the group?"

Oops. Wrong question. This lunatic was a tightly wound ball of fury. "I don't know. You told us to sign that suck ass deal. What do you think happened?"

Danny all but groaned out loud. Like he had time for a first deal sob story. Everybody knew that virgin signings were practically slave contracts. Royalty rates were for shit, and the artist had to earn back everything from recording expenses and marketing fees to tour overhead and video costs. The best way to generate real cash was to blow up big and bring in a pit bull to renegotiate. Ask Toni Braxton. She was once bankrupt *and* a household name.

The current industry climate was a dangerous tightwire act. If your first CD didn't move, you got dropped. End of story. The days of nurturing performers along until they found an audience were over. Had Paul Simon started his career today, he would be singing in coffeehouses and glad to have the work.

"It's a tough business," Danny said, trying to avoid a patronizing tone but not really giving a fuck. He glanced around for Leo's bodyguard. Just in case this nut job started getting physical again. "We do the best we can for new artists. And we *definitely* explain to them what they're getting into." He threw out the last line considerably louder to drive the point home.

Danny couldn't believe this retard with the serious pass-the-blame issues. Come on! If there was a poor rock star wannabe on earth who wouldn't blow the entire naval academy to sign with a major label, no matter how one-sided the contract, then Danny hadn't met him yet.

The apparently *former* member of Aunt Brenda's Garage said nothing. He just stared death rays from drunk, angry eyes.

Danny still didn't know the guy's name. He couldn't even

remember whether he played lead guitar, bass, or drums. "Listen, I'm sorry it didn't work out for you. Really. Is the group still together?"

No response. Just that cold psychotic stare.

Danny, truly beginning to fear for his physical safety now, started to inch away. "Maybe another band will come along."

He gave Danny another violent shove. "Fuck you, laundry boy!"

A racial slur was all he could come up with? No wonder the group had tanked. Suddenly, and with great relief, Danny caught sight of the bodyguard approaching the anger management case from behind, this time flanked by hotel security.

As they strong-armed him toward the exit, Danny peered through the crowd, looking for Leo, ready to get out of there. He spotted Leo hanging on King's every word. The place was loud and packed with people graffiti. Maybe he should just leave on his own. Make Leo wonder about him for a change. From across the bar, Danny heard shouting and bustling. He turned to look.

There was no time to duck. A flying glass smashed into his forehead. The room dipped and swayed. He sank down on both knees and felt a warm liquid oozing.

"What happened?" a voice said.

"Look! That guy's bleeding!" another shouted.

For long seconds, he couldn't move.

Then Joel appeared at Danny's side and helped him into a chair. "Somebody call the paramedics!" He moved around to face him, gripping Danny's face in his hands. "Shit! Are you okay?"

Danny nodded vaguely, feeling woozy. "I . . . I think so."

Joel screamed at the bartender to toss him a wet towel. One came sailing through the air. He caught it with one hand, applying it to Danny's wound with gentle pressure. "You're gonna need stitches, dude. Are you sure you're okay?"

Danny shook his throbbing head yes. "What happened?"

"Some asshole chunked a glass at you. There's an ambulance on the way."

"I'm fine. I don't need—"

"Let them decide that," Joel said forcefully. He laughed a

little. "What does a lawyer know about head injuries anyway?"

"I got it," Danny said, taking over the task of holding down the compress. He tried to stand. Wobbly at first, but he managed.

Joel smiled at him. "You know, none of this would've happened if you'd just gone to Friday's with me."

"Why? Did *you* throw the glass?"

"No. He did."

Danny followed Joel's pointing finger to see the stalker of the night being handcuffed by a pair of uniformed NYPD officers.

Everything happened at a blistering pace. First, he gave a statement to the police. Next, the paramedics arrived and treated him at the scene before taking him to the Lenox Hill emergency room for stitches. He only needed a couple, and they were sewn just above his hairline, which made them barely visible.

Joel stayed with Danny throughout and insisted upon seeing him home. By this time, the clock had ticked past two in the morning. At the door of his Third Avenue rental duplex in a Trump high-rise, Danny finally asked the question that had been burning up his brain stem. "Do you have any idea what happened to Leo?"

"He left with King Jackson just before the paramedics came." There was a faint I-told-you-so glint in Joel's eyes.

"I owe you a dinner at Friday's," Danny said. And then he stepped inside and went straight to bed, cursing himself for wanting Leo the cheating runaway more than he wanted Joel the dashing hero.

But that was the tricky thing about desire. It had a mind all its own.

22

Cock Tales

Nathan's ass was screaming. It belonged to Panther now, and if that sexy beast wanted to brand his name on both cheeks with a hot iron, Nathan would be game.

But right now more pressing matters monopolized his time. Tonight marked the opening of Stella Moon's debut show at Frankovich, "Cock Tales." Ignoring his tender bum, Nathan stood in the center of the expansive gallery, taking everything in with a critical eye.

Twenty new pieces. Each one pure Stella Moon. The showcase might not earn Frankovich raves from the *New York Times* and *Artforum*, but it would definitely get people in the door and red dots on the wall. At the end of the day, his boss would gladly take a critical drubbing for buzz and bucks.

Stella had truly outdone herself this time. Deep down, Nathan had to admit that, initially at least, he harbored a hint of doubt, wondering if magic could actually strike twice. After all, Stella had made quite a splash with fruit cocks. Would a vegetable series be viewed as merely a desperate act to cash in on a phenomenon already croaking out its last breath?

The answer was a resounding no. If anything, the new show would eclipse the old one. Who could resist *Fried Green Tomato Cock*? Not many, apparently. The largest canvas in the show had sold for seventy-five thousand to a collector who had slipped in for a quick peek just as they were hanging it. Within hours, three other early lookers had spotted that red dot and reacted with crushing disappointment. But they recovered soon enough, wasting no time in claiming owner-ship of *Sweet Potato Cock, Creamed Spinach Cock,* and *Summer Squash Cock.*

Nathan's heart was thrumming. The positive vibrations for this event were off the charts. His prediction: every piece would find a buyer—tonight. That would mean a sell-through of one hundred percent. The big bonus John had been promis-ing might actually materialize.

He stepped over to observe the audio/visual tech gearing up the flat screen and DVD player for Stella's film installation. Another stroke of brilliance from the indomitable Ms. Moon. Her costar in the short was none other than Emma Rose, a ju-nior socialite and something of a Manhattan celebrity along the lines of Estee Lauder heiress Aerin Lauder. The society clique would turn out in droves to see one of their own swap *Cock Tales* with a controversial artist. Such a naughty, sub-versive move would be the talk of the season and generate ink in all of the columns.

The bonus possibility came swinging back into Nathan's mind. If it did happen, the first thing he planned to do was get his own apartment. Living with Rob had lost its appeal, pri-vacy being the key issue. Besides, he didn't need Rob like he used to. The same could be said for Danny and Carson.

A familiar anger stirred. Nathan hadn't spoken to Carson since their argument at the Cosi Sandwich Bar. The judgmen-tal jerk had sent a few e-mails, but Nathan simply deleted them on sight. If Carson wanted to apologize, then he could pick up the phone or show up in person. E-mail was too god-damn easy.

Maybe it was better that he distance himself from the group anyway. He tried to imagine bringing Panther along to one of the gay summits. Right away, he started to cringe. What a horrible union that would be. Worse than Eminem's rumored tryst with Kim Basinger. Just an awful combination. Panther had no patience for jaw flapping about clothes and movie stars and pop relics from the eighties.

Perhaps the biggest barrier of all was this: Panther would

not get on well with Carson. In a moment of frustration, Nathan had told him about the big scene at brunch. Panther had simply sneered and said, "Fuck that motherfucker."

Hmm. At the time, Nathan had believed that to be a searing indictment against Carson. But now that he really thought about it, Panther offered those same hostile words to so many people.

The slow bartender at the Warehouse. "Fuck that motherfucker."

The cab driver on Second Avenue who didn't stop. "Fuck that motherfucker."

The sleek fashionista giving him a fearful look on the sidewalk. "Fuck that motherfucker."

The younger brother who asked to borrow twenty dollars. "Fuck that motherfucker."

Apparently, this was a phrase applicable in a wide variety of situations. Nathan vowed to start employing it at once. Doing so might raise his street credibility. He would definitely need some to hold on to a man like Panther.

Nathan's ass tightened at the thought of him. His groin stiffened, too. That bald head, those big hands, the coal black skin. Oh, God, he felt primed for him right now. He could almost feel the steel sheeting of his bull-like chest, taste the coarse, dark, wiry hairs that sprouted conservatively from Panther's Adam's apple to just below his navel. There was an uptick of adrenaline, and Nathan experienced a sudden heat. Shit! He was almost panting. Did he have it bad or what?

Even if Nathan never saw Panther again (and the mere idea of that was agony in its purest form), he would never forget Panther's body. The exotic erotic image was permanently tattooed on his brain. Most men had muscles; Panther had steel knots. Nathan stood in awe of the way his skin stretched so tightly around his hulking frame, every inch of him corded, hard, and defined.

And then there was Panther's amazingly thick cock. One look at it and Nathan had wanted to turn and run. No way was *that* going inside him. But it had. Half an inch at a time. Over and over again. Sometimes Panther would stop his incessant pounding and pull out to linger at Nathan's core until he heard enough begging. Then—and only then—would he continue fucking him.

Audrey and Patrick Williams had raised Nathan to be proud. In fact, he never would have believed that he was capable of such shameless pleading, squirming, whimpering, and clawing—for sex. But Panther had him doing all of that and more. The need he inspired was savage. Every encounter had left Nathan drained and astonished. It was like the discovery of a whole new world, a world which Panther ruled with an iron cock. And Nathan was just happy to be one of his loyal subjects.

The wild trip had started the night Nathan had scored the crystal meth from Stella's creepy dealer. He'd taken it straight to the Warehouse, where he found Panther leaning against the bar on the first floor, hanging tough, looking rough. Nathan had presented him the little bag of glass like a child at the beach showing a pretty seashell to his parents.

"Let's go." That's all Panther had said.

Nathan had struggled to keep up, trailing him out the door. Next had come a short discussion concerning where. Panther had two roommates. Nathan had one. A train ride later they were checking into the Paramount on the Frankovich corporate American Express.

The front desk clerk had been a snotty white queer who demanded to see everything but blood and urine for identification. Two black men in a swanky hotel with a Gold card? How could it be? *I'm a Vassar grad, bitch,* Nathan had wanted to hiss. *And he's a contemporary artist represented by a major gallery.* But he'd let it go, taken the key, and hustled toward the elevator. They had been given a room on the sixth floor, thank God. The shorter the ride the better.

Once inside, Nathan had stood there awkwardly, fumbling with his hands, even as his body crackled with electric lust.

Panther had taken a violent sniff of the crystal meth, then offered the bag back.

Nathan had shook his head no. "I'm good." The intent had never been to feel himself on the drug. He wanted to feel

Panther on it. *You haven't been fucked until you've been fucked with a crystal dick.* Those crude words had been haunting his darkest fantasies ever since they were spoken in that grimy stall at the Warehouse.

Panther had flicked on the cheap stereo and twisted the knob until he found an urban station on a music sweep. "What's Luv?" by Fat Joe and Ashanti had come out blasting at maximum volume, the bass thumping so loud that Nathan thought the speakers might explode. Certainly any guest on their floor had been ready to. It had been late at night. No doubt the noise had woken some light sleepers. Nathan had felt trapped between good breeding and bad yearning. One simply didn't behave this way in a fine hotel.

At that moment, it had dawned on Nathan how destructive desire could be. He didn't drink, but he had sucked down rum and Cokes at the Warehouse. He didn't do drugs, but he had scored a quarter gram from a street dealer. He didn't steal, but he had just charged this room on the corporate card without approval. When Panther had given him that ravenously horny look, Nathan no longer cared if everything that he knew to be right and proper and safe got kicked out the door.

Panther had gone after him like an animal, peeling off Nathan's shirt, pushing down his pants, and lifting his legs over those impossibly broad, rock-firm shoulders.

"I've got condoms," Nathan had murmured.

"I don't use rubbers," Panther had fired back. "Not with somebody I trust. You trust me, don't you?" His eyes had narrowed to near slits as he dared him to answer, slipping off Nathan's silk Bergdorf Goodman boxers, cupping his ass and squeezing it with exquisite force.

Nathan had fallen silent.

"This is special. I'm going to hit it raw."

And then Panther had taken him like a cruel pirate lover. Either that or Nathan had given himself up. He couldn't remember which way it had gone.

The Bang & Olufsen phone purred, the slinky ring demolishing his castles in the air. Nathan moved quickly to answer. It could easily be Stella on the verge of a nervous breakdown.

He might have to talk her out of showing up for the opening in a Vicodin stupor. "Frankovich Gallery."

"Nathan! I'm staring at the most vulgar invitation I've ever had the displeasure of receiving!" Audrey Williams screamed.

"Mother? What are you talking about?"

"Your father and I have just returned from a ten-day trip to Greece. I'm going through our stack of mail, and I find this . . . this *filth!*"

Nathan almost started to laugh. But he fought back the impulse. Dr. and Mrs. Patrick Williams had been added to the Frankovich mailing list. Obviously, his mother had stumbled upon the invitation heralding the "Cock Tales" opening.

"I . . . I . . . I can't even say it," Audrey sputtered. "This is sick promotion for some *person*—I won't say *artist*—who calls herself Stella Moon. Appalling!"

"The opening's tonight," Nathan teased. "Are you coming?"

"Is this why we sent you to a top school, Nathan? So you can sell paintings of genitalia?"

He decided then and there that Panther's "Nubian Nights" show would be the death of her. Mental note to remove his parents from automatic mailings. No point in gaslighting the poor woman. "It's called contemporary art, Mother. Sometimes it can get . . . provocative."

"I think you mean to say disgusting."

Nathan smiled as he announced, "Not everyone thinks so. I've sold four pieces, and the show hasn't even opened yet."

"Don't be smug, Nathan. There are crazy people out there who will bid good money for an old smelly sock on eBay, too."

He paused, grinning, actually enjoying sparring with her for once. "New York society will be turning out tonight. Emma Rose is actually in the show." His voice trilled, savoring every syllable like a precious nectar. "She appears with the artist in a short film."

Audrey Williams gasped.

Nathan knew that last announcement would drive her crazy. His mother didn't just read *Town & Country;* she studied it as if an exam would be given at her next symphony league meeting.

"*Emma Rose?*" Her voice was soaked with incredulity. "It must be another Emma Rose, probably some strumpet from New Jersey, certainly not the Roses of Fifth Avenue."

"I've hired a photographer for tonight. I'll send pictures and copies of coverage in the papers. You'll see for yourself that this is the same Emma Rose who cochaired the Fire and Ice Ball last year."

There was a damning silence. "I hope you didn't invite Tia Elliott to this pornographic debacle. She could get the wrong idea about you."

"Oh, she has a pretty good idea already."

"What does that mean? I thought dinner went well. I spoke with her mother, and she said the two of you had a lovely time."

Nathan felt strangely emboldened today. Maybe it was the show's instant success. Maybe it was the haze of sexual aftershock. "I can't stand Tia, Mother. I've never met a more insufferable bitch."

"Nathan!"

"It's true. We didn't even have dinner. She got a call from the office and left me in the restaurant to eat alone."

"There must have been an emergency."

"Then it was the second one that night. She was thirty minutes late, too."

Audrey Williams huffed. "Well, that's just plain rude."

"No, the rudeness came after she arrived. Believe me."

"I might have a word with Suzanne about this. Perhaps it's that nasty Wall Street environment. Women get in there and start behaving like men to prove their worth. It happened to Faith Jordan's daughter. Her company shipped her off to one of those Bully Broad seminars."

"Who cares?" Nathan said easily. "Fuck that motherfucker."

"*Nathan!*"

"I have to go, Mother. There's still a lot to do before the opening. We'll talk soon." He hung up and checked his e-mail.

John was pressing the flesh at a bigger show for his London gallery and might have written for an update on tonight's details.

Nothing but SPAM—porn, debt consolidation, penile enlargement, mortgage offers. And one new message from Carson. The subject heading was "Emergency." If it was a real one, he should call 911.

Nathan clicked the DELETE button.

23

Who's Your Daddy?

"These tests are stupid. Why do we have to know this stuff anyway?" Tiffany DeCaro pelted the question with typical teenage scorn.

Rob shifted through the career campus quiz pile until he found her paper. Easy to spot. She had big curvy handwriting and substituted little hearts for dots. He gave it a quick scan. "It's important to know who the current mayor is, Tiffany, particularly if you work at a PR firm that handles political clients. Might come in handy."

Tiffany rose up in surprise. "Did I get that one wrong?"

"Giuliani is gone," Rob said wearily. "Bloomberg's in office now."

There was a collective groan from at least half the class.

Tiffany rolled her eyes and began to apply peach lip gloss to already glossy lips. "Isn't he the rich guy?"

"Good, Tif." He made a quick notation. "I'll give you half credit for that." Hey, it was something. You had to meet kids in the middle. There was a new national panic about students' knowledge of history. Rob worried about their grasp of the present, too. He knew students in this class who remembered the names of all the *Survivor* winners but were blank on the fact that Hillary Rodham Clinton represented their state in the U.S. Senate.

Oh, well. That's why he drilled them with these career campus tests every week. You chip away a little of the iceberg each day. What else could be done? And there had been some noticeable improvement. Several had become hooked on the Internet news sites he directed them to.

"Those are more interesting than the chat rooms," Skylar, a pretty senior, had announced last week. "I get sick of people saying, 'I'm bored' or 'Who wants to go private and cyber fuck?' I'd rather read the news. Now I can really argue with my dad. He's a total conservative. But Rush Limbaugh says the same thing over and over, so I've been kicking his ass at the dinner table."

Moments like that were the reason Rob continued teaching. It made amends for the crappy salary. He glanced up to see Brad slumped down in his seat, sleeping like a baby. There was even a bit of drool on the corner of his lip. No telling why he was so exhausted. Probably up all night with a pair of strippers from Scores.

The fourth period bell jangled, and thirty-one bodies lurched up in acknowledgment of the first lunch that lasted all of twenty-seven minutes.

Rob preferred eating in the cafeteria to one of the faculty lounges. Better to hear a teenager's amusing autopsy of the previous weekend than to listen to a gaggle of science teachers bitch about staff parking.

Cricket, a withdrawn senior who spent half her school day at one of the big accounting firms, approached him on her way out. "Mr. Cahill, can I talk to you for a minute?"

"Sure, Cricket. What's up?" Many students sought him out for advice, even those he didn't teach. Word spread quickly about which teachers were cool and approachable. Rob enjoyed listening to kids and passing out whatever wisdom he could offer. That they chose to confide in him seemed to be a measure of his influence. It had become a great source of pride. Besides, he was young enough to remember high school, or, as he liked to call it, the demented lab of self-invention.

"I've got a friend, and she's, like, really depressed," Cricket said. "Her boyfriend broke up with her, and she's, like, only making five ninety an hour at this video store, and they won't change her schedule. She's got to work, like, every Friday and

Saturday night, which is why her boyfriend broke up with her in the first place. Anyway, she wants me to give her some of my Zoloft, and I, like, don't know if I should or not."

Rob gave Cricket a kind smile. "Where did you get your prescription?"

"From my doctor."

"Then that's where your friend should get hers. Zoloft is a serious medication, Cricket. Your dosage might be too strong for her or she might have a chemical reaction to the drug and end up in the hospital. You can't pass it out like Tylenol."

Cricket smiled faintly. "Thanks. I knew that. I just wanted to hear someone else say it." She gave him a hint of a grin and disappeared into the hallway.

Rob swept the room for any belongings left behind. He spotted an MP3 player in the last row. Suddenly, the sight of Brad, still zonked out at his desk, startled him. He went over to nudge him awake. "Rough night at the Playboy mansion?"

Brad's eyes fluttered open.

It continued to amaze Rob how much he looked like David, as if they were twins eighteen years apart instead of father and son.

"Sorry." Brad glanced around. "Shit, I really was out. Where is everybody?"

"Probably in line for pizza and cheese fries by now."

"Oh, man." Brad rubbed his tired eyes. "I was up all night reading *Heart of Darkness* for English. Joseph Conrad's a fucking wack job."

Rob laughed a little, sliding into the desk opposite Brad's. As a senior, he'd hated that book, too.

"Last year a buddy of mine just watched *Apocalypse Now* and got a C. But old Mrs. Spoto is hip to that now." He yawned and stretched, focusing in on Rob with a secret smile. "So how are *you* feeling today? Pretty good, I bet."

Rob felt his face flush. He knew it was all over his cheeks like a stain of blood.

"I never figured you for a screamer," Brad said. "But you've got a set of lungs on you, man. Say, we could use you at the pep rally on Friday." He laughed at his own joke. "By the way, he's *my* daddy."

Rob stared at the wisecracking teenage Adonis as if his head carried the snakes of Medusa.

" 'Who's your daddy? Who's your daddy?' " Brad mocked, doing a dead on impression of David. "I heard him yelling that at two in the morning. And I heard you holler out 'You are!' at least ten times. Don't worry. I'd be confused too if someone had their dick rammed up my ass."

This time Rob found himself laughing. His heart was light, and he realized that he couldn't care less. Brad's life was an *American Pie* movie that never ended. Sex acts, sex jokes, sex talk. Rob would just have to deal.

"You know what sucks?" Brad asked.

Rob hesitated, wondering if this was a trick question.

"That hot girl in PR at The Janssen Group I wanted to bang found out I was in high school. She refuses to go out with me now."

"There will be other girls, Brad," Rob told him. "And given your track record, probably by fifth period." He stood up. "You better run get something to eat while you still have time."

Brad smiled. "My dad's got a surprise for you."

"Another one?" Rob cracked.

"Don't get excited. It's not a secret basement with a leather sling."

"Well, damn. It can't be very good then."

Brad rose up, a tower of testosterone, strength, and an amazing gene pool. He stared at Rob earnestly for a moment before speaking. "I hope you guys stay together. You're good for him."

Rob searched for a neutral response. "We'll see what happens."

"No pressure . . . *Papa*." Brad snickered and started out.

"So what's the surprise?" Rob called, curiosity killing him now.

"I can't say. But you better pack a weekend bag." Then, from somewhere down the corridor, he yelled out, "And sunscreen!"

Rob felt an involuntary smile play around his lips. The Hamptons maybe? Granted, David wasn't rich enough to have a house there, but he was a top producing advertising executive. Certainly he rubbed shoulders with clients who did. What about Grand Bahama Island? USAirways offered nonstop service from JFK. It was only two hours away and not overdeveloped like Nassau and Paradise Island. There were still secluded romantic spots to get lost in.

Suddenly, it dawned on Rob. Perhaps he *was* good in bed. Otherwise, why would David want to steal away with him for a weekend? A move like that meant sex all the time. Shit, there was so much to do. He needed new underwear, swimming trunks (not a Speedo, God, no, but David could get away with one), a back waxing (a tuft of hair beyond his reach that drove him crazy), a trip to the dentist. Yes, definitely that. He could try out that hour-long teeth bleaching procedure. All the coffee over the years had left his smile a little dull.

All the excitement effectively murdered Rob's appetite. He stayed in his classroom, drank a bottled water, ate half a banana, and made lists of everything he should do for the trip. For things that seemed too expensive, he wrote down BORROW FROM CARSON. Designer sunglasses, for example. They were expensive as hell, and Carson had at least ten or fifteen styles. Parting with one for a weekend wouldn't kill him.

The twenty-seven minutes had ticked down to four. Rob wired up his iBook to check e-mail before the natives got restless and began storming the halls. The dial-up connection was agonizingly slow. Finally, the AOL screen flickered to life, and the voice of Jon Bon Jovi (downloaded during a special promotion) sang, "You've got mail!"

There was one new message.

FROM: CarsonWuzHere
TO: RobCTeaches
SUBJECT: Emergency
Help! My life is falling apart. I'm sitting here in a suite at the TriBeCa Grand (the robes are fabulous, by the way) because it was the site of Mariah's breakdown, and that's what's happening to me. A total meltdown. This morning I

didn't even apply toner and moisturizer. Just a quick swipe
of gel cleanser. I've never let myself go like this. But I just
don't give a fuck. I'm a home wrecking bitch! Yes, that's
what I am! Call me Monica Lewinsky, only I swallowed
(Gil's tasted like salty Brie—yum) so no stain worries. Wait
a minute. Call me Marla Maples. She's thinner and much
prettier. I don't know what I'm going to do. I'm about to
hit the streets with my Hello Kitty boom box. I have the
eleven-minute version of Cher's "Strong Enough" (Future
Anthem Mix by Club 69). My plan is to press REPEAT
PLAY and walk until my Prada soles are nothing but shreds
of high-tech rubber! Unless I get tired. And then I'll stop
and come back to my room. It's very posh here.

Rob laughed and composed a quick response. As break-
downs go, this was not the stuff of strait jackets, electric shock
therapy, and ice baths. Carson would survive until school let
out.

24

Paging Mariah Carey

"Okay, that's it. You can go now." Carson rolled away from the Brazilian muscle escort.

"Don't you want me to shoot my load?"

Whateverrrr. Carson had been sucking and fucking that eight-and-a-half-inch uncircumcised cock for almost an hour. To no avail. "I gave up that dream about forty-five minutes ago. I figure Morgan Fairchild will have a comeback first."

"Hey!" Austin Grey protested, managing to pull off a look that was pissed off, hurt, and challenged all at the same time. Did daytime television know about this guy? Hazel eyes blazing, he started to jack himself off with righteous indignation, pumping like a madman.

Carson scarcely paid attention. He was too busy checking the cash envelope to make sure the proper amount was there. Two hundred sixty dollars for a one-hour out call. First order of business tomorrow—a reimbursement from *Throb.* After all, it had been Gil's big idea to road test one of these New York escorts for the first Boyfriend Material column, a comparison shopping exposé of East Coast/West Coast high-end rental studs.

Austin moaned triumphant, soiling the bed in short, white, hot bursts.

"Great," Carson snipped. "The maid's already been here today."

He jumped up to his full five-foot-nine height, posture ramrod straight, no doubt helped along by that ripped six-pack.

Whoa. This guy really did have a spectacularly solid muscular body. Not to mention a model-perfect face. One click of a Hasselblad and he would be ready to smolder in a Versace ad.

"You know what? My satisfaction rate is one hundred percent. I've never had a client like you before. Are you sure that you're gay?"

Carson thought it stood out like neon, but the blessed bastard before him wanted official confirmation. What a sweet thought. If only his enemies from high school could hear this. "Very. But thank you for asking." He slipped another twenty into the envelope.

Austin shook his head and started to get dressed. "It's your money."

Suddenly, it hit Carson what this must feel like for an escort whose self-concept was wrapped up in his work. It would be akin to some cretin using a brand-new issue of *Throb* as fish paper. An insulting blow to say the least.

Now Carson watched Austin with guilty eyes. The well-hung sex toy was angrily flinging on his clothes with violent tugs.

"It's not you," Carson said. "It's me."

"Yeah," Austin snapped. "Thanks for clearing that up. For a minute there I saw my career going down the drain." He rolled his eyes and took the money, stopping at the door to count it.

"I think I'm having a nervous breakdown."

Austin Grey nodded. "I think you're right. Good luck with that." And then he walked out, leaving a cloud of Aramis behind him.

Carson shuffled over to his laptop, hoping someone had responded to his cyber S.O.S. His heart soared. Danny and Rob had reached out. Yes!

FROM: DannyK
TO: CarsonWuzHere
SUBJECT: Emergency
I'm buried in Four Deep's new contract today. I'll get there as soon as I can. Moving into the TriBeCa Grand is hardly self destructive, so I'm sure you'll be fine.

FROM: RobCTeaches
TO: CarsonWuzHere
SUBJECT: Emergency
I can't leave until school's over. But let's review here. I'm in a sprawling brick and stone building with over 1,300 teenagers, and you're in a suite at the TriBeCa Grand. Who needs to be rescued exactly?

Carson couldn't believe it. Those smart-ass bastards! What time were they coming? He checked the bedside clock. Oh, thank God. Any minute now. It occurred to him that Nathan had failed to respond. Fine. He didn't need Connie Selleca to do an infomercial about it. Point taken. Nathan was writing him off after one lousy catfight.

Carson fumed, stepping into the shower to loofah away the scent of Aramis. He hated that fragrance. Cheap hooker. The nerve of him! Nathan now, not Austin. The gigolo had put in his hour and taken the cash. As expected. But that crab infested gallerino was actually ignoring him. He scrubbed with a crème brûlée body wash until his skin was practically raw.

As if Nathan was so *above* a Mariah moment. Yeah, right. Once the escapade with Tiger, Lion, Panther, whatever the fuck turned ugly—and it would, *that* was only a matter of time—then Nathan would be pulling a total Lisa Nicole Carson. Yes, he could see it now. The very second the clock struck midnight after the "Nubian Nights" opening, Nathan was in for a very rude awakening from that spray painting gangsta.

Without warning (Christ, he wasn't even thinking about him), the urge to call Gil's cell phone rose up within Carson like a rash of poison ivy that had to be scratched. He jumped out of the shower, dripping wet, and darted for the bedside table. Just a quick hello. *Hi. How are you? Divorced yet?* Something like that. The receiver felt as heavy as a brick. Oh, God, he couldn't do it. The mini bar beckoned. What if he got drunk first? Finally, his sensible side began elbowing its way into his mind. *Forget him, Carson. It's over. Or wait for him to call you. Then you'll know it's back on.*
This train of thought only mollified him briefly. Why

should he sit around waiting for a call? Gil had given him his private cell number and encouraged him to use it. *If you've got a question about anything or just want to run an idea by me, pick up the phone.* Those had been his exact words.

Of course, that declaration had come *before* the fateful call from Mrs. Gil Bellak. One thing was certain: that bitch could stand a rainy afternoon cozied up with the latest Letitia Baldridge guide. *Are you the faggot who's fucking my husband?*

At first, Carson had just stood there, frozen, speechless, like a statue in the park. But soon enough his wits had come railing back. "No, darling, you've got it all wrong. Your husband is fucking *me.*" And then he'd proceeded to lecture her on the distinctions between tops and bottoms.

Satisfying? Oh, yes. Though only for a teensy weensy moment. Because Claire had started whimpering in his ear, crying in heaving jags, fretting about losing her husband, and accusing Carson of destroying their perfect family.

Naturally, Carson had felt like the lowest form of life on the planet. Not quite as bad as Joey Buttafuoco and Tonya Harding. But very close. So he'd backpedaled, apologized profusely for reacting like a soap vixen, and explained that nothing was what it appeared to be, that Gil had been merely curious, as so many straight men are. He'd put a hard sell on this creative version of the truth, going on about the sexually charged, homoerotic atmosphere at *Throb.*

Jesus, that had been a real stretch, as the incompetent Plum was a stick-thin girl (a *real* one, with a vagina) and the art department spilled over with average boys who always seemed to have food stuck in their teeth. And it's not like the writers and photographers could ever hope to light an erotic fire. They were freelancers who rarely made it into the offices. Everything was done over the Web now.

Anyway, the emotionally distraught Claire had bought this story. She'd even cited a *Cosmopolitan* article about husbands and boyfriends who experiment with homosexuality once and only once. Thank God for Kate White! What a gem of an editor to green-light such a panic piece for the final edition. Of course, it was total bullshit. There was no *one time* for a man when he got his cock sucked until his eyeballs fell out. Those guys went looking for it again the very next day. But Claire had wanted to believe in this rubbish, so Carson cheered her on.

And it hadn't ended there. The subject of Gil's body had come up. Carson had decided to detail for Claire all the reasons she should be worshiping this delicious hunk of a man. So tedious. Most women really had no idea about male beauty. Sure, they screamed behind the velvet ropes for Matt, Ben, Jude, Josh, and all the rest, but once the ovaries began to twitch, they would march down the aisle to a handlebar-moustached big-bellied buffoon if he could pay the mortgage and splutter out sperm that got the job done.

By the time they signed off, Carson had even given Claire a few oral sex tips to drive Gil insane, like wrapping her warm mouth around his cock first thing in the morning, even if he was still sleeping, running her tongue along that sensitive ridge just under his fat mushroom head, and holding an ice cube underneath his balls seconds before he climaxed. A bitchy move, yes. But she deserved a push into the pool of bedroom insecurity for all those pesky calls.

Telling Gil about the encounter had not gone quite as well. The fact that he'd been saucing up downstairs in the Hudson Bar was partly to blame. The poor man had actually cried. Seriously. He'd sat down on the edge of the bed and wailed as if he were twelve and someone had stolen his bicycle. Then he'd packed like a speed freak and called to book the next flight to Chicago. It'd been standby only. But Gil hadn't cared. He'd simply wanted out of there as fast as possible.

So there'd been no show stopping good-bye. Carson had wanted the gay version of *Casablanca* but instead got a tepid "I'll be in touch." And that had been all. No kiss, no hug, no last tumble in the sheets. Not even a goddamn handshake. Now, it felt like Gil had banished him to Siberia. Had a discreet e-mail arrived? Hell, no. Flowers? Keep dreaming. A small trinket to symbolize their time together (say, a travel kit from Hermes or maybe the new cologne by Mark Birley)? Get thee to *Fantasy Island*.

Carson could almost feel the steam rushing inside his skull.

He had a mind to call Claire and tell her what an asshole she was married to. An awkward proposition, yes. But right now she was the only person who'd truly understand. He'd been there for her. Why couldn't she do the same for him?

A rhythmic knock rapped the door.

Carson looped a towel around his waist and dashed to answer.

Moral support had arrived! It was Danny (fiercely suited up in Armani) and Rob (a walking love letter to the Gap). He accepted their hugs in the manner of a fragile recent widow and pulled them inside. "I'm going out of my mind. I feel just like Jessica Lange in *Frances*. Except my mother's not crazy and played by Kim Stanley." He sighed dramatically and flounced onto the chaise.

Danny's voice was calm. "Start at the beginning."

"But leave out the explicit sex," Rob added. "We know what goes where. No need to sensationalize." He stepped over to the bed, hesitating before sitting down. "Is that what I think it is?" His accusing finger zeroed in on Austin's pretty mess.

Danny pulled a face.

"It's not mine!" Carson wailed.

Rob and Danny traded worried looks.

"I'm doing a column on escorts in the city, so I booked a guy. I thought losing myself in work would help. I didn't enjoy it at all. I'm serious. I had more fun watching *Vanilla Sky*."

"God," Danny said. "He must have been awful."

"That's how I know I'm heading for Mariahville on the Connie Francis Express." He pointed to his laptop on the desk. "See for yourself. His name's Austin Grey. He's got his own dot com."

Rob got there first and rubbernecked a look back to Carson. "Austin Grey was in this room, and you're not smoking a cigarette? Maybe you are insane." He typed fast.

A few seconds later, Austin, all one hundred ninety pounds of that Brazilian sex god, downloaded to life.

Rob's breathing became labored. "I've had this man tacked up on my refrigerator. I'd hire him, too, but I can only afford fifteen minutes. He's got this dumb policy about one hour minimums."

Danny couldn't take his eyes off the screen either. "Are you actually standing here and expecting us to believe that you didn't enjoy him?"

Carson nodded with total conviction.

Danny went for the cell phone attached to his hip. He turned to Rob. "I'm calling Silver Hill Hospital. You arrange a car service to meet us out front. We're taking this basket case to Connecticut."

Carson practically jumped up and down. "This isn't funny!"

"It really isn't," Rob said, his gaze glued to the computer as he scrolled through Austin's photo gallery.

"He actually looks better in person," Carson said. "Those pictures don't do him justice."

Danny groaned and raided the mini bar for a Snickers that probably cost five dollars.

Suddenly, Carson noticed the thick bandage pushing up his hairline. "Oh, my God! What happened to your head?"

Danny tried to shrug it off. "It's just a few stitches. I got hit with a glass at Thom's Bar."

Carson couldn't believe it. This sounded like something that would happen in the Bronx. "At 60 Thompson?"

Danny nodded.

Carson turned to Rob in a state of alarm.

"He says it doesn't hurt," Rob said, shrugging. "Nobody flipped out when I broke my wrist playing basketball."

"It wasn't your face!" Carson snapped. He gazed at Danny in horror. "What if it leaves a scar?"

Danny opened his mouth to answer.

But Carson cut him off. "Dermablend. It takes practice, but it works. Your skin tone will be tough to match, though." He sighed again. "Okay. We can't sit here and talk about you all day. I'm the one with the emergency."

Rob had returned to Austin's Web site.

"Turn that off!" Carson screamed.

Rob closed the computer and faced him. "Mind if I grab a beer for this?"

"There's a pack of good peanuts in there, too," Danny mumbled, his mouth full of Snickers.

Carson trudged through the whole story—his blissful days with Gil, their last dinner at Hudson Cafeteria, the call from Claire, that wretched good-bye.

"I don't get it," Rob said. "Why didn't you just hang up?"

Carson wanted to push him in front of a bus. Honestly. Sometimes Rob could be so simple. He looked at Danny expectantly.

"It sounds like this went down as well as you could hope for." Danny's voice, oozing practical reason, was balm for the soul. "Did you really want him to abandon his kids and move to New York to be with you? I wouldn't want that on my conscience."

"Yeah," Rob agreed. "But why didn't you just hang up?"

"I don't know, Rob," Carson answered impatiently. "I felt cornered and under attack. I just lashed out."

"Like a skunk," Rob put in. "You felt endangered, so you sprayed."

Carson huffed and inspected his nails. The manicurist at the hotel was great. Best one he'd had all year. "I'm not thrilled with your analogy. But, yes, I guess it was an animalistic reaction."

"What can you do about it now?" Danny asked rhetorically. "This was doomed from the start. A married man with three kids? Come on. Just be thankful you got out alive."

"But I love him." Carson hadn't intended to just blurt it out like that. And now he was crying, tears streaming down his face, ruining the under eye concealer he'd so carefully applied to mask a night of no sleep.

Danny darted into the bathroom to grab a box of Kleenex.

Rob moved over to the chaise and patted Carson's knee. "It's going to be okay."

Carson accepted one of the tissues and blew his nose. "God, I'm a mess. Do you think Julia Roberts gets this way every time?"

Danny tilted his head to mull the thought. "It had to have been hard to watch Benjamin Bratt marry Talisa Soto."

"What's all this?" Rob asked, his gaze falling on the stack of Boyfriend Material entries from Los Angeles that were spilling out of a FedEx envelope.

Carson dabbed at his eyes. "We're going ahead with that trading card idea."

Rob began to flip through the possibilities. "Look at this one."

Carson stared into the Nordic blues eyes of Koren Brillstein, a shockingly cute Jewish doctor (plastic surgery, too—money *and* convenience) who loved Cher, Bally shoes, and Tom Ford's Gucci designs. He was short but knew how to dress. For example, he didn't go for the buttoned-up look. Instead, he paired a tight crewneck with a smart sport coat. A real winner. It didn't even matter to Carson that he played racquetball and watched *Meet the Press* with Tim Russert.

"One day you're going to look back on this and go, 'What the hell was I thinking?'" Danny said.

Carson shook his head. "I'll never say that. Gil is smart and accomplished. He's a dead ringer for Owen Wilson. And we *clicked*. There was real chemistry. No, I think he'll always be the one who got away." He sniffled and inspected Koren the bachelor again. "If I ended up with this guy, though, maybe I could get free Botox injections."

Rob finished his Coor's Light and downed the rest of the peanuts. "I think you're off the critical list. You've already got your mind on a rebound guy."

Carson was tired of ignoring the fact that the intervention team had shown up one member short. "Where the fuck is Nathan?"

"He's probably at the gallery," Danny said pointedly. "Tonight is Stella Moon's opening. Remember? I'm sure he's crazed."

"Oh," Carson mumbled. *I guess the world really is still turning.*

"Get dressed and come with us," Rob suggested. "David will be there. You'll get a chance to meet him."

Carson didn't bite. "I'm not ready to venture out."

"This is a big night for Nathan," Danny said. "You should

be there. I'm sick of this standoff anyway. Someone has to be the adult and put an end to the bullshit."

Carson stood up. "Are the two of you really my friends? The last thing I need to look at is a dick, and you're dragging me to an art show called 'Cock Tales.' "

25

Flavor of the Night

Stella Moon was a storybook blonde. Her wide-set eyes sparkled as she surveyed the crowd, standing rock solid on impossibly high heeled, bone-colored leather boots, her birdlike frame sheathed in a kaleidoscopic print mini dress by Missoni.

Nathan watched her in awe, stunned by the turnout. Gooseflesh spread up and down his body. People were queued up outside as if waiting to see the biggest event on earth. Maybe "Cock Tales" was. It certainly seemed that way.

Assembled here was the kind of mob scene that would drive the suits who deal in demographics to the breaking point. New York in a blender. Uptown chic, downtown trash, Wall Street smarm machines, East Village desperados, and every other clique, group, and category that could slither in between. The usual art world suspects were definitely outnumbered tonight.

Stella sidled up to him, sniffing her nose and tipping back a Bellini. "I would give up my second born to sneak into the bathroom for a line of coke right now."

"What about your first born?"

"Honey, I bartered that away a long time ago." She giggled. "How many pieces have sold so far?"

"Eight." Nathan smiled. "And it's still early." Once more, he took in the swarm of people, suddenly reeling back at the sight of an alarmingly seedy pack admiring *Stuffed Mushroom Cock*.

"Oh, look, there's Heaven," Stella remarked, waving at one of them from afar.

Heaven smiled back, revealing a bad overbite and flashing cheap gold from neck, wrists, and fingers. Her enormous breasts were packed into a midriff baring Lycra top, and her skirt (Nathan was being generous; technically, it should be classified as a sock with the toe snipped off) rode up so high on her legs that you could almost catch an eyeful of the hollow over her hip joint. Add to that super hooker boots that stopped mid-thigh.

"Who are these people?" Nathan asked.

"Honey, every pimp, prostitute, and pervert in New York will probably show up tonight. I like to think of them as . . . my people. They can't afford my work, but they want me to succeed." Stella giggled. "Look at Emma Rose over there talking to that fat man with the bushy beard. He's got his own porn company, you know. Extreme stuff like gang bangs. And she's hanging on his every word like he's the director of the Whitney Museum. I hope one of the photographers is getting that."

"Don't worry," Nathan said. "There are a few here tonight, all of them well trained on VIPs."

"Imagine if that ended up in *WWD*." Stella curled her lips with devilish glee. "I'd have it framed."

"Forgive my rudeness," a man cut in, cupping Stella's elbow with a beautiful hand, a Chanel J12 sports watch gleaming on his wrist, "but I have to steal away the beautiful and brilliant artist responsible for this cultural cluster fuck."

Stella's lips parted open in lustful wonder. The woman never at a loss for words was speechless now.

The same could be said for Nathan. This charmer had arrested his attention at art shows and salons for months. Alessandro Imperiali was an Italian prince and headed up the Junior International Club. He was dark, lean, more handsome than any man had a right to be, sexy as hell, and famous for telling an interviewer with the *New York Times* "Sunday Styles" section that he had to make love twenty times a week to avoid splitting headaches.

He extended his free hand to Nathan. "I believe we met at

one of Kristine Bell's events. Alessandro Imperiali." The gorgeous name tripped off his gorgeous lips like powdered sugar.

"Nathan Williams." He shook fast, feeling an electric current of desire from the touch. It shocked him.

"Honey, don't be modest," Stella told the intoxicating intruder, back on her game now. "It's *Prince* Alessandro Imperiali."

He laughed a little. "As a matter of full disclosure, I must confess. The title doesn't mean that much. I actually work for a living."

"You poor, poor thing," Stella cooed.

"But enough about me." He extended his arm as if taking in the whole room. "I have to know what inspired you to do this."

"You already know about my series of fruit cock paintings, right?"

Alessandro gave her an amused nod.

"Well, I got too drunk one night and was throwing up when I thought, 'What about artichoke cock?' That's really all there was to it."

Nathan excused himself, leaving the shock artist and faux royalty to their mutual seduction. He searched the gallery for Panther. Still no sign of him. He had a disturbing habit of disappearing for hours or simply not showing up for plans and offering no explanation. Nathan huffed. He bet Alessandro would never do something like that. But then the prince was probably dignified in bed, so unlike Panther, who fucked like a demon.

He remembered their first encounter. Right here at Frankovich. It had been like an explosion. One look and Nathan had known it was fatal. Panther worked so strongly on him. For Nathan to keep his life his own was a minute by minute struggle. And, yes, it was exquisitely addictive, the thumping orgasms that seemed to go on forever, the way he felt so utterly complete when Panther impaled him. But the sexual obsession had thrashed around in pursuit of more, claiming the spiritual and emotional as prisoners, too. Nathan had given up everything it seemed, his common sense, his intellectuality, his will . . . even his friends.

"This is what passes for art these days?"

Nathan turned to locate the familiar voice and came face to face with Tia Elliott. "There's more to the field than the Henri Matisse poster print you probably have tacked up in your cubicle."

Tia scowled. "It's a Marc Chagal. Besides, I'm only here because my assistant dragged me at gunpoint. One glass of cheap champagne and I'll be back at the office."

Nathan iced her with an up and down glance, his gaze lingering on her shoes. "We only serve top brands, sweetheart. The only thing cheap around here is those Payless pumps."

Tia stuck her nose in the air. "Look at some of your patrons, Nathan. They freeze up every time one of the photographers comes around. Must bring up bad memories of having their mug shots taken."

"You'll have to excuse me, Tia. I see someone who wants to pay thirty thousand dollars for *Cabbage Patch Cock*." He started to go.

"That was a shitty thing to tell your mother."

Nathan stopped in his tracks.

Tia was staring daggers. "She went whining to my mother, who in turn called me at work at least ten or fifteen times today."

Nathan thought back. The whole crazy day was a blur. He could hardly recall what he'd told his mother about Tia.

"The receptionist blabbed about it to everyone," Tia went on. "My boss got wind of it, and by the end of business I got an official memo about incoming personal calls."

"Shouldn't you be telling this story to your mother?"

"I thought we had an agreement."

"My mother was about to push for us to go out again. I had to tell her the truth."

Tia folded her arms. "Funny how the truth only involved me being a rude bitch, not you being gay."

"That is the truth, Tia. Even if I were straight, I still wouldn't want to date you."

Tia stopped a passerby and robbed him of his champagne. "You don't mind getting another, do you?" she posed acidly after the theft had been completed. And then she tossed the drink in Nathan's face.

He remained stoic, betraying nothing, licking his lips to taste the bubbly liquid. "Ah . . . Cristal. I told you we served the best."

Tia was fuming. "I would love nothing more than to out you to that smug, smothering mother of yours. But if I've learned anything from Christian, it's to respect people's privacy on such matters. Sorry to disappoint you. I'm not a total bitch." She pushed the empty flute into his hand and made a beeline for the door.

Nathan watched her go, cleaning himself up with a handkerchief, refusing to feel guilty for giving someone so awful a dose of her own medicine.

"Seven point five on the diva scale," Carson said.

Nathan looked up to see his estranged friend just a few feet away.

"Not bad, considering your youth and ignorance. I'd say you have a promising future ahead of you."

Nathan thawed instantly. Tonight he wore D&G from head to toe. So did Carson, the collateral damage from their SoHo shopping spree on the weekend Danny had jetted off to Miami to be with Leo. Rob avoided retail therapy altogether. Having Carson all to himself that day had been a blast.

"Tasting the champagne was a nice touch."

Nathan smiled at him. "Glad you approve."

"I almost didn't come tonight. Gil's wife found out about us."

Nathan searched Carson's face and saw real hurt in his eyes.

"The only difference between me and Mariah Carey lately has been my lack of vocal range and the questionable state of my finances. I can pull off the outfits and strange behavior."

Nathan opened up his arms, and Carson fell into his embrace.

"I'm sorry," Carson whispered. "I was a complete asshole, and I can't promise that I won't be one tomorrow. Maybe even later tonight. I haven't started drinking yet."

Nathan squeezed him tighter, glad to have this fool back in his life where he belonged. "What about me? I said all those terrible things. As if I had the right to talk. I'm obsessed with a thug."

Carson drew back and adjusted Nathan's tie. "Just don't do anything stupid, like get involved with drugs or let him fuck you without a condom. That way you can safely parachute out and never look back, if it comes down to that. But who knows? Maybe it'll work."

Nathan stood there, listening to his own racing heartbeat, sweat prickling, his every synapse registering the cautionary words. But it was too late to heed them.

Carson gave him a quizzical look. Why did Nathan seem like he'd just left Earth on a lunar mission? Before he could ask, the flavor of the night crashed their reconciliation.

"Honey, is he not the most *delicious* man you've ever seen!" Stella Moon squealed, clutching Nathan's arm with both hands. "Italian men are trouble, but that's okay. I know the drill. First, I'll get swept away. Then I'll learn some horrible truth about him. Like he uses the same lines with all women or he forces his girlfriends to get abortions. But then I'll just say, 'Fuck it,' give in to the moment, and let him make love to *me* twenty times a week." She sucked in an excited breath. "Oh, my God! Honey, if we got married, I'd be *Princess* Stella! Can you imagine? Everybody in New York would shit. But I don't care if he has to work or not. I'd make them address me by my proper title."

Nathan gestured to Carson. "This is one of—"

"Carson St. John!" Stella cut in. "I know you." She bit down on an acrylic, French manicured nail. "Somebody was talking about you the other day. Who was it? Oh, that's right. Your assistant. She's named after a fruit. Kiwi?"

"That would be Plum."

"Plum. Yes, that's her. She didn't have very nice things to say about you."

Carson rolled his eyes. "That doesn't surprise me."

"Well, she skipped out early and left us to pay for her drinks, so, hey, I'm on your side. Anyway, I read *Throb* all the time." She laughed. "I'm a bit of a fag hag, flame dame, whatever you girls call us now. I've got a bone to pick with you, though. I love, love, love Ryan Law, and you put him on the cover all dressed up like he was an Eskimo!"

Carson wondered how many substances this woman was on. "He modeled beachwear."

"Yeah, those long baggy suits that surfers wear! You should've had him in a Speedo or standing there holding a washcloth over his dick. Give me some skin, honey!"

A thought surged into Carson's brain. Another one stumbled on top of it. At last! The final piece of the puzzle. "May I kiss you right now?"

Stella gave Nathan a strange look as if to say, "What's up with your friend?" Then she shrugged. "Okay, honey, go for it."

Carson planted a hard, bruising, passionate kiss on Stella's mouth, only coming up for air when he felt her squirming for breath. "You just gave me a fucking fabulous idea!"

Stella's blood red of the sunset painted lips were freshly crushed. "Are you sure that you're gay?"

Carson laughed. Twice in one day. Who would ever believe it? "Yes, and you better watch out because I'd steal that prince away from you faster than a David E. Kelley show can run out of fresh plots."

Stella lengthened her spine. "Do you know Alessandro?"

"Not personally," Carson said. "But you said that he's handsome Italian royalty. What else is there to know?" Suddenly, Carson was attacked by a rogue impulse to talk to Gil. He turned on Nathan. "Is there someplace private I can make a call?"

Nathan pointed to the rear of the gallery. "Use John's office. He's in London. What's up?"

"I'll tell you later." And then Carson power walked to his destination, stopping once to air kiss Emma Rose. Last year they'd cochaired an AIDS Walk together. The poor twit was beaming like a Hollywood screen goddess, as if appearing in Stella's silly dick chat short made her the next Ashley Judd. So pathetic. Rich people were never satisfied.

He reached the secluded office, slipped inside, pulled out his cellular, and punched in Gil's number. It started to ring . . .

* * *

Danny stood in front of *Hearts of Palm Cock* and won-dered why anyone would pay thirty-five thousand dollars for it. He didn't like navigating these events alone. What he knew about art wouldn't get him through a three-minute conversa-tion.

He spotted a man who was either a pimp or a serious sucker for anything in the Sean John collection. Maybe they could huddle and chitchat about fur coats on men. At least that would kill five minutes.

"I have a question for you."

Danny spun around.

Joel was giving him that intense runway stare. "Are you re-sponsible for any dead end careers in this room?"

"None that I'm aware of."

"I suppose it's safe to stand next to you then." The square jawed eye candy grinned. "How's your head?"

Gingerly, Danny touched his bandage. "Not bad. Sometimes it hurts at night." It startled him to realize how glad he was to see Joel. "What are you doing here?"

"I like art. I like vegetables. I like cock. How could I lose?"

Danny laughed. "When you put it that way . . ."

His cellular phone jingled. He started to ignore it, then re-considered. Four Deep had a new megabucks contract with Rhapsody. Ten million for three new studio albums. The ne-gotiation had gone down earlier that afternoon. Someone might be calling with a question on one of the deal points. He gestured for Joel to stay put and picked up. "Danny Kimura."

"Danny, this is Walter. Where are you?"

He'd never heard Walter Orloff, the managing partner of the firm, sound so grave. "At an art gallery in Chelsea."

"We need you back at the office. Joseph and Clint are here, too."

"Is something wrong?"

"Just get in a cab. Now." *Click.*

Danny dropped the phone from his ear and gave it an odd look. "I have to go," he murmured distantly.

"Me, too," Joel said. "I need to pack for a photo shoot in

Mexico. I leave in the morning. Here's fair warning: I'm col-
lecting on that Friday's dinner when I get back."

Danny, still distracted, managed a weak grin. "Yeah . . .
sure." His hands turned cold as an ominous dread moved
through him. Something was very wrong, or . . . he felt a
flood of relief as he closed the taxi door and called out the
firm's address to the driver.

Of course! They were fucking with him. Shit, why hadn't
he thought of that right away? Today he closed a ten million
dollar deal. This was partner time, baby! Walter Orloff,
Joseph Dayan, and Clint Ross. Those sneaky sons of bitches.
Danny could see them now, laughing at Walter's terrible stab
at acting. Don't quit your day job, sir. Face the fact. You're no
Jack Nicholson.

He laughed to himself, peering out the grimy window as
the city he loved slipped past. Absently, he shifted in the cab,
his hand hitting foam. Glancing down, he shook his head and
called out, "Hey, does every taxi in New York have a rip in
the backseat?"

The driver with fifteen consonants in his name said nothing.

Danny groaned, mostly pleasure, just a whisper of pain.
After all, Joseph would break out those stinky cigars, and he
would have to pretend to enjoy it so as not to offend. Oh,
well. To be the youngest partner in the firm's history, he could
handle that much. Besides, the Scotch would be good.

He let the driver keep a twenty on a nine dollar fare. Why
not? He could afford it now. And he could *definitely* afford it
tomorrow. Humming "Girl, You're in My Heart," he signed
in at the security desk, rode the elevator to the sixteenth floor,
and headed straight for Walter's office, the plush corner one
with the killer views and the decadent square footage. The big
man's door was closed.

Danny knocked twice and turned the chrome knob. He
stopped half-way in. No cigars. No Scotch. Just three powerful, wealthy white men with their fingers on the button of his
future staring back at him as if he'd bilked a debt-ridden
widow out of her late husband's life insurance policy.

"Have a seat, Danny," Walter said.

To Danny's sense of alarm was now added an overwhelming sense of doom. "What's going on?"

Walter looked at Joseph and Clint.

They gave the resident bad cop a cold, affirmative nod.

And then Walter spoke again. "Are you sexually involved with Leo Summer?"

"Seeing all these dicks is making me horny as hell," David said, gazing at *Corn on the Cob Cock*.

"Yeah, well, seeing the prices on them is making me sick," Rob countered. "The big paintings go for more than I make a year."

David grinned and put an arm around Rob's shoulder. "If it were up to me, I'd pay you a million dollars to do what you're doing."

"That's sweet," Rob said. "But there's no reason to blow smoke up my ass. You're going to get lucky tonight."

"A saint in the classroom and a whore in the bedroom. I could get used to you." He raised his empty glass. "Mind if I get drunk on the free champagne?"

Rob passed David his flute. "Not at all. As long as you help me do the same."

There was a quick step forward, and then David was standing close enough to breathe Rob's breath. "Are you sure that you want to get drunk around me?" he whispered thickly. "Because I'm liable to take serious advantage of you."

Rob's mouth itched for him. "I'm counting on it."

David left in search of Cristal, and Rob watched him work the room. He was so goddamn sexy, the way he moved with such confidence and upbeat charm, never opening a conversation with the verbal napalm of "what's new" or "how are you," always more clever than that.

They were well into the night now and still no mention of the weekend getaway. The suspense was driving Rob crazy. He couldn't even remember the last time he'd been on a real vacation. Summers were spent teaching for extra money, and Christmas break usually found him doing holiday retail duty for the same.

When David returned, he decided to just come out with it. "Brad mentioned that you had a surprise for me."

"That little fucker." David pretended to be annoyed, but there was laughter in his eyes.

"He suggested that I pack a weekend bag and stock up on sunscreen."

David paused for a leisurely sip of champagne. "My son can't keep a secret for shit, but at least he gets his facts straight."

Rob sighed his frustration. "I'm dying to know."

David smiled and seemed ready to relent. "Okay. I'll give you this much: we're going away this weekend. Make arrangements to take Friday off."

"What do you mean *this* weekend?" Rob's words sprayed about like spit. "I can't just up and—"

"Get a substitute," David said matter-of-factly. "Or call in sick. It's just one day. Manchester High will survive. We'll be back late Sunday night."

"Where are we going?" Rob demanded.

David clamped his mouth shut and made a pantomime out of locking his lips and throwing away the key.

"I have to know so I can pack!"

"Just bring basics. Anything else you might need will be provided for you."

"At least give me a hint. Is there sand involved? I've always wanted to scuba dive, you know."

David grinned. "Trust me. It's an experience that's going to change your life."

26

Infidelity as Sport

"It's me."

Gil's stony silence on the other end stretched on for long portentous seconds.

"*Carson.*" Maybe they had a bad connection. Or perhaps Gil didn't recognize his voice.

"This isn't a good idea. For us to talk. It's better that we just—"

"Pretend it never happened?" Carson finished. He sighed. So typical of a married man who cheats. To get all he needs out of an affair and then return home with a vengeance to play husband/father of the year until the next irresistible piece of ass comes along.

"Yeah," he answered coolly. "That's how I plan to deal with it."

"Relax, Gil. I'm not calling to give you the standard mistress gripe about not getting you on holidays. This is business regarding *Throb.*"

Another booming silence. "I talked to Matthew today and recommended another consultant. Her name's Carly Stone. She's one of the best. Turns out I'm going to be booked solid for the rest of the year."

"How sudden."

"Not really. A few clients were in the works, and they just firmed up."

Carson didn't need to flick on the Weather Channel to know this was an ice storm. Gil was doing the Mr. Freeze bit better than Schwarzenegger in that wretched Batman movie. The plan had never been for him to continue on in an official capacity. Matthew had caved on bigger budgets for writers, photographers, and paper quality only with the understanding that Gil would exit early.

"I'm just fulfilling my promise," Carson said tonelessly.

"What's that?"

"To call this number if I had an idea to run by you."

"Well, now I'm asking you to break it. I'm sorry about the way things turned out."

Carson gripped the cell phone tighter. He wanted to break it over Gil's skull in answer to those patronizing words. Gil might be sharp as a knife on the job but trying to maneuver from back home in suburbia dulled the blade.

I'm sorry about the way things turned out. His voice carried the distinct ring of someone reading from a TelePrompTer. A gut thing told Carson that this wasn't the first time he'd played the brutal good-bye game.

What a fucking fraud. Claire, too. The poor wife, just trying to keep her family together, always the last to know. Carson saw it so clearly now. The bullshit alarm was blaring. *Are you the faggot who's fucking my husband?* Only a woman who'd gone ten rounds with a Gary Condit type would have the balls to call from out of the blue and ask that. Gil and Claire were dysfunctional people playing sick games with each other. They deserved to rot miserably in Chicago.

It infuriated Carson that Gil would dish out to him the same arctic brush off and canned apology that he likely kept on file for some stupid model. After a week of boardroom and bedroom games, the sleazy bastard should have known to take his act up a notch.

And to think all this time Carson had harbored the secret notion that Gil Bellak was a superior being to himself. Now he knew better. Granted, there were real feelings there, emotions that wouldn't disappear overnight. But melancholy faded, and squeaks of pain subsided. One day you wake up to discover that the so-called lost love who had you living life to a Joni Mitchell soundtrack has suddenly been downgraded to windshield bug status.

Carson didn't need Gil anyway. He could make his own goals and hammer balls through them. In all truth, Gil had taught him how to think magazines on a higher plane. But the ideas were all Carson. The Boyfriend Material trading cards, the column, the calendar, and the club nights. Sure, Gil had coached him behind the scenes, but it was game day, and Carson St. John intended to grab the glory. Stella Moon's talk vomit had unintentionally provided the missing link for *Throb*'s metamorphosis, that essential ingredient to turn a ho-hum facelift into an oh, wow makeover.

"I'm sorry, too, Gil," Carson said easily, employing the tone of a person just finding out that a distant cousin can't make it to their birthday party. "I learned a great deal from you professionally and hoped we could stay in touch, but given all that's gone down, I can understand and respect your decision to cut things off. No hard feelings."

Once more, Gil's silence filled the line.

Carson smiled. Out there people were laughing at the dicks on the wall. In here he was laughing at the dick on the phone. His heart banged on the turnaround. Gil's ego wasn't craving this kind of food. Deep down he wanted drama of the fatal attraction variety. "Are you still there?"

"I'm here," Gil said tightly.

"Listen, I've kept you too long. I'll let you go. Take care of yourself." Carson hung up and dialed Matthew's cell straightaway. He checked his watch as it rang, feeling certain the man would still be knocking back drinks at the Royalton.

"Matthew Redmond."

"Hi, it's Carson. How drunk are you?"

"How drunk do I need to be?"

"Order a double."

"Why?"

"Because after you hear what I'm about to tell you, you're going to need one."

"What the fuck are you talking about?"

"I'm talking about the magazine formerly known as *Throb*. As of this moment, it's over. Way over. More over than the Spice Girls."

27

The Most Famous Fag in the World

"Excuse me?"

"Are you sexually involved with Leo Summer?" Walter repeated.

The question rocked Danny. He paused to let it stalk the room.

Walter, Joseph, and Clint were all eyes. Hard eyes. Angry eyes. Exterminating eyes.

"Did one of the secretaries bring in the *National Enquirer* again?" His voice sounded so hoarse it surprised him. He tried to smile, but his lips were frozen.

"This information didn't come to us from a tabloid," Walter said.

Danny's armpits went hot. He was churning with fear, guilt, and paranoia. Who knew? Who told? His heart began to pound, so loud that he thought these men might hear it . . . and instantly know the truth.

"Late today I received a call from Paige Fisher," Walter said. He paused. And then he dropped the nuclear bomb. "Leo's new attorney."

Danny felt a jarring sense of personal holocaust. "I don't understand."

Walter's gaze was unrelenting. "You still haven't answered my question."

He stood stock-still, motionless, holding his breath. What the hell was happening? How could Leo be represented by one lawyer at four o'clock and another one at five? And why

Paige Fisher? Her name being thrown into the mix scared the hell out of Danny. She was one of those media barracudas, a young Gloria Allred type, always turning up on *Larry King Live* and *The O'Reilly Factor* as the legal battering ram of record behind the high profile sex scandal of the day.

"Yes," Danny said. "The answer is yes." As soon as the words passed his lips, he wanted to pull them back from out of the ether. But deep down he knew that coming clean was the only way. Lying would only delay the inevitable. Besides, he had no fucking idea what lurked behind the curtain.

Walter, Joseph, and Clint exchanged intense looks.

The air was thick with damning consequences, and Danny knew that it was over for him at Ross, Orloff, & Dayan. The realization vibrated in his bones. So did the sense of betrayal. Danny couldn't sort it out logically yet, but he felt certain that Leo had saved his own ass and left him to burn.

Walter tented his long, slim fingers and regarded Danny as if he were a mess on the side of the road. "How could you be so goddamn stupid?"

Danny, feeling drained of all energy, simply sank down into one of the plush chairs. He made no attempt to explain himself to the holy trinity standing before him. They were hardly distinguishable as individuals now. Instead, he just saw one disapproving knot of expensive suits.

"Count yourself lucky," Walter said. "You're only part of the shit storm."

Danny glanced up.

"Leo's been outed. It'll be splashed across the cover of tomorrow's *Star*. Some beach boy in Bali sold the story. There are pictures, too."

Danny bit down on his lower lip. The fog was clearing. "I suppose Leo made a change in management."

Walter nodded primly. "My understanding is that he signed with Tully Dunne."

Danny was savvy enough to connect the dots now. Leo had managed an escape trick worthy of David Copperfield. No doubt the *Star* had attempted to reach him for comment, tipping him off to just how much carefully crafted image blood would be shed. A beach bimbo yakking for cash was one thing. Incriminating photographs were quite another. That Leo had ditched the ICG Management team to join Tully Dunne told Danny all he needed to know. The pictures were career anthrax. At least for the one Leo had known up to today. Obviously, a reinvention was afoot, which explained Paige Fisher's presence.

First, she would have the court render the new Rhapsody deal null and void. Danny shivered in acknowledgment of the humiliation to come. There were enough ethical breaches on the table to fill up a whole season of *The Practice,* and Paige would be waving the American Bar Association's Model Rules of Professional Conduct and Responsibility with all the gusto of a bible bitch at a pornography rally.

Danny struggled to find a silver lining. There was only one that he could see. His good name might get dragged through the muck, but at the end of the day, the worst case scenario would be a public reprimand from his peers. He'd live on to practice law. Of course, not at this firm.

"We had big plans for you, Danny," Walter said. "This is a sad day for all of us." He gestured to a file box near the door. "I called Suzanne back in to collect your personal belongings. If you sign the resignation letter on top, we're prepared to give you a ninety-day severance package. It's more than fair."

He stared blankly at Walter, who held an envelope in his right hand. It was such rich stationery, the heavy weight and smooth texture of the paper, the raised bumpiness of the firm's embossed logo. Danny could remember sitting at his desk and staring at the letterhead, praying for the day his name might be in the firm's title, too. But that dream was officially dead.

Wordlessly, he scribbled his signature, accepted the check, lifted up his box, and walked out. And then it dawned on him. How amazing it was that one phone call could so quickly destroy a life.

He glanced down at the MGM Grand coffee mug clattering against the Shore Club shot glass, souvenirs from his secret getaways with Leo. Feeling a rush of anger, he tossed them into the nearest bin. For a long second, he lingered over the garbage. Soon he was disposing more. Like he needed to

tote around this shit. Finally, in one vicious movement, everything got dumped. Fuck it. And then the tears came. Hard and
bitter ones.

How could you be so goddamn stupid?

In the heat of the moment, when your heart beats a fast
double step, when the sweet danger is right there for you to
see, touch, and taste, in that single voluptuous moment, no
risk is too great. Sex had that destructive power. *I'm not stupid. I'm merely human.*

He thought about a cab but discarded the idea and started
walking in the direction of his duplex. Thoughts of Tully
Dunne smoked his brain. Leo's new manager had a P.T.
Barnum mentality, a gift for marketing the most out of extreme situations. You didn't have to be Faith Popcorn to
know what he would throw over the pop cultural transom.

Tomorrow, as Danny set out to salvage what remained of
his career, Tully would begin building Leo Summer into the
most famous fag in the world.

28

There's No Such Thing as Safe Sex?

"That ungrateful son of a bitch," Stella fumed. "If it wasn't for me, he wouldn't even have a show. And then he doesn't bother coming to mine."

"Fuck that motherfucker," Nathan said.

Stella laughed at him. "Honey, don't take this the wrong way, but you sound like a complete idiot. Nobody wants to see Sidney Poitier all hardcore and thuggish, and nobody wants to see you that way either."

Nathan blanched.

"Panther has really done a number on you, honey. I hate that I ever introduced you to him."

"Too late." Miserably, Nathan slumped back in the hard leatherette chair in front of his sales desk.

Stella sat atop it, legs crossed, Missoni dress riding up to places Prince Alessandro desperately wanted to go. "Oh, Nathan, take it from me, honey, any man you get down with in the bathroom of a club is not a man with whom you'll have a long lasting relationship." She paused to reflect on her own words. "Hey, that was pretty good. Maybe I should write one of those dating books."

Reluctantly, Nathan's lips curled into a hint of a smile. He sat up straight. "Fuck . . . excuse my French . . . who cares about Panther? Look around this place. How many red dots do you see?"

Stella slid off the desk and began prancing around the room, counting all the way up to twenty like a two-year-old who had just learned her numbers from Barney and Baby Bop.

Nathan felt himself perking up. Stella's absolute glee was infectious. "Cock Tales" had enjoyed a one-hundred-percent sell-through. The show turned out the non-arts crowd in a way no other gallery in New York had ever been able to pull off. Media reps had pushed themselves on Stella, wanting a quote on this, an opinion on that. In one night she'd become more than just another artist pushing paintings. She was something of a guru now, a personality.

The funniest part of the night had been her altercation with Ethan Elgort, a highly respected artist who, naturally, saw very little in anyone else's work. He'd soaked his mind with champagne and accosted Stella in front of a Page Six stringer. "This show is a joke! How dare you call yourself an artist!"

"How dare you call yourself a *man,* honey. I've heard about that pinkie finger you call a dick."

There had been titters from the gaggle of direct observers, and as the story had passed around the room, laughter geysers shot up in quick turn. In this gallery full of people, spilling over with New York names, Stella Moon had been the center of attention, the star!

"Honey, I want this thing with the prince to work," Stella was saying. "I deserve some real happiness. My game plan is to not fuck him until our third date. I just hope I can hold out."

Nathan felt anxiety rise. The questions surrounding Panther were getting all cranked up again. Where was he? Who was he with? Why wasn't he answering his phone or pager?

On a gut level, he knew the answers would provide no satisfaction. Panther was the kind of brother who played ball, talked shit, and did as he damn well pleased. To push him for more would be to push him away. The sensible part of Nathan knew he should do the latter. After all, where could this relationship go? Panther could never be a true partner. He was like the husband of a famous movie star. Great in bed but the rest of the time just in the way and/or downright embarrassing.

"I hate that I care so much about what he's doing," Nathan said. He looked at Stella and realized that he wanted to hear her thoughts.

"Oh, honey, it'll pass. You just need to learn a little discipline. My therapist says that before you do anything that might have the tiniest chance of fucking up your life, you should stop and ask yourself, 'Is this healthy for me?' Then you should play that Mary J. Blige song, 'No More Drama.' If, after all that, you decide to go ahead, then it's probably a positive thing for you."

Nathan couldn't imagine Stella doing any of that. "Do you actually go through with this ritual?"

She took both of Nathan's hands in hers. "Honey, please. You know I only listen to rock stars who I want to sleep with. I *should* be following that ritual, but I don't. There's no point. I've been drinking and drugging and screwing since I was fifteen. I don't know any other way. Besides, I'm street smart. I can handle myself. *You,* on the other hand . . ."

Nathan stiffened.

". . . are simply not built to tangle with the Panthers of the world. You've got too much to lose. They don't have *shit* to lose. Somewhere out there is a nice light skinned black boy who was sent off to summer camp just like you. Save yourself for him. Ya'll can sit up in bed and talk about things like how you're both mad at your mamas for throwing away those comic books that would be so valuable now."

Nathan laughed in spite of himself. He *was* angry at his mother for that. She'd thrown away all those near mint issues of *Spider-Man, Daredevil,* and *Fantastic Four.*

"I love you, Nathan," Stella went on. "I really do. You're smart and sweet and great at what you do and a dream to look at. Panther doesn't deserve you. At best, you'll only get a small part of him anyway. Right now he's probably with his family in New Jersey."

"I thought he grew up in the Bronx."

"He did. But he's got a girlfriend and a kid in Newark. The boy's two, I think. His name's Jay-Z. You know, after the rapper. And Panther's always on and off with some actor guy. I can't remember his name. But he's been on *Law and Order* twice. Once as a carjacker and another time as a rapist. He's scary looking. I hold my handbag closer every time I see him."

Nathan's heart bolted in his chest. An inner panic consumed him. It was in the pores of his skin. It was in the very marrow of his bones. Stella had a cruel sense of timing to announce this after Carson's call to arms. He felt the urge to flee. There was something he had to do. Right now. Tonight. Or the fear of the possible would never give him a moment's rest.

Getting Stella out of the gallery was no small task. She wanted more champagne. She wanted to do an instant replay of the night. People who were there. What they wore. Things they said. Finally, he ushered her out and into a taxi, then locked up and secured his own cab for St. Vincent's.

Part of him felt like a fool for being there. The waiting area of the emergency room was swollen with serious cases—fight wounds, kidney stones, toddlers stricken with dangerously high fever, teens sweating out the results of a friend who fell out on a club drug.

He sat for hours, wringing his hands, thumbing through a tattered issue of *Redbook,* scolding himself for ending up here in the first place. A sickening wave of shame stormed through his nervous system. No amount of pleasure was worth this.

"Nathan Williams," a tired nurse called out. The Latina woman with the thick barrio accent led him to a room and closed a flimsy curtain. "What seems to be the problem?"

"It's extremely embarrassing," Nathan whispered faintly.

The nurse didn't even blink. She scribbled something onto the chart. "No problem. You can wait for the doctor. He'll be with you shortly. Take off your jacket. I need to check your blood pressure."

He removed the D&G number, folding it carefully beside him.

The nurse strapped the thick band around his right arm and worked the pump like she'd done probably a million times before. A loud hiss filled the sterile room. "You must be nervous. It's high." And then she was gone.

Nathan wrinkled his nose at the hospital odor. For a long

time he held his cell phone in hand, finger lightly dusting the number pad. He wanted to call Rob but knew his roommate and best friend was cozy in bed with David. There was no doubt where Danny was—off playing with the pop star. And Carson had left Frankovich as if the sky were falling. Something about the end of *Throb*.

A middle-aged man in black framed glasses and a gleaming white coat stepped inside. "I'm Dr. Siebel." He glanced at the chart, extending his hand as he read, "Mr. Williams." His shake was firm and fast. "How can I help?"

"This is embarrassing," Nathan said in the same faint whisper.

Dr. Siebel gave him a kind smile. "Relax. I'm not here to judge. Tell me why you're here."

"I've had unprotected sex. Gay sex."

"How long ago?"

"Several times over the last week or so."

"How many partners?"

"Just one."

"What kind of sex?"

"Oral and anal."

"Active or passive?"

"Passive."

"Any reason to believe that your partner was HIV positive or carrying a sexually transmitted disease?"

"No . . . I don't know. He gets around. Apparently."

"Any symptoms?"

"None I'm aware of."

"Urination problems? Pain? A need to relieve yourself more?"

"No."

"Sore throat?"

Nathan felt his Adam's apple. "A little, I guess."

"Fatigue? Flulike stuff?"

He shook his head.

"Any rashes, itching, penile or anal discharge, blisters, or swelling in the groin area?"

"No," Nathan said, reeling from all the horrible possibilities. He started to announce the crabs incident from several weeks ago but held it in reserve, afraid that Dr. Siebel might think him disgusting.

The doctor stepped closer and examined Nathan's glands. "Open your mouth as wide as you can and stick out your tongue." He peered inside with a small, lighted instrument. "Pretty red back there. I don't see any sores, though." He reached into one of the cabinets and pulled out a small kit. "I'm going to take a throat culture."

Nathan practically gagged as the swab touched down, creating a slight burning sensation. Just as quickly, it was over.

"This will test for chlamydia, gonorrhea, and syphilis. The nurse will draw blood for the HIV test. I assume you want one."

Nathan nodded.

"Testing takes several days, depending on the lab. The nurse will call you with the results." He reached for a prescription pad and began jotting in a hard to read scrawl. "I'm giving you a shot, followed by a few days of a strong antibiotic. That throat worries me. If it is oral gonorrhea, this approach should clear it right up."

Nathan swallowed hard.

Dr. Siebel clocked him with a ray gun gaze. "Do you want my safe sex lecture?"

"This won't happen to me again," Nathan assured him.

"There's no such thing as safe sex. Unless two virgins marry and remain eternally faithful. But how often does that happen?" The doctor smiled. "Condoms, condoms, condoms. For anal and oral. No exceptions. Lifestyle has a mint flavored one that doesn't taste so bad."

Nathan silently vowed to never give in to his lowest animal appetites again. Not at the risk of his health. Not at the risk of his *life*!

Dr. Siebel started to exit. "How about some free, nonmedical advice?"

Nathan shook his head yes.

"Find a nice guy you can trust, get checked out together, and settle down."

29

Saving Private Cahill

The gun was inches from Rob's face.

"Try to make a move. You've got about five seconds before I blow your brains out."

Arms raised above his head, Rob rocketed into action, slapping the gun with his right hand. But he forgot to pivot. *Shit.*

His assailant pulled the trigger. *Click.* "You just got shot in the neck," Kane Grubbs spat. The Army Special Forces veteran's irritation was showing. "It's slap, pivot, push barrel up, and in with your left." He demonstrated for the rest of the group. "You've got *one* chance in a situation like this. Don't end up six feet under like Randy here."

"It's Rob, actually."

Kane laughed at him. "You're dead! I don't think it matters all that much."

This earned Kane a big laugh from the benchwarmers waiting to take their turn.

"Hey, let's give him a hand for giving it his best shot," David bellowed, clapping heartily.

This earned Rob some tepid, scattered applause.

"Pike!" Kane yelled. "Get your ass up here and see if you can take me down."

Cheers, whistles, and dog woofs exploded from the peanut gallery. Everybody idolized David. They merely put up with Rob.

Same routine, different soldier boy.

Only this time Kane Grubbs ended up flat on his back with his own weapon pointed into his mouth.

"I wanted to try something different," David said eagerly, helping the fiftysomething vet up to his feet. "That works, too, right?"

"Yeah, Pike," Kane coughed, trying to regain his breathing. "I'd say that's a pretty effective move you got there."

They were somewhere on the outskirts of Tucson, Arizona. A former Army Air Corps base. In the desert. Under the brutal sun. Millions of miles away from Rob's beach fantasy.

David's surprise had been a weekend of terrorist attack training at Operation: Dead or Alive, a make-believe camp for paranoid CEOs, lawyers, doctors, schizo entrepreneurs, and anyone else willing to pay the four thousand dollars for a few days chockablock full of war games.

It drove Rob crazy to think about all the money David had spent on this bullshit. Eight grand. Plus travel. They could've gone anywhere in the world for that much. And taken the five star route.

The only entertaining part of this nightmare had been observing the reaction to David's carefree attitude about his homosexuality. He was so open about his lifestyle and proudly introduced Rob as his new lover.

At first, the motley assortment of macho, Master of the Universe executive types had kept a disapproving distance. But then David's true masculinity had been on display in hand-to-weapon combat, hostage rescue, and every other test of lethal skill that the big gut Grubbs bastard could dream up.

Drill by drill, David put everyone else to shame. He was Rambo to their Beetle Bailey. But he managed to do it without offending them. Instead, he became the proverbial big man on campus. Guys competed to laugh the hardest at his jokes. And, after giving their all to a covert ops mission, getting a thumbs-up or a slap on the back from David Pike seemed to be the equivalent of a Super Bowl ring.

It didn't surprise Rob that these men never warmed up to him. After all, he was sharing David's bed. If Rob were to fall into a ravine, no fewer than forty trigger-happy fools would step right up to be queer for a weekend with David.

Now back in the barracks after a second full day of tough training and bad food, Rob wondered if it would ever end. David, freshly showered and smelling of Old Spice Pure Sport, lay next to him, muscular arm looped around Rob's shoulder. The lumpy twin sleepers had been pushed together to create one bed, so they couldn't move around much.

"Isn't this just the fucking best?" David asked, smiling up at the cracked and molding ceiling.

Rob rose up slightly to blast a look at him. "No. As a matter of fact, it's fucking awful."

David was genuinely stunned. "What do you mean? You're having a great time."

Rob shook his head. Did David live on another planet? Had he not noticed him vomiting up breakfast after this morning's first evasive driving exercise?

Deep lines furrowed into David's brow. "You're not?"

"No. *You* are."

"Is this because Grubbs called you a pussy? He said that to anyone who tapped the brakes in the target car. Don't take it personally."

"This has nothing to do with that. And by the way, I don't even own a car, so why do I need to learn how to avoid being run off the road by kidnappers?"

"It's fun."

"Yeah, for one of us. Guess which one?"

"This is because Grubbs called you Miss Cahill for never nailing the Rockford."

Rob buried his face in his hands. "Again, when will I ever need to negotiate a three-point turn at full acceleration? Oh, yeah, I remember now. In case I get that job doing stunts in the next Paul Walker movie!" For emphasis, he placed his hands on David's bare, hairy, firm, finely sculpted chest. They felt very much at home there. "Listen. Grubbs doesn't bother me in the slightest. He's just like my old gym coaches. 'Ladies first, Cahill. The ball won't hurt you, Miss Cahill.' I'm used to that. In fact, it's been like old home week."

"So what's the problem?"

"All of this! I thought I'd be whisked away for a beach view, nice restaurants, lazy days by the pool, drinks in hollowed out coconuts with little paper umbrellas. And here, Jesus Christ, I feel like an extra from *Black Hawk Down*!"

"But I thought—"

"I know what you thought. And I can't let you go on thinking it. This sucks. I hate it. I hate it more than Regis Philbin."

"What's wrong with Regis?"

"That's not the point. David, come on. This is too extreme for me. I don't care about learning any of this stuff." He drew back, removing his hands. "And admit it. You would've had a better time here alone."

David started to remonstrate.

"You're embarrassed for me."

"What kind of shit is that? I think you're doing great. You're out there. You're trying. Okay, getting carsick was a little nelly, but I thought it was cute."

Rob grinned. "Really?"

David propped himself up on one elbow and reached out for Rob's hand. "Adorable, in fact. And for as much as you've hated it, I've got to admire you for being such a good sport." He smiled. "Up until a few minutes ago at least." His eyes crinkled. "I guess you've reached your limit, huh?"

"I think it was the teargas drill that pushed me over the edge."

David pulled Rob closer and kissed him hard on the mouth. "I'm going to make this up to you. Next time, we go anywhere you want. Name the place."

"That's not how I want it to be. I'd rather plan trips together. What's the point of another one if you end up faking *me* out about enjoying yourself?"

David shrugged. "I like physical things. I'm an athletic guy."

"Well, I'm not. I was always among the last to be chosen for sports in P.E. Usually, it was me, the really fat boy, and a kid with bad asthma named Myron who got dumped onto the team that lost the coin toss."

David laughed. "I'm sorry, but the way you put that was pretty funny."

Rob pretended to be hurt. "Are you making fun of me?"

David couldn't stop laughing. "No . . . okay . . . maybe just a little."

"Look, I'm not a complete spastic. I enjoy physical activity. We could go on a hiking trip. Or snorkeling. Skiing! I love to ski. I'm not so great at it, though. I stick to the bunny slope with all the kids."

"Rock climbing," David put in.

"You just lost me. I'm afraid of heights."

David pulled Rob onto his chest and wrapped his arms tightly around him. "River rafting."

"Ever since I saw that Meryl Streep movie with Kevin Bacon, I've been a little freaked out about it. But I'm game. Only for you, though." He breathed in David's musky smell and felt infinitely content.

"Ice fishing."

"Too cold," Rob murmured, feeling the weight on his eyelids now.

"Hot-air ballooning."

"Some friends of mine did that in the Napa Valley on their honeymoon. They said it was amazing." Rob yawned deeply and began to drift under the realization that he'd never felt so comfortable in another man's arms.

"Sailing."

"I'm . . . so . . . there." Sleep was almost upon him.

"Running with the bulls."

Rob's eyes fluttered open. "You're trying to trick me."

David kissed the top of his head. "I was just checking to see if you were asleep or not."

"No, I think you were trying to slip that one under the radar."

"Speaking of slipping one in," David said thickly. "I would love a blow job before you fall asleep."

Rob groaned. "I'm too tired. Plus, I've got a crick in my neck from all that defensive driving. I need a break, stud. Grubbs seems to be pretty sweet on you. Maybe he'll help you out." He laughed at his own joke.

David laughed, too. "That is a truly disgusting thought." Gently, he rolled Rob onto his back and placed two pillows under his head.

"What are you doing?"

"I'm taking care of my baby. You got a problem with that?"

Rob's mind filled up with soupy longings. He opened his mouth to speak, but nothing came out.

"Is that too much elevation?"

"No . . . it feels great," Rob managed.

David loomed over him, face on face, body on body.

Rob experienced a high floating calm and brought David's head down. Their tongues intertwined and turned liquid. He pushed his hips upward, pressing his rapidly arousing cock to David's already hard and insistent one.

In one fluid movement, David slid down and enveloped Rob in the hot, velvet receptacle that was his mouth, working fast, slow, and fast again.

Rob shut his eyes, allowing the pleasure to surf over his nerve endings. It was the first time David had gone down on him. Now he saw David's hand on his own cock, stroking himself in perfect rhythm to Rob's growing excitement.

"We're going to come together," David said, rising up, one hand on Rob's cock now, the other hand on his own, working them in unison like they were joysticks to the most erotic game ever invented.

Rob quivered, finding himself lost in the silken folds. He bucked down and reared up, watching David, seeing the strain of his biceps, knowing that each stroke was full of motive. His own release. And Rob's release, too. The zenith of sensation hit. Oh, God, it was mind melting. Rob's feet flew up.

They were both ready to blow now, and this cramped room wouldn't be enough to contain them. The rumble started at the back of their throats. Gasps at first, then moans, and finally a chorus of deep and soul burning growls.

"Fuck," Rob breathed. "That was amazing."

"When I take care of my baby, I take care of my baby. Don't go anywhere." David wet a washcloth and cleaned them up, then tossed it to the floor and climbed back into bed, spooning into Rob, their bodies interlocked like two pieces of a child's puzzle. "Hey, you know what I was thinking about?"

"What's that?" Rob murmured, already feeling sleepy again.

"You'd never fired a gun before today, right?"

"That's right."

"You did pretty damn well at target practice. Especially on those human silhouettes."

"Thanks."

"You must have had someone in mind to kill."

"I did."

"Who was it?"

Rob sighed the sigh of the satisfied. "Your travel agent."

30

Madonna Has Balls

"Twelve-year-old Sherry from Nebraska doesn't give a fuck what Leo puts in his mouth—a dick, a stick of dynamite—as long as he sings. So if you let those brainless shits cancel this show, the full weight of this will be on your ass!" Tully Dunne slammed down the phone. "Goddamn schmuck." He lit a Marlboro Light and dragged deep, blowing curls of smoke up toward the ceiling in his cramped Upper West Side office. "Sorry about that. Where the hell were we?"

Carson sat there, repulsed by the man in front of him known to dress in the worst Versace had to offer. Today he lived up to the hype, looking like a chubby bowl of neon rainbow sherbet dusted with chocolate designer logo sprinkles. Any minute now he could be channeling thunderbolts from the platform of an Elton John temple. But he gave good management to embattled, seemingly radioactive stars. The network TV drama queen who last year had been acquitted of murdering her gambling addict husband would agree. She was back on top with a seven-figure book deal, Emmy buzz for her best season ever, and offers to jump to features.

Leo Summer's outing in the *Star* had careened the world of pop music and spun it off its axis. This was more than the recycled unsubstantiated rumor hemorrhage that dogged every sensual golden fox from Ricky Martin to Lance Bass. The tabloid had offered up visual proof that spelled out GAY with all the subtlety of a Times Square billboard for Calvin Klein underwear.

The image was now the stuff of Internet shrines. Leo washed up on a beach in Bali. His Indonesian lover on top of him. Arguably the most talked about gay kiss ever. And the tabloid rag had already been replaced by another week's worth of busted celebrity marriages and rehab woes. But buzz on the boy-boy kiss thundered on. It was *From Here to Eternity*. Only Burt Lancaster had dumped Deborah Kerr and was rolling around in the sand with a hunky soldier.

Each day of moves and countermoves had kept the rabid media mutts foaming at the mouth. They were still scratching at the gates, panting and howling for any new drop of scandal blood.

LEO SUMMER TO EXIT FOUR DEEP
BANDMATES REFUSING TO TOUR WITH
GAY SINGER
LEO INKS NEW MANAGEMENT,
SOLO RECORDING DEAL
'HE WASN'T GAY LAST MONTH!'
SAYS NUBILE GROUPIE
SUMMER STILL SILENT ON GAY CONTROVERSY
LEO TO DEBUT FIRST SOLO SINGLE ON
MTV'S VMA SHOW IN NY
'MY MUSIC WILL SPEAK FOR ITSELF,'
VOWS LEO SUMMER

The final dates of Four Deep's "Twice Shy" tour had taken the idea of *denial* to the moon and back. Leo refused to talk, freezing out former management, his bandmates, and the media. No matter what threats of cancellation surfaced, the few remaining shows had to go on. After all, there were signed contracts to consider, not to mention nervous promoters with megabucks on the line and lawsuit ready attorneys on speed dial. So the guys took the stage and went through the slickly produced show, which had been choreographed down to the last nanosecond. Even the stage banter was scripted syllable by syllable.

Carson had scored a ticket for the Atlanta date on eBay, cashed in frequent flyer miles, and watched the surreal scene unfold from a mid-level seat in the stands. Before and after the show, vicious gay jokes had sprayed around the arena. But when the lights went down, the pop idolization went up.

Leo crooned "Girl, You're in My Heart" and, on the last note, let twin tears fall from his languid bedroom eyes. The screaming girls were devastated.

Leo moved his hips so salaciously that it made Shakira's boom boom sensuality look like a jig from Dana Carvey's old Church Lady act. The screaming girls needed oxygen.

That's when the art of the possible had hit Carson. Right there in the Philips Arena. During the Dionysian tribal humping dance break of "All My Love 4Ever, Girl." The idea had touched down like the storm it was. *Hurricane Leo.* Carson's solar plexus had vibrated in acknowledgment of what could be a master stroke. If Tully bought in, the launch of the remixed, remade, and remodeled *Throb* would be publishing gold.

So here he was, sitting before Leo's vaguely queeny, thick jowled crisis manager, lobbing his proposal over a Pig Pen desk, surprised to see that a half eaten donut had survived the morning mastication.

"Why should we do your magazine first when *Rolling Stone* is ours for the taking?" Tully demanded.

He gave the panjandrum gatekeeper a cool smile. If this was the best counterattack, then the deal was all but done. Carson wanted this so fucking bad that when he opened his mouth to speak, it was with the compulsiveness of a horny high school boy explaining why sex was good to an ambivalent date.

"Because you can't trust *Rolling Stone.* Somewhere in the world there's an exclusive cemetery for all the cover subjects who've been butchered by their so-called rock journalists who had axes to grind."

Tully shrugged. "I'll get writer and editorial approval."

Carson's response was instant. It was easy sparring with this intellectual minnow. Dense models had better verbal cut and thrust. "Maybe you can bully them into letting you choose the writer. But *editorial* approval? Never. Britney will go unplugged first."

Tully Dunne puffed on his cancer stick.

"I'll protect Leo," Carson said. "His first interview should be with a gay magazine that understands how important his next move is. Mine does. Leo Summer could be the first openly gay pop star to see his popularity soar instead of sink. George Michael got arrested in that Beverly Hills outhouse about ten years too late. It was already over for him. Leo has a shot at becoming a revolutionary figure. He's an icon in the making."

"Tell me something I don't know," Tully half chortled, half grunted.

How about this, you fat fuck. That son of a bitch almost turned my best friend into Neely O'Hara. But Carson held this back. He had to separate the business from the personal.

Danny had gone down but not for the ten count. The inner sanctum of the entertainment industry knew his role in the saga, but within a week so much more had happened that already his involvement was the stuff of vague memories and scratched heads. Danny Kimura was to the Leo Summer scandal what the first bimbo on screen was to the slasher flick—cut up quickly and then forgotten.

"Get me access," Carson said, leaning in with a ferocity that astonished him. "I'll have this issue on stands the same week of the MTV Video Music Awards. A magazine cover, a live performance, a single to radio. Leo Summer will *own* the media."

"I'll get back to you." Tully cocked his head to one side. "After I go over the offer with Leo."

Carson squirmed in his seat, only slightly, though, not enough for Tully to notice. *Shit.* He wanted to leave with more. "How soon?" His tone was casual. But desperation was pumping wildly in his heart.

"Later today."

Carson rose to exit. "How far is Leo willing to go?"

Tully Dunne grinned. "This kid has bigger balls than Madonna."

31

Boy, You're in My Heart

Danny tried sinking into a *Valley of the Dolls* drug haze, but his heart simply couldn't go there. That he spent hours researching prescription drug side effects and online addiction stories told him all he needed to know. Elizabeth Taylor just home from hip surgery he was not.

Protecting himself from the Leo Summer coverage had been next to impossible. By nature, Danny sought out entertainment news. It was as essential as the blood pumping through his veins. And a new wrinkle in the scandal seemed to break every day. There was no escape.

The Urge Lounge, a gay bar in the East Village, turned out not to be the early afternoon refuge he hoped for. Minutes into his gin and tonic, the bartender broke the ice with, "Heard the news about Leo Summer?"

"Yeah," Danny said quietly. "It's been brought to my attention."

"Hope he saved his money."

"Why do you say that?"

"Because. It's over for him." There was a hint of smugness in the bartender's voice.

Danny sensed a ghetto centric crabs in a barrel mentality. "But he just signed a solo deal," he argued, feeling oddly protective of the guy responsible for his personal Waterloo. A gay singer with speed outing skid marks on his back couldn't get props in a gay bar? What the fuck?

"Lisa Marie Presley has a solo deal, too. Think we'll ever

see *that* album?" The bartender laughed. "Anyway, I don't think Leo singing '*Boy,* You're in My Heart' will play in Peoria. The world just isn't ready for that. Sad but true."

Danny drank up.

"Want another round?"

"No thanks." He paid the tab and hit the door, wondering if the barkeep's opinion was the general attitude being swapped around. If so, Leo could flop fast. In a few years, he might end up on one of those *Where Are They Now?* specials, looking chewed up and spit out, yammering contradicting bullshit about not missing life in the spotlight but planning a comeback just the same.

The truth was, Danny didn't want that for Leo. He actually wished the scheming bastard all the success he desired. Maybe that was his conservative upbringing. The house of Kimura had been oppressive to say the least. Personal responsibility ruled.

For instance, it wasn't part of Danny's cellular makeup to understand an idiot who could smoke for twenty years and then call up a lawyer to sue Philip Morris after the cancer dragon started to roar. He expected more from himself than that.

Leo Summer had more warning labels than Tommy Lee had tattoos. But Danny had lit the match. So if he burned up his career in the process, then it was his own fucking fault. He shook his head. The things you do for lust.

And Danny did have to give the scandal twink some credit. He knew how to jump the *Titanic* and live to tell about it. For sure, Paige Fisher and Tully Dunne were wise to smooth maneuvers, but Leo was driving the car. He probably had taken one glance at the *Star,* knew they had his balls tangled up in barbed tabloid wire, and calculated the damages faster than an actuary.

Leo had known instinctively that Rhapsody would want to ride out the storm, protect the Four Deep catalog, and shove Leo so deep into the closet that he might meet the ghost of Rock Hudson there. Enter Tully Dunne. He always knew when to pounce. Or maybe Paige Fisher. She did, too. It really didn't matter who had come first. They played tag team often.

Pushing Danny onto the legal guillotine had been something straight out of *Cruel Intentions*. So how fitting that Leo sweated Ryan Phillipe vibes directly from his pores. Regardless, the move had loosened Rhapsody's grip, inched enough room for Emperor to slip in an offer, and left Chad, Damian, and Greg with no lead singer, no brainchild, and a very iffy future. Danny likened their fate to the idea of Bon Jovi soldiering on without its namesake, the guy with the raspy rock voice, golden tan, and great hair.

Danny jumped into a cab and directed the driver to his duplex. No more city wandering games. The pity party was over. He needed to shave and put on a suit and start thinking like a killer deal maker again. Maybe get on with another firm or hang his own shingle. Anything but drinking in the middle of the day.

The taxi was sitting idle in a traffic fuck when his cellular jingled. "Danny Kimura."

"I never thought they would fire you," Leo said without preamble.

Danny's laugh was hollow. But the sound of Leo's voice didn't completely surprise him. "If you had only run the plan by me first," he said, his tone merely part acid, "I would've let you know otherwise."

Leo hesitated. "I fired Paige Fisher."

Silence. A Sheryl Crow song drifted in the cab. Something about soaking up the sun. It sounded so carefree. Danny tried to sort out the facts. He never imagined that this would be part of the script. Leave it to the insolence of the young and too famous to keep things interesting. "She's a strong attorney. You could do worse."

"I want better. I want you. The deal with Emperor is done, but there's more. Book publishers are calling Tully about a memoir. Other offers are coming in." He snarled at his own situation. "Some magazine wants me to bare my soul and most of my body. Come on, Danny, I need a voice of reason in my camp."

Even as Danny dismissed the offer, a voice in his mind said, *Why not? What the hell's stopping you?*

The cab jerked back into motion, and a T.G.I. Friday's

slipped past. Danny rubbernecked a look until the eatery's familiar signage faded to nothing. He thought of Joel, who was back from Mexico and waiting for his junk food binge. It only took a heartbeat to come up with a new game plan.

With his heart he said yes to the model.

With his head he said yes to the pop star.

What did he have to lose?

32

A Very Good Christian

"It's *enormous.*"

"I've never seen one that big. It looks like a nightstick."

"How do they walk around with those things in their pants all day?"

From behind a velvet rope, the Chardonnay crowd gawked at the nude, oil slick bodies posing in front of Panther's black canvases.

Without the name recognition of Stella Moon, not to mention the oomph of her marketing machine, the turnout for "Nubian Nights" was, to be kind, less auspicious than it had been for "Cock Tales."

The critic from the *New York Times* had already left in a huff, calling it an "instantly forgettable pseudo-event" and "not even worthy of the time it would take to pan it."

Nathan felt certain that, after this was over, Panther's show would live on only in the mind of Panther. Electric fingers played on Nathan's spine. What a difference a cab ride to St. Vincent's could make. The rich fuel of obsession had sputtered out, and erotic longing had given way to practical avoidance.

The time spent waiting for those test results had been like standing on the lip of a landslide. Nathan had brokered a new deal with God about every few hours. He couldn't remember all that had been promised. But he definitely needed to find a church and start tithing ten percent of his income. Finally, a nurse had called to deliver the news. Everything had shown up negative with the exception of the gonorrhea throat culture.

That worthless, shit talking, fuck-anything-with-an-orifice closeted *homey*-sexual had given him gonorrhea! Thankfully, no further treatment was necessary. There had been the shot in his ass on the initial visit plus the swallowing down of the other antibiotic Dr. Siebel had prescribed for safe measure. But the fact that his body had already been cured of the disease did nothing to make Nathan feel less grimy. It was unbelievable! Somewhere in the city was a street hooker shuffling home after a hard night who didn't have half the health problems.

First crabs from Mike. Now another STD from Panther. He sure could pick the guys. Something had to give, though. It amazed him that Carson had bedded down two male escorts and the master of philandering yet pranced around as clean and healthy as one of the Von Trapp children from *The Sound of Music.* That fool had all the luck.

Initially, staying away from Panther had been easy. It was never his custom to call or stop by. No, Panther was too cool for that. *You* had to chase *him* down. And Nathan had simply refused to do it. Fuck Panther! But then the yearning for the satisfaction of blasting him right to his face had become unbearable.

So off Nathan had gone to the South Bronx. *For the last time.* He hated the Warehouse. He hated the cheap decor. He hated the fifteen dollar cover charge. And once inside, he hated pushing through the thug types in search of Panther most of all.

Suddenly, Nathan had come face to face with the same hard-ass who had told him he belonged upstairs on his virgin visit.

"You're Panther's bitch, right?"

Panther's bitch. The moniker steamed up Nathan's brain. "I'm nobody's bitch. You must have me confused with your mother." The words had dropped. It was too late to pull them back.

"I must be hard of motherfucking hearing or something. Because I thought I just heard you talk shit about my mother.

And if I'm right, then you're looking to be Panther's *dead* bitch, nigga." He'd taken a menacing step forward, standing close enough to graze Nathan's lips with his own. "But first I'll make you bitch out for me like he says you do for him. You'll like it, too. Because I can wax that ass a whole lot better than that motherfucker."

Nathan had recoiled from the *Oz* reject's sour breath. If that had been intended as a come on, it missed the mark entirely. But it had also offered up the go-ahead for a little manipulation 101. "Have you seen him?" He'd shouted above the thumping Busta Rhymes song and given this husky loser the benefit of pleading eyes. Possibly *grateful* eyes. They said, "Give me what I want, and after the Panther drama plays out its final act, maybe I'll come back here and be *your* bitch."

The crime statistic smiled for the first time, revealing platinum in his teeth. Talent scouts for Crest spots would not be calling. Nathan hadn't been able to determine who was responsible for this—a bad dentist or a bad jeweler.

Ultimately, Nathan's eye play had done its handiwork, the suggestion working from bull neck to crotch (after all, no brain to start with) to get this bar trash talking. "He's been kicking it at the Plaza with Baller X."

The name rang familiar. Nathan had seen the rapper's video. His hit, "Bomb Ass Bitch," was assaulting the industry, robbing radio airtime and stealing allowances from white suburban kids. It added up that the music star for a day had chosen to meet the sunrise in Trump's hotel. The hip-hoppers loved it there. Page Six had even tattled about Missy "Misdemeanor" Elliott's tacky habit of never tipping the staff.

Nathan had tried to get the hell out of Dodge, but it was slow going. The Warehouse had been packed that night, every square inch of space bulging with Panther clones running on short tempers, making the exit crawl interminable. Wedding parties left congregations at a faster clip.

Finally, he'd reached the street, and the fresh air had been pure oxygen. Once in the taxi and speeding back toward the city, Nathan had started working the cell phone. Job or no job, Danny was a baby Clive Davis with an industry Rolodex that earringed A&R guys would sacrifice a kidney for. All

Nathan needed was the fake travel name for the poor man's
Ja Rule. Stars used them for safety reasons. It'd taken about
ten minutes for Danny to hit pay dirt: Baller X had most likely
checked in under the name John Shaft.

The cab had squeaked to a stop on Fifth Avenue, and
Nathan swung out of the dented door more determined than
Mary Wilson on a stealth mission to bitch slap Diana Ross.

Inside the glamour oasis he'd felt right at home. Silver
spoons and golden goblets were his world. He was young,
pretty, dressed in designer duds, and already earning appre-
ciative glances from other guests. So unlike Baller X and Panther, who, upon entry, had probably inspired secret hopes for
Jodie Foster's *Panic Room*. He'd laughed at the thought.

Nathan had located one of the house phones and paused to
savor the moment in the making. He could've done this from
a coin operated booth on Mars, but he'd wanted to be at the
scene of the crime, to watch Panther scamper out of the posh
surroundings like the subway sewer rat he was.

He'd dialed the operator and asked her to connect him to
John Shaft's suite.

A deep, masculine voice had picked up on the fourth ring.

"Hello, Baller X?"

"Yeah."

"Is Panther there with you?"

"Who the fuck is this?"

"If I were you, I'd be less concerned about me and more
concerned about the medical history of the man you're in bed
with."

There had been a long second of worried silence.

"Don't be alarmed," Nathan had assured him. "It's nothing fatal. But you will have to get poked in the ass with a nee-
dle and pay a visit to the pharmacist. Ever heard of a nasty
little disease called gonorrhea? I bet some serious bling bling
that your new friend Panther has infected you with it." *Click.*

Nathan had watched the elevators.

Minutes later, Panther had tumbled out of one, half dressed
but fully freaked out, his obsidian eyes cursing the ritzy hotel
for not thinking of an on-site health clinic for oh shit moments like this one.

Nathan had felt none of the painful lust that normally gnawed and twisted at his body whenever Panther was in view. Maybe the bad boy monkey had finally jumped off his back. The desire meter reading had all but confirmed this. That walking health hazard with the crazy shady life was flatlining. Not even a blip.

Panther had loped out of the hotel, onto Fifth Avenue, and off to God knew where. Back to his baby's mother in Newark? To the small-time actor who gave good gangbanger on episodic TV? To the hardware store for more spray paint to finish up the color blocks he called art? As if any of the answers mattered. Ambivalence was climbing up the vine. Fast and furious. Too bad, so sad. Panther who?

Nathan had briefly toyed with the idea of yanking the plug on "Nubian Nights," but Panther's roughneck impulses made such aerial bombardment a tricky proposition. It seemed more civilized to just host the show as planned. Besides, the ball was already in play. Invitations had gone out, and the boutique publicity firm had done its media work.

So here they were, the prince and the thug, holding court at the art world's biggest non event of the year. For Nathan, this night would be viewed as a minor lapse of judgment. He was still coasting on the superleaded fuel of the "Cock Tales" phenomenon, and instant forgiveness would come tomorrow when the press release went out announcing Stella Moon's next show, "Mascara," a limited series of makeup pencil portraits using Park Avenue society mavens as subjects. For Panther, it would be viewed as so much more. A monumental failure by a minimal talent. The career that never was would never be. The gallery gossips crunching on his laughable debut like a lizard on a roach had already seen to that.

Nathan's eyes were glints of malice. Panther had no idea about his call to Baller X. Or the *Got Gonorrhea?* flyer he'd printed up with Panther's picture and circulated all over the South Bronx. The thrill of going out a winner unleashed a fountain of fine feelings within.

"Nathan Williams. What would your mother say about this?"

He spun around and found himself staring into the sparkling eyes of Christian Elliott. The room seemed to explode into phosphorous starbursts. Every muscle twitched. It took less than a millisecond for the dream of yesterday to become the dream of today. "Before or after she fainted?"

Christian laughed.

Nathan hugged him, taking hold of both shoulders as he drew back to make certain the vision was what it appeared to be. "Tia told me you lived here. I've been meaning to look you up."

"This is the first time in months that I've been in town for more than three days at a time."

"Mr. Celebrity Trainer. Always in demand."

Christian shrugged modestly. "Things are going well. I've been lucky."

Nathan wondered how anyone with Christian's supreme body, angelic face, and Denzel-perfect overbite could call it luck and not divine intervention.

"In my career, at least."

The qualifier stunned Nathan. His eyes asked the question.

"Relationship trouble," Christian explained.

"I'm sorry." But Nathan wasn't. With superhuman effort, he held back a smile. This news called for a parade, the kind with big floats and marching bands.

Christian glanced around at the black rectangles and the hard bodied nude models in front of them. "Tia told me your exhibits here were . . . *different*."

"How is Tia?" Nathan tried to sound pleasant.

"A bit hostile, actually. She made me promise to throw a glass of champagne in your face."

Nathan laughed playfully, not wanting to put Christian in the middle. He belonged on top. "That Tia can be so crazy."

"She was serious," Christian said. "But let's not and say that I did."

"Sounds like a plan."

"Tia can be very high-strung. You should only pay attention to about half the stuff she says."

"Half? Really? I haven't been paying attention to any of it."

Christian chuckled. "That's my sister, man. Give her a break. She's a black woman on Wall Street."

"You know, I've never thought about it that way. Poor girl. She's down on two counts before the first bell rings."

"Who knows? Maybe she'll relax after she makes her first million."

"I've only known people to get worse. Tia with a million dollars? That's scary."

"Don't worry. I'll protect you."

Nathan's attention was gridlocked onto Christian as the semantics thickened. His cheeks were burning. He wanted chapter and verse on this safety plan. And nothing else existed but the strangely stirring possibility that tonight he was finishing it up with Panther and starting it up with Tia's brother.

33

Son of a Preacher Man

The launch party at Damage for the magazine formerly known as *Throb* had brought out the pretty boys of New York. And if they weren't pretty, then they were definitely state of the trend.

Rocco did his thing on the raised DJ platform, jamming a monster mix of Geri Halliwell's blistering remake of "It's Raining Men." The music didn't lie.

It was.

On the better side of the velvet rope, Carson extended a freshly chemical peeled cheek to a fellow VIP. He knew his skin, like his career, was glowing, and he arched his back to send the muscles rippling down his stomach.

Matthew Redmond's kiss was *Godfather* inspired. "I don't give a fuck how much this night costs. You deserve it."

"That's the same bullshit you dished out at last year's Christmas party, and then you went insane when the bill showed up after New Year's."

"Ancient history," Matthew insisted, laughing heartily. "I've never seen a first issue go gangbusters off the newsstand like this. We must be a goddamn Oprah pick!"

Carson turned back to take in the massive enlargement of the inaugural cover. The *Throb* masthead was gone. And in its place, three big letters, flush left.

BFM.

The magazine was oversized, like *W*. But instead of cover copy graffiti stacking up like bricks, only one headline existed here, and it existed for the sole purpose of trumpeting the cover subject, which, in this case, happened to be Leo Summer on the beach.

Nude. Shockingly nude. Temptingly nude. Gloriously nude. Save for a large playing card (the queen of hearts, mind you) that he held over his unmentionable. And the headline screamed

LEO: POP'S OBJECT OF DESIRE GOES ONE ON ONE WITH STELLA MOON ON BOYS, BALI, & BREAKING UP

It seemed only fitting that Stella be given a role in the metamorphosis. After all, her prattle had sent *BFM* into motion with her take on *Throb*'s Ryan Law cover: *You should've had him in a Speedo or standing there holding a washcloth over his dick. Give me some skin, honey!*

The obvious had smacked Carson between the eyes. His high concept could be summed up in two words: *Nude Hunk.* But not just any hunk. The blandly handsome, next-stop-gay-porn-stud need not apply. Nor the designer underwear beefcake who made a run for the sock drawer seconds before Herb Ritts gave him the signal to contract his abs. Carson wanted famous guys. *Hot* famous guys. Hot famous guys willing to strip down to nothing more than a strategically placed hand. It was hardly revolutionary. Hell, at best, he was a shameless Johnny-come-lately.

Already there was *FHM, Stuff, Controversy,* and *Maxim,* the sex, sports, and fast car publishing circle where top female actors, models, and music stars sought out cover privileges as if they were the passport to heaven on earth. Halle Berry, Rebecca Romijn-Stamos, and Jennifer Love Hewitt had all posed in fabric scraps or less for the horny guy set.

But what about the gay boys and straight girls? They had cash to burn, were demographic dreams, and would scoop up a glossy monthly that stopped one breath away from *Playgirl* faster than Melissa Rivers could send them dive bombing for the remote control to obliterate the E! channel.

Carson had known the idea would have media buyers

doing slalom dashes across Madison Avenue to stake claim on advertising. A well established magazine hoped for one thousand ad pages a year. *BFM* had one hundred fifty in the first issue. And that was pre-buzz.

Every new journey needed a Christopher Columbus to lead the way. *BFM*'s was Leo Summer. The photo session had produced visual dynamite, every image of him liquid sex personified. Even Carson's first look at the proofs had resulted in a dropped jaw and a face wiped clean of expression. It didn't seem possible that the creamy voiced singer of banal pop ditties fresh out of a mediocre boy band could conjure up a look so deliciously seductive. Leo's fuck-me-I'm-famous pout was just right, bubbling all the way up to the rim but not boiling over.

The text was hotter than July, too, thanks to Stella Moon's hands off the wheel approach to conversation. Selecting pull quotes had been pure hell. By comparison, *Sophie's Choice* was no big deal. The whole piece was a powder keg. People were calling it the yummiest celebrity interview since a pre-superstardom Jennifer Lopez opened fire on Hollywood bitches and bastards in *Movieline*. Nothing was off-limits.

Leo on his former Four Deep bandmates: "I was the star. We could've replaced the other guys with orangutans. Once a roadie filled in for Greg because he was too wasted to go on. Nobody noticed."

Leo on the subject of his sexuality: "I hate labels. For me, sex is fluid. I never know what I'm going to do. If I see a hot couple out at a club, I might fuck the girlfriend or suck off the boyfriend. Depends on how I feel that night."

Leo on other boy bands: "The Backstreet Boys are a bad joke. Have you ever heard them sing live? They suck. *NSYNC might stick around, but O-Town will be carrying my luggage in two years. Bet on it."

Leo on his future: "I plan on doing it all—recording my own music, starring in films, writing a book, maybe even developing a sitcom. Everybody wants a piece of my fine, tight ass."

Beyond the nuclear effects of the Leo piece, the rest of *BFM* was earning raves—Carson's cheeky column, the trading cards, the city-by-city club roundups, plus the edgy fashion and lifestyle features. Out of this world comparisons had been tripping off lips for days. "He's the queer Candace Bushnell," one said. "*BFM* is the gay *O*," another proclaimed. Bonnie Fuller, the take no prisoners editrix who'd blazed a trail from *YM* to *Cosmopolitan* to *Glamour* to *Us Weekly* told Carson to start making notes for his speech at next year's National Magazine Awards.

Ironically, the biggest praise of all had come via Gil. Just days after the national lay down, a FedEx packet had arrived from Full Picture Associates. Inside was a handwritten critique of *BFM* from industry doyenne Helen Gurley Brown done up in her trademark chatty style. Gil knew her well and had called in the favor. Helen said the cover was "scrumptious," that the column on the East/West escort trade was "naughty fun," and that the tradings card concept should "save boys oodles of time in their search for Mr. Wonderful." For Carson, it was the equivalent of a devout Catholic getting a personal letter from the Pope. He almost found himself feeling melancholy about Gil, but in the end he held tough and refused to look back.

"Tomorrow's my wife's birthday," Matthew was saying, shouting to be heard over Geri and pulling Carson back into the earth's orbit at the same time. "See if you can get Max and Manzie to wish her a happy day on the air."

"No!" Carson said emphatically. "I can't eat up precious seconds with boring birthday wishes. I'll be lucky to get three minutes to sell the magazine. *BFM* comes first. Call up one of those oldies stations. They love to do that sort of thing."

Max and Manzie were the hosts of *Manhattan Morning,* a younger, hipper *Regis and Kelly* type talk show just beginning to gather up steam. Tomorrow he was booked during the program's first half hour. He did his tap dance after Max and Manzie's banter, immediately following Tony Danza's song, and just before the Culkin brothers reunion.

"This is crazy!"

Carson flipped to the right to see Rob, Gapilicious as always, and his swoon inducing boyfriend David, creeping up in years but still as hard bodied as a twenty-five-year-old gym addict. He gave big hugs to both, swinging from side to side as Rocco faded out Geri and whipped the room into a frenzy with Hex Hector's reworking of Britney's "Don't Let Me Be the Last to Know."

"Guess who's here?" Rob screamed.

Carson couldn't begin to guess. Damage was hundreds deep with the gay elite.

"Remember that plastic surgeon? We looked at his BFM card at the TriBeCa Grand."

Carson raided his mental file. "Koren Brillstein! He likes Bally shoes, *Meet the Press,* and Cher. Not in that order, I hope."

"I saw him getting a drink at the bar," Rob said. "He's cute. Looks better than the picture."

Carson smiled. "Are you his agent or something?"

"I just thought you'd want to know."

"I invited him. He's in the next issue, and all the top bachelors for the first few months got the star treatment. But this guy screamed at Plum for booking him a window seat. Too high maintenance."

David glanced up at the floating screen broadcasting the MTV Video Music Awards. "What time's the main event?"

Carson checked his watch. "Any minute now."

The plan was for Leo Summer to do his live bit and then shoot over to Damage to play guest of honor. The heat regarding his first appearance as a solo artist had become the stuff of burning forests. The VMAs singled out one breakout performance each year, and the list of past superstars who'd earned subject marquee time at next-day watercooler confabs read like *Billboard*'s all-time greatest hits.

Madonna, before cementing her icon status across two centuries, writhing on the stage in her wedding dress hiked up to there as she warbled "Like a Virgin."

Britney Spears, pushing her stripper, trailer tramp act to dizzying heights with a vampy, flesh-colored bodysuit and thong clad reading of a heavy metalized "Satisfaction"/ "Oops . . . I Did It Again" medley.

Michael Jackson, emerging from boy love exile to herald the release of the laughably titled *Invincible,* a super bomb outsold in the states even by preteen pipsqueak Aaron Carter, turning up on stage to muscle in on *NSYNC's action with a herky-jerky dance slash seizure routine made all the more frightening by his liquid paper skin and circus freak plastic surgery.

Tonight the A team was split to cover all the action.

Rob and David were hanging tough at Damage, enjoying their inner circle status and providing instant calm for moments when Carson thought the Xanax blood had stopped pumping.

Danny, Leo's off-again/on-again attorney, had taken supermodel Joel to the pop cultural train wreck at Radio City Music Hall.

Nathan was there, too, as the guest of Christian Elliott, the body guru responsible for every cut, curve, and ripple of Leo's physique envy. Thanks to *BFM,* the trainer's after shots were being shoved in the faces of magazine browsers everywhere.

Stella Moon held court as well, with Prince Alessandro in tow, both there as Leo's special guests.

It was almost time.

Carson waved Rocco to a stop with a slice-the-neck gesture. He didn't mind putting his ex-boyfriend number whatever into the role of hired hand. This was the food chain at work. Rocco always was and always would be plankton.

The tribal dance beat at Damage went down.

The screams at the VMAs went up.

Leo had just been introduced by a stringy-haired Kid Rock and the hepatitis case with booty club boobs also known as Pamela Anderson.

The beat was funky, urban, and nasty, nothing like the Swedish pop candy hooks of Four Deep's best known material.

"Jimmy Ray was a preacher's son . . ." Leo growled in a raspy voice that revealed more soulful range than the gay troublemaker had ever hinted at with his old cronies, who were already heading for Corey Haim Town with a series of embarrassing arrests, public scenes, and drunk driving accidents in Florida.

The club talk at Damage stopped dead. Every face was on the screen, watching history in the making.

This take on Dusty Springfield's "Son of a Preacher Man"

was in full swing, complete with leather baby go-go–clad back-up dancers and a shirtless, oiled down Leo squeezed into a pair of pink hot pants that left nothing to the imagination.

"The only boy who could ever teach me . . ."

Leo Summer sang. Leo Summer danced. Leo Summer preened.

"Was the son of a preacher man . . ."

Carson watched in awe. He knew to expect something that would shock and titillate. But not this. The *Star* had outed Leo against his will, pressing quick cash into the dirt poor palm of the Balinese bimbo. But Leo was in control now.

Rob and David flanked Carson on either side, equally shell-shocked.

The third chorus was taking Leo's solid voice to the rafters, and the sensual dancing and crude gyrating probably had the censors in the control booth sweating buckets, nervous fingers hovering on the seven-second LIVE TAPED DELAY button.

"And here I thought the *BFM* interview was career suicide," Rob said. "But *this* . . ."

"No," David disagreed, watching intensely with advertising/creative concept savvy eyes. "This guy knows *exactly* what he's doing."

Carson stopped breathing as the number swelled to an abrupt stop.

What would the jackals in the VMA live audience do?

The answer was deafening. They were on their feet, the rumble of approval for Leo's fuck you attitude and shock you capability so powerful it could have powered a rocket mission to the moon.

Leo Summer had triumphed.

The clarion call was loud and clear. Madonna had grown up. She was scheduling play dates at parks and bulldozing her way onto the London theater scene.

Pop music had a new controversy stirrer to deal with, and the music world would never be the same again.

Max Stover was doing a spot-on imitation of Tony Danza from the *Taxi* years, while Manzie Mosbacher fixed her hair, her microphone, and her blouse.

The *Manhattan Morning* set, down to a thirty-second count from a two-minute commercial break, tensed for readiness. A producer scribbled on white cue cards. The cameras shifted into position.

"We're back!" Manzie exclaimed. "Oh, my God! Do I sound like the little girl from *Poltergeist*?"

"More like Linda Blair," Max cracked. "Can you spin your head around, too?"

Manzie shivered. "Ugh. Don't remind me of that movie. *The Exorcist*. I had nightmares. My nightmares had nightmares."

The producer windmilled a hand through the air to encourage Max and Manzie to wrap up the banter and stay on schedule.

"Speaking of nightmares . . ." Max intoned, clearing his throat.

"What kind of a segue is that?" Manzie scoffed.

"Oh, I don't know," Max said. And he really didn't. "I imagine the singles scene sure must be one."

"For gay men, too. It's tough out there."

"I wouldn't know about that."

"But our next guest does," Manzie chirped. "He's the editor of a new magazine called *BFM*. That's short for boyfriend material, and I'm definitely interested in some of that. The first issue features a *very* personal interview with former Four Deep singer Leo Summer." Manzie flipped the mag around to display the cover. "Not leaving much to the imagination there, are we? And I think we have a clip of Leo's performance on the MTV Music Video Awards."

Oohs and whistles bounced off the studio walls as the scorching *BFM* cover and Leo's VMA burlesque act steamed up the monitors.

"Please welcome, Carson St. John."

Polite applause.

Manzie shifted the issue of *BFM* onto the coffee table and began flipping through it. "So this is your baby."

"In a word, yes," Carson began. "I feel like I gave birth to it."

"Look at this," Manzie said excitedly, pulling out one of

the trading cards. "It's like a baseball card for dating. If only this man was straight!"

Titters from the audience.

Manzie turned on Carson. Her expression was fairly serious. "Do you find it difficult to meet men in the city? Is that why you dreamed all this up?"

"It's not difficult to meet them in general. Just this morning one tried to sell me a fake Prada wallet on my way here. Men are all over the place."

Manzie grinned. "So it's all about finding a *good* man."

"I'm not picky. I'll settle for one I don't want to push in front of a bus after the third date."

A smattering of supportive audience cheers. They could relate to that.

Max leaned in to join the conversation. "Let me ask you something. How do you approach another man?"

Manzie laughed. "Are you asking for lessons, Max?"

"No, I'm just curious. I have no idea how this is done. Say, for instance, I was sitting in a bar. How would you make your first move?" He laughed a little. "Assume I'm not wearing a wedding ring."

"Oh, that doesn't make a difference," Carson said easily. "I just broke up with a married guy."

Manzie sucked in a breath. "No!"

Max gave the audience a quick comic double take.

"I'm not proud of it. But this sort of thing happens all the time." Carson turned directly to the camera. "Wives of America, listen to me very carefully. Nobody plays *that* much golf. Think about it."

Laughter rocked the studio.

Manzie paused a moment to allow the audience time to settle down. "Now this has turned into an entirely different interview." She rubbed her hands together. "Give us some hints, Carson. Help out our female audience. What are the warning signs that your husband might be seeing another man?"

"If he becomes self-conscious about body hair and stops asking for oral sex, it's time to get a lawyer."

More laughter.

Max and Manzie exchanged a glance, then gave Carson a look, as if discovering him for the first time.

Once more, Manzie picked up the copy of *BFM*. "You've written a column that talks about your experience with male escorts, right?"

"First, let me say that it just happens to be part of my job. I have a duty to fully inform my readers." He smiled as if to say, *You're not buying this, are you?*

Manzie grinned. "Okay, enlighten us. What's the difference between a male escort and a plain old hooker?"

"A better job title and a stronger commitment to exercise. Our hookers are really letting themselves go. It's such a tragedy." Carson's tongue rolled around the one liners with considerable ease. The audience was digging him, and the thrill of their response was something he could get used to. Sparks were in the air.

They rushed the segment to a close and went to another commercial break, buzzing around the set to rearrange for the Culkin brothers reunion. Carson wandered out, feeling vaguely depressed, wishing the chitchat could have gone on.

He returned to what they called the Green Room (he didn't know why—it wasn't that color at all) to grab his things and start off for the office.

A producer stopped him on his way out. "You were great today. You really mixed things up with Mike and Manzie quite well."

Carson smiled. "Thanks. It was fun."

"Would you be interested in coming back on a regular basis?"

The question caught him off guard. "To talk about the magazine?"

"Maybe. Or just dating in general. We're looking for a relationship expert who's not of the book pushing, pop psychobabble variety. You fit the bill."

Ever the sly boots, Carson instantly thought of the way this opportunity could push the brand. "Could we call the segment *BFM* and model the reports after features in the magazine?"

The producer smiled. "I don't see why not."

34

No Frills Love

It was a real date.

Nathan and Christian met early at Fiamma on Spring Street to enjoy an Italian feast, then headed for Broadway to take in *Mamma Mia,* their center orchestra seats a gift to Christian from one of his regular clients. Now they were on a horse and carriage ride through Central Park, sitting shoulder to shoulder, Christian still humming "Dancing Queen." *This* was romance.

"I had a really nice time tonight," Christian said.

Nathan sighed his agreement. "But nice is too neutral a word. I vote for amazing."

Christian laughed. "Okay . . . amazing. That sets a high bar for the good night kiss, though."

Nathan shook his head in marvel. "I still can't believe that I'm here with you. Do you have any idea how huge a crush I had on you in high school?"

"Are you serious?" Christian seemed genuinely stunned.

"Oh, God, I was *sick* for you. I never bothered to keep score at the basketball games. I just watched you run up and down the court."

"Why didn't you ever say anything?"

"Oh, sure, *that* would've gone over well at Highland Prep."

"Do you remember Karl Sessums?"

Nathan scanned his brain. "He ran track, right? Tall, big teeth?"

Christian nodded. "We sort of had a . . ."

The realization hit Nathan and popped like a firecracker in his mind. "No!" he thundered incredulously, pushing Christian in the chest to drive the point home.

"Easy, man," Christian laughed, almost tumbling out of the carriage. "Don't kill me."

"Karl Sessums?"

"I'm not proud of it."

"I want details."

Christian smiled, shaking his head. "Okay . . . it was spring semester of our junior year. We used to kick back at his house and watch videos. Both his parents worked. He was an only child." A diffident shrug. "One thing led to another. We both had girlfriends by the summer, so it just stopped. I don't think either one of us considered ourselves gay at the time." He gave Nathan a strange glance. "Why do you look so devastated?"

"Because!" Nathan whined. "I was *aching* for you, and there you were fooling around with that skinny, goofy Karl Sessums. He was in remedial English. Did you know that?"

Christian laughed. "We didn't talk about school very much. If it's any consolation, I would've much preferred making out with you."

"A lot of good that does me now."

"Think of it as saving the best for last."

Nathan turned to him, still having trouble believing the turn of events. "There is the matter of your sister."

"Tia won't be a problem. She's too busy taking over Wall Street to interfere with us." His gorgeous lips curled into a wry smile. "Think about it. Our mothers are the real obstacle."

"It's not exactly the match Audrey hoped for," Nathan said, his tone almost gloating. He thought about Panther. "But she should be grateful. I could've brought home a nightmare walking just a few weeks ago."

"That bad?"

"Trust me. You were involved recently, too, right?"

"Yeah, he plays for the Knicks. A pretty cool guy but a

paranoid closet case. He never wanted us to arrive at or leave a public place together. Finally, I just couldn't deal."

Nathan gave him a quizzical look. "Tia gave me the impression that you were pretty deep in the closet yourself."

Christian rolled his eyes. "Don't listen to my sister unless she's giving you investment advice. I'm not in the closet. But you won't see me waving from a float in the Gay Pride Parade either. I guess I'm somewhere in the middle."

"Me, too," Nathan said.

The horse clopped to a stop.

Christian paid the Willie Nelson lookalike and helped Nathan onto the pavement. "Do you mind if we call it a night?"

Nathan was taken aback and began to play back the evening at hyper speed, searching for something he might have done wrong. "I don't understand."

"I have a history of moving too fast," Christian explained. "And I don't want to do that with you. When we wake up together for the first time, I want us both to feel good about it . . . to know that it's right."

In that moment, Nathan knew without a doubt that Christian was someone with whom he could spend endless amounts of time without disagreeing much.

Nathan kissed him, and he could have done so until the corners of his mouth were cracked and raw.

Finally, Christian drew back, his eyes hungry for renegotiation. "Fuck it. Let's go back to my place."

Nathan laughed. "Good answer. I've waited long enough."

35

A Different Kind of Love Song

Biceps were screaming at Sports Club L.A. in Rockefeller Plaza, just a few floors down from the studio where *Manhattan Morning* was airing live. Carson's first regular BFM segment was up after the break. A voice in his inner ear mike gave him the count.

"Thirty seconds."

He nodded and moistened his lips with a sweep of his tongue, heart bolting in his chest.

"You'll do great," Keri, his field producer, assured him. "Just be yourself."

Cruz, a Spanish dream who for reasons unknown chose to *operate* a camera instead of *pose* for one, gave Carson the thumbs-up sign.

He tried to scan his notes, but under the feverish pressure of live television, suddenly the words made about as much sense as a Ted Kaczynski Unibomber manifesto. Just letters on a page.

"Stand by for Manzie. And ten . . . nine . . . eight . . . seven . . ."

Keri grabbed the pages and gave his hand a supportive squeeze.

"Hi, Carson!" Manzie chirped.

"Good morning! I'm seeing you on this tiny monitor, and I have to say, the new hair is working for you. Love it straight, Manzie."

"Thanks. It only takes three hours. So it looks like you're at a gym. What's going on? Are you getting buff?"

"Manzie, please. You know I only do heavy lifting after a big sale. I'm here at Sports Club L.A. for the first *Manhattan Morning* BFM report. That's short for boyfriend material, by the way. And I'll be scouting the hot spots to find out exactly what is on the minds of single New Yorkers. Standing next to me—or should I say *over* me, this man is at least six-foot-two—is Justin. Very strong, I can attest. He's been doing curls with forty-pound dumbbells. So, tell me, Justin, do you consider yourself boyfriend material?"

"Sure, why not?" Justin began, his voice smooth and self-assured. "I've got an awesome body, I'm great at my job, and I've never had any complaints in the bedroom."

"Maybe you're a bad listener. Have you ever thought about that?"

On the ear mike, Carson heard Manzie, Max, and the studio audience lose it.

Justin blanched. "Uh, no."

"Straight or gay?"

"Straight," Justin said, jutting his chest out a bit. "Totally straight."

Carson reached over to smooth a hand over one of Justin's impressive pecs. "Hmm. You get your chest waxed. Personally, I think this is a sign that you're borderline. If the right guy came along . . ."

A burst of laughter on the *Manhattan Morning* set.

Carson was nailing the segment. It looked that way. It felt that way.

Justin chuckled. "Sorry, man. It's a done deal. I'm into chicks, not d—"

"Okay, time to move on. We're also joined this morning by Freesia, who's been putting everyone to shame in the spinning class. And she's got the butt to show for it. Hi, Freesia."

"Hey, can I say hi to my mom?"

"Freesia, trust me," Carson cut in. "We don't want Mother to watch this. I plan on having you reveal some very personal things that she knows nothing about."

"Oh." Freesia giggled. "Sorry."

Carson turned back to Justin. "I'm going to put you on the spot, okay?"

Justin smirked. "I told you, man. I'm straight."

"No, I'm through with that," Carson said, waving a dismissive hand. "It's between you and your therapist now." He pivoted toward Freesia. "What do you think about Justin here as boyfriend material?"

Freesia played with the scrunchie in her hair and eyed Justin up and down. "I think he's hot. But I didn't hear anything about a house in the Hamptons, so I guess I'm on the fence."

"No house of my own yet," Justin chimed in. "But I've got an in on a cool summer share."

Freesia seemed impressed by this.

"I think we have a love match!" Carson said exuberantly. "You're not so picky," he said to Freesia, giving her a playful nudge. "Apparently, all it takes to please this woman is a sexually confused young man with big muscles who has the possibility of getting stuffed into a summer rental with thirty other singles."

Carson gave Justin a clap on the back. "Please don't hurt me."

More explosive laughter on the set.

"Okay, Carson, give us your thoughts as we go into another glorious New York weekend. What do *you* consider boyfriend material?" Manzie asked.

Carson St. John saw the sparkling eyes of Keri and the deep dimpled grin on Cruz. The energy from the *Manhattan Morning* set crackled with excitement. He could hear it in the baby mike, see it on the mini monitor. His expression turned serious, but not too serious.

"The qualities I look for have changed at different stages in my life. Right now, the perfect guy for me would be an invisible one." He looked directly at the camera and smiled. "A real man would just get in the way. I'm having too much fun."

36

Like a Virgin

"Honey, you are too scrumptious," Stella said, clutching Brad Pike's muscular arm. "If you even think about turning fag, I might just have to hunt you down and fuck your brains out until you come to your senses."

"Actually," Brad began, leaning closer to Stella. "I've been having these dreams about some of my football buddies . . ."

David swiped off Brad's Janssen Group baseball cap and hit him over the head with it. "The only dreams you've been having are about the cheerleaders."

"Yeah, and they've all come true," Rob added.

Cafeteria on Seventh Avenue rocked with laughter.

The informal gay summit had mushroomed into something like *Eight Is Enough,* at least for today's brunch. There were the original cast members—Carson, Danny, Nathan, and Rob—plus new additions Joel, Christian, and David, as well as special guest stars Stella and Brad.

The raunchy artist and budding writer waved her fork in the air. "Carson, this is just too ironic. You're the new It Guy with *BFM,* and you're the only one at the table without a boyfriend."

Brad, sandwiched between Carson and Stella, scooted closer to Carson, wrapping an arm around his shoulder. "I'm in the same boat. What do you say?"

Carson locked eyes with the teen stud who obviously believed in equal opportunity flirtation. His sculpted arm, hard from pumping iron and sun baked brown from practicing on the field, connected to an even better body. The intoxicating attitude of physical self-respect clung to him, much like his clean laundry scent—Tommy by Tommy Hilfiger—which rained down as if from heaven. "I say . . . ask your father if you can spend the night."

Those pouty Pike lips, which had once been a teasing invitation to a hot party, compressed into a single line. Brad was shocked, and he looked it. "I was kidding. You know that, right?"

"Not so fast, son," David said. "Maybe you should go. It could be an important life experience."

Brad froze up.

Stella moved in to rescue him from the fire he started, extending a silken cheek to Brad's freshly shaved one, smothering the idol of youth and virility in her arms, mimosa eyes raking over him. "Leave this boy alone. He just might be the last straight man in Manhattan. After Prince Alessandro, of course." She giggled.

Brad practically drooled. The babe magnet had met his match.

The rest of them laughed again and attacked their plates, even though food was always secondary at these gatherings. Usually the waiter had to drag orders out of them like secrets from a spy coup.

Suddenly, Rob clinked a butter knife against his juice glass. "I have an announcement to make."

"Let me guess," Joel said. "All this time you've been using the father to get closer to the son."

Rob gave him the reassuring smile of a psychopath with a chain saw. "No, Joel, but given your line of work, I'll excuse the confusion."

Joel did a cute injury scene, a pantomime of the walking wounded. "Dumb model jokes from the shop teacher. I'm crushed."

Carson's laugh was real. The preppie Adonis knew his way around a one liner. Danny had definitely traded up from the gay Madonna with tunnel vision locked on fame.

Stella squealed in delight. "This table's bitchier than Thursday night supper at my old sorority house. And I was a Delta Gamma. Any minute now I might start checking for dicks. I can't be the only one here with a vagina."

Nathan's grin smacked of an inside trader who had a tip that could translate to millions with one rogue buy. "You're certainly the only virgin among us."

Danny nearly choked on his French toast. "I'm sorry. I thought you said virgin."

"He did," Stella answered, shooting faux daggers at her confidant. "Is that so hard to believe?"

"There's really no safe answer for that one," Joel said.

Nathan summed it up for the group. "Stella has been, how should I put this . . . I guess the word is . . . *revirginized.*"

"That's right," Stella clucked proudly. "In fact, it's inspired me to do a new show. What do you think about Star Fruit Pussy?"

Brad summoned up a dazzling smile. "I would love to see this work in progress."

"Excuse me," Carson said, putting a halt on the proceedings. "But what does it mean to be revirginized?"

"In Stella's case, it used to mean going without sex for more than three days," Nathan explained. "But medical technology has advanced."

All heads boomeranged to Stella. The collective mood of slightly confused, slightly guilty curiosity made this look like a parlor game of guess my piercing with Christina Aguilera.

"Oh, fuck!" Stella caved. "But if I tell you, it doesn't leave this table."

Eight fast nods of agreement sealed the deal.

"I don't want every slut in New York jetting off to Dr. Matlock just so she can wave her new cherry in Prince Alessandro's face." A deep breath. "I had myself a little procedure done called hymenoplasty."

Danny leaned in toward the center. "What?"

"*Hymenoplasty.* At the Laser Vaginal Rejuvenation Institute."

"Let me help," Brad offered with a laugh. "Besides you, I'm the only one who's fluent in pussy here."

"Oh, thank you, honey," Stella gushed.

"She's talking about hymen reconstruction," Brad said. "Matlock stitched her cherry back."

Carson grimaced. "Okay, I just got this creepy image of Andy Griffith between Stella's legs, and it's really freaking me out."

"Honey, this man is brilliant. Alessandro actually believed that he had deflowered me. There was blood on the sheets and everything."

Rob pushed his plate away. "Why do I even bother trying to eat with you people?"

"And if he asks me to marry him, I'm going to do it again, so I'll be a virgin on our wedding night. It only costs about five thousand dollars."

"Just think, boys," Brad posed. "They might be able to do that for asses one day."

"Okay, who brought the straight guy?" Carson bellowed.

"Wait a minute," Rob said. "I was about to announce something before Stella started in on her gyno history." He clinked the juice glass once more. "I'm putting my apartment on the market."

Carson noticed David's hand snake underneath the table to claim Rob's knee. He bounced a look over to Nathan, who was grinning the grin of a man tipped off early to a buddy's big life change news.

Rob beamed at David. "Looks like I'll be moving in to David's brownstone."

"Oh, my God! Honey, that is so sweet. Ya'll make the cutest couple. I can totally see the two of you in one of those gay Ikea ads." Stella leaned across Brad to address Carson, her breasts firm, braless, and full right underneath the senior's jackpot eyes. "What's his name again?"

"Rob," Carson whispered.

"And who's the Chinese guy with the model?"

"That would be Danny. And he's Japanese."

Stella nodded approvingly. "I like their food better."

Rob was still talking machine guns about the move.

"So Brad," Joel elbowed in, a fun trouble smile resting on his famous lips, "I guess this makes Rob a stepfather of sorts."

"I'll probably still go to my dad for sex advice. No offense, Rob, but Stella tells one story, and you can't even finish your breakfast."

"I don't know what your father could do for you," Rob said. "Even Dr. Ruth would have to study up."

"Where does that leave you?" Danny asked. His eyes were on Nathan.

"I've started looking for my own place."

"Oh, honey," Stella wailed dramatically. "You are in one *serious* situation. If I had to look for an apartment right now, I would just have to kill myself."

"I've got a place," Christian said. It was his first real utterance. It was a big one.

Nathan's eyes swiveled toward him. The expression on his face said this was breaking news.

"It's large enough for two," Christian reasoned. "And half the time I'm traveling with clients and not even there." His body to the stars rippled with serious crush vibes. "I wouldn't mind coming home to you."

"Okay!" Nathan spoke out brightly. He laughed at the speed of his acceptance. It was all happening so fast. Fresh from the Panther apocalypse he was starting it up with an adolescent fantasy that had clung to his psyche like Garfield to a back windshield. But there were no secrets between these two. The genuine affection was right there for the whole world to see.

"You know," Joel started, allowing ample time for the congratulations to Nathan and Christian to simmer, "I get the feeling that we're just not making a commitment to each other." The model god's fashion glory face was all over Danny as he rolled the dice of the words onto the Cafeteria table. "I have an important question to ask you, and I want you to think about it very carefully before you answer."

Danny's nod was deadly serious.

Hilfiger's hottest hunk paused a second for effect. There were sixteen eyes glued to him, and he knew it. "Can I have some space in your bathroom for my hair gel?"

Everybody laughed together as only great friends can. Another round of mimosas kept the good times going.

"Okay, bad eighties hits for five hundred," Danny blurted out. He had the Dick Clark bit down. The interjection was way off point but already subjects had run the gamut from virgin blood to real estate nightmares.

Rob pushed his face into David's rock of a shoulder. "Oh, God, I hate it when they do this."

"Whatever happened to that Taco guy?" Danny asked.

Nathan bounced up and down in his seat. "I remember him! He sang 'Puttin' on the Ritz.' It's, like, a medley of his hit."

Christian reared back and pointed an accusing finger at Nathan. "Wait a minute." He was laughing now, showing off perfect teeth that could glow in the dark. "You did a routine to that song in a neighborhood talent show!"

The forgotten baggage of yesteryear rose up on Nathan's face like a brand-new morning. "Oh, shit! I can't believe you remember that!" He buried his blushing face in his hands.

Carson eased up to his feet, shelling out more than his share of the brunch damage. "Okay, I'm out of here before somebody starts arguing about how to spell Apollonia's name. Just one P, by the way." He kissed Stella's cheek, squeezed Brad's shoulder, and stood over the table to study the group.

Danny with Joel.

Nathan with Christian.

Rob with David.

He smiled. The algebra was looking good here. Definitely BFM. And with Stella and Brad in the equation to keep things lively and unpredictable, you had to love mathematics like this.

Carson walked out on a cloud of happiness. He was off to a colonic center to get flushed out with two quarts of purified water. Tomorrow he returned to *Manhattan Morning,* with a new segment, and the treatment would drop a few pounds and flatten his stomach.

He wanted to look *good.* You never knew who might be watching.